CW01496423

THE POPPY

THE POPPY

BY

K.M.KNIGHT

Cover photographs by Zoe. F. Knight
I.T. support by Zachary Ulm
Original painting by K.M. Knight

Chapter 1

Old William Martin awakened, cold and disorientated, as the sun was setting. He had been dreaming about the past, when he was young and robust, surrounded by his noisy family, the little rickety house invariably filled with the aroma of stew and hot bread. His wife's singing and laughter had been slowly quelled by the relentless deaths of the children. Four had died from malarial fevers. Nursing the two youngest through the prolonged agonies of smallpox took the greatest toll upon her and he never heard her laugh again. William had outlived his wife and six of his nine children. Tears welled up in his eyes as he creaked forward in his old chair and threw a log onto the fire, which had failed to warm the house since his beloved wife Ellen Rose had died of grief and hard work. His beautiful daughter Lily had married above her station and moved away, he had not seen or heard of her for fifteen years. His two remaining sons, John and William had married and were raising their own families. John named his daughter after his sister Lily and at twelve years old young Lily's beauty was unnerving, and it was she who found her grandfather dead of forlorn loneliness in his decrepit chair the following morning, still staring into the cold fireplace.

Lily lit the fire and sat beside William, she

covered him in an ancient moth-eaten blanket and held his old gnarled hand that had worked the land and tended sheep for over fifty years, and whispered to him. She could hear his responses in her head, a conversation that was to continue for the rest of her life. That was where her father found her several hours later, concerned when she had failed to return home.

William was buried in a woolen shroud, beside his wife and children, in the long shadow of the majestic flint church that had dominated the village for five hundred years. The year was 1740.

Lily was a quiet solitary child. She had been a difficult birth and her mother Mary had traumatized her husband, the neighbours and the livestock by screaming in terrified agony for four days and nights, clawing the sheets and the old midwives to shreds. Eventually, John burst into the room and dragged the child into the world in the same way he saved stuck lambs. The baby was blue, thin and weak. The old midwives shook their heads sadly, but John put the feeble little scrap of life inside of his shirt and took it downstairs and sat beside the fire until it shuddered and emitted a tiny, feeble cry. Mary barely survived and never forgave Lily, who after the unspeakable torturous nightmare was only a girl. She had initially believed the child dead and felt no emotion, and when John brought her upstairs, pink and breathing, she was horrified by the stare that the child fixed her with. She never conceived again and slowly, layer by layer, became mean, embittered and cold.

Grandfather William had loved Lily and he carved little wooden animals for her, burning on the details with a hot knife. She would sit and watch him, as her father had done before her, as tiny sheep and cows emerged from the wood. She grew into a pretty, delicate child with thick dark curly hair like her grandmother Ellen Rose and eyes of an unusual deep violet hue. The more beautiful Lily became, the further her mother withdrew from her, and struggled with teaching her the skills she would need in later life. Lily failed to demonstrate any skills in the kitchen, and her needlework lessons consisted of her gazing out of the window at the weather. She much preferred to walk the marshes and woodlands with her grandfather, or sit quietly with her father whilst he minded his sheep. Her mother despaired of marrying off an unaccomplished, withdrawn girl, despite her beauty. A man needed a skilled, tireless wife, not some kind of ornament. When Lily began constantly whispering to her dead grandfather, it was the last straw. Mary believed she was possessed. This belief was exacerbated by Lily's fascination with herbs and wild plants and their curative properties gleaned from her grandfather on their long walks.

Lily's closest friend was her cousin Joseph, one of the numerous sons of her Uncle William and Aunt Isabel. Uncle William worked on the land like his father and Aunt Isabel, a jolly plump woman, cooked, washed and ran around tirelessly trying to control her ever-expanding brood of boys. She laughed and sang and walloped the boys with a wet cloth. Lily was scared of her and unable to believe that Aunt Isabel and her own mother were members of the same species. Joseph was a dark, thoughtful boy, unlike his riotous brothers, Edward, Thomas, Charles, Henry, William and Ernest. He and Lily would spend hours in each other's company, rarely needing to speak.

Word arrived that Mary's mother had been taken bad with malaria, rife in the village due to the boggy marshes. She packed a small bag, adamantly rebuffing Lily's offer of a herbal remedy for the fever, and stalked off through the village to nurse her mother and tend to her father's needs. Few people in the village acknowledged the passing of the tall thin figure, with a once pretty face ravaged ugly by years of rancour and jealousy, with more than a curt nod. Within a week, her mother was dead, willingly giving up on a life with a husband who, years before had chosen the drink over his family. Mary stayed to cook, clean and nag her father to death.

John and Lily's combined culinary skills did not stretch beyond cooking the eggs that Lily collected daily from the chicken coup. So Aunt Isabel cooked stew and bread for John and Lily, that Joseph carried round to them at mealtimes. Mary was not greatly missed, the little house took on a quiet untidiness and even the two sheepdogs plucked up the courage to come inside and doze contentedly in front of the fire.

On Sundays, the family would meet at church and Mary would visit and cook the dinner, tidy up and startle the dogs, who bolted outside, tails between their quivering legs. She would mutter and complain in a whining monologue that lasted the entire afternoon. She bemoaned the fact that her husband was uncaring, that he preferred the company of sheep and that he had failed to support her and improve their situation. She rued the day she had married John and wished she had accepted the proposal of marriage from the short, fat Clarence who was now a man of means living in the town. And as for her useless daughter who allowed dust and grime to invade the cottage and spent her time wandering around alone asking to be deflowered by any man who felt so inclined. That her poor dead mother had suffered years of slaps and kicks and misery at the hands of yet another uncaring, selfish man. That she was now doomed to look after the ungrateful drunken wretch, to clear up his vomit and wash his filthy clothes and breathe the wretched stink of him day after day. John invariably invented a reason to visit his flock, leaving with the relieved dogs scampering at his heels. Lily would talk to her dead grandfather or insist on returning Aunt Isabel's dishes and go for a walk with Joseph. After several months, Mary's visits became more infrequent and then stopped. She contented herself with relentlessly reducing her drunken father's life to abject misery. By then, Aunt

Isabel had managed to teach Lily the rudiments of cooking and washing and she and her father settled into their life of peaceful disorganization and meals of a random quality.

Mary's father's rage that had simmered for months, finally boiled over during a particularly cruel tirade from his daughter and he caved her head in with the poker. He sat beside her and finished his jug of ale, dispassionately watching the blood darken on her pulverized, silent head, then he hung himself from a beam directly above her. No one noticed their absence until the dogs and maggots had reduced their remains to a few bones and a vast cloud of flies above the cottage.

The remaining bones were interred in the churchyard in a poorly attended funeral on a mild autumn day. The cottage was burnt to the ground as no one could imagine living there and the dogs were killed, as no one trusted creatures that had fed solely on human flesh for several weeks.

Chapter 2

John worried about his daughter. At almost 18 she remained unmarried. Families matched up their offspring with suitable husbands and wives and their children generally accepted the arrangement. He had hopes that she would marry one of her numerous cousins, she had always been close to Joseph, but when he mentioned the subject Lily had admonished him with stare that had upset him for days.

She was content to keep house for her father and roam the woods, marshes and shoreline, collecting her plants, making potions and ointments. John frequently watched her walking the sea wall as he tended his sheep, her long dark curls buffeted by the wind from the estuary. He watched her solitude, her vulnerability, and feared for her safety, he had witnessed the hungry eyes that ravished her on their visits to church on Sundays. Lily appeared not to notice this, as she strolled gracefully on her father's arm, her violet eyes smiling as she greeted neighbours. She was almost as tall as John and her dark curls reached below her slim waist. Her clothing was plain, drab and bore the scars of her explorations of the countryside. Her humble attire did not detract from her beauty, but greatly intensified it, reducing the other young women to jealousy and the older ones to wistfulness. John walked proudly beside her, but it was a pride tinged heavily with the weight of responsibility for her striking appearance.

Lily had no interest in marrying, her experience of marriages having been severely blighted by her parents troubled disharmony and her Aunt's permanent state of pregnancy and nursing. She preferred to be free to wander the land, constantly aware of the seasonal changes and the bounty they produced. Her remedies were popular in the village and she kept the pennies she earned in a jar on a shelf in the kitchen.

Thomas and Charles joined their Uncle John, learning the shepherding trade. It was a profitable time for shepherds, wool was more popular and the sheep were breeding well. Lily collected a pile of lambs fleece and spent weeks scraping the skins, salting, drying, washing, oiling and washing them numerous times until she had achieved a mound of soft fleeces, enough to make a sturdy winter coat. Her father's sheep came in different shades, from pure white to darkest brown. Her favourites were the mottled fleeces, with patches of greys and soft light browns. She shaved the hair from one fleece and cut the leather into thin strips for thronging the skins together. The finished coat was a patchwork of shades, she constructed it with the wool on the outside, as the sheep wear it, rather than like her father's coat, who preferred the wool on the inside. The coat was long and hooded and enabled her to stay warm during the snow and the biting winds of winter.

Lily was still wearing her heavy coat in early spring, due to the persistent icy wind that blew in from the estuary. She was searching for seaweed on the shore. A strange, uncanny sensation enveloped her, she found herself holding her breath without any evident reason why. Perplexed, she stood up and turned around, scanning the horizon, the uncannily pleasant apprehension intensified and she struggled to breathe normally. She climbed to the top of the sea wall and saw him immediately. He was leading a black horse along the path below the sea wall and stopped as she appeared. Although the distance between them remained considerable, some hundred yards, she was overpowered by his proximity and paralysed, stupefied and still. He began to approach slowly, his horse's steaming breath the only sound she could hear. His black hair was as long as his horse's tail, and when he was a matter of a few yards from her, he stopped and bowed low, then rose slowly and smiled at her before resuming his journey. Lily was aware of a sweet warm aroma as she watched him walk for half a mile until the bend in the riverbank obscured him and his horse. She had not moved throughout the interaction and suddenly realised that her mouth had remained open since her initial gasp. She sat down on the grassy sea wall, her body still shaking.

'Grandfather.........what was that?' she stammered.

'That, my dearest Lily........is Love!

Lily was never quite the same again, she burnt the bread, forgot to collect the eggs and found it impossible to sleep without vivid dreams which woke her breathless and exhausted. Her father thought she was 'sickening for something', whilst she sat staring vacantly into the fire. She was unable to tell anyone, apart from grandfather William, and after a few weeks of walking the shore looking for him decided that the   dark stranger with the dark horse had been an apparition. Her sense of balance gradually returned, until the warm May morning when Lily and her father were walking to church. She felt the familiar breathlessness and began to tremble, she held tightly to her father's arm. As they turned the corner she saw the stranger standing on the cobbled path leading to the church. She could feel her cheeks flush as they approached, whereupon the stranger bowed to her and nodded to her father as they passed. Enveloped by the same warm sweet smell, Lily could feel her father's eyes on her as they entered the church where she gratefully sat down before she fell.

'Who was that man in the churchyard?' John asked Lily as they walked home.

'I have no idea father, I saw him once before at the shore, I have never spoken to him.'

Alarmed, John lost no time in making enquiries as to the man's identity as Lily reverted to daydreaming and forgetfulness. No one in the village knew of him, so John set off for the dock at the bend in the estuary. There were several ships moored off the jetty, a mix of villagers and strangers were unloading their wares and piling the goods onto carts for transportation to the town. John walked around the carts, unsure of where to start his enquiries, when he saw the stranger disembarking from one of the ships. He approached the tall dark man responsible for his daughter's recent disquiet.

'I'm John Martin.......' he said and then had no idea what else to say.

'I am Aziz Shadi Rashad Salamar Badr al din, and I am honoured to make your esteemed acquaintance Mr John Martin.' the stranger bowed and proffered his hand, which John shook, not knowing what else to do, having already forgotten his name.

Sensing John's abject confusion and discomfort, Aziz Shadi Rashad Salamar Badr al din invited him to take refreshment. John accepted as he still did not know what else to do and followed him along the jetty onto a ship. John had never in all of his life set foot on a ship.

Aziz Shadi Rashad Salamar Badr al din ushered John into a room with sumptuous furniture and invited him to sit. John had not imagined rooms on ships and was entirely out of his depth. He observed the surroundings, the brightest colours he had ever seen, polished wood, books, a desk with large sheets of paper covered in weird patterns. John was a quiet man, but always thought of himself as strong and resourceful. Now, for the first time in his life, he felt shabby, threadbare and fervently wished he had not embarked on this venture. A large green parrot sat on a perch.

'Inshallah!' it said at regular intervals.

Refreshments arrived, consisting of a tall glass pot and two red glasses with gold decorations and a plate containing unusual cakes or biscuits that John was unfamiliar with. Aziz Shadi Rashad Salamar Badr al din poured a brown steaming liquid from the tall pot and offered a glass to John. The liquid was hot and very sweet, this was John's first taste of tea, but he was none the wiser, and continued to sit like a dumb fool.

'You are, I believe Mr John Martin, the most fortunate father of the most beautiful woman that I have ever seen!' said Aziz Shadi Rashad Salamar Badr al din.

' Ermm.....er.....I...yes.' answered John eventually, not feeling very fortunate.

'I would beg your most gracious permission to marry your daughter, subject to her full agreement, and after a suitable length of time has elapsed. In the meantime, please accept these gifts as a token of my integrity and honesty. Peace be with you Mr John Martin.' announced Aziz Shadi Rashad Salamar Badr al din, much to John's astonishment. He passed John two parcels wrapped in thick brown paper and escorted him, still speechless, back to dry land. John wandered back to the village in a very similar state to which his daughter had latterly been suffering. At home, he stared at the packages for a while, wondering if he should have accepted them.

Then he opened them, the first one contained a pair of exquisite leather boots, the quality of which he had never before witnessed. The leather was thick and soft and embossed with extraordinary patterns. The second parcel contained a bolt of the finest, softest fabric he had ever touched. It was a deep violet colour and shimmered in the light and he had no idea that the thin fibres had been made by caterpillars.

Chapter 3

John was still sitting staring at the gifts when Lily returned from her walk with a basket of herbs and an armful of bluebells.

'Father.........what?' her eyes widened as she caught sight of the packages on the   table.

'That man, the one outside of the church, he wants to marry you.' muttered John.

'You've   seen   him?   ...who   is he?..............what....?'

'I don't know.'

'FATHER ...you must know who he is if you've spoken with him!'

'Well I don't. He's not from around these parts.....and he doesn't sound like the Irish and his name was the strangest thing I've ever heard!'

Eventually, John managed to explain what had happened. Neither of them knew what to do next. Lily's sensible side wanted to know a lot more, but when she remembered his smell she wanted to run and find him. Her father desperately wished she was five years old again and he went off with the dogs to sit with his sheep and think.

Aziz Shadi Rashad Salamar Badr al din, a well travelled individual, proved much more resourceful. A week later, a seamstress arrived with orders to transform the violet silk into a dress for Lily, with instructions that the acceptance of the service held Lily under no obligation whatsoever. A week later, a messenger arrived at John's door, with a small package for Lily and a verbal request for John and Lily to have dinner with Aziz Shadi Rashad Salamar Badr al din on his vessel, a carriage would be sent for them on the following Saturday at seven o'clock.

Lily was beside herself with mute excitement. Her father hoped he was experiencing an unusually vivid dream. The entire village had got wind that a foreigner was trying to steal away the Martin girl. Many were scandalized and blamed John for his failure to marry her off to a village lad and for allowing the unfortunate motherless girl to wander about unsupervised and meeting all sorts of strangers and causing a calamity.

On the Saturday evening, when John saw his daughter resplendent in her violet silk dress and the amethyst necklace delivered by messenger, her violet eyes shining and her dark curls spilling around her shoulders, he abruptly left the room to hide his tears. He could see why the foreigner wanted her. John wore his Sunday clothes and felt obliged to wear the new boots, which squeaked as he walked.

The carriage, pulled by a majestic black horse, drove through the village of twitching curtains and into the marshes towards the dock. The setting sun cast a warm gold hue across the land and lit up the mast of the ships. As John stepped from the carriage, Lily heard the stranger's voice for the first time.

'Ah, Mr John Martin, I am your humble servant.' Aziz Shadi Rashad Salamar Badr al din spoke softly, bowing his head.

When Lily appeared from behind her father, Aziz Shadi Rashad Salamar al din fell to his knees, he took her hand and kissed it, tears rolling down his cheeks. 'Lily.' was all he said. At that precise moment, enveloped in his enchanting perfume, Lily lost her heart and John knew he had lost his daughter.

Aziz Shadi Rashad Salamar Badr al din was a rich, successful merchant. He traded in silk, tea, porcelain, hides, jewels, gold and spices. John learned that the large sheets of paper were navigational charts, showing where countries with names such as China, India, Turkey and Africa were in the world. As he told them fantastic stories of his voyages, Lily felt her world becoming unfathomably large. John just felt his become insignificantly small. Aziz Shadi Rashad Salamar Badr al din had gone to great effort with the meal, and his cooks, led by Mustapha, had valiantly attempted to produce a traditional English meal of roasted lamb and vegetables. After the meal, they sat on large bright cushions in hammocks slung across the cabin, swinging gently as the tide turned. They drank hot, sweet tea and liked it. Lily felt completely at ease and talked of her fascination with herbs and remedies. She watched Aziz Shadi Rashad Salamar Badr al din closely as he talked to her father about his sheep. His eyes were the darkest brown she had ever seen, his skin a deep olive brown. He wore a short moustache and his beard was trimmed into a thin line down both sides of his face, joining at the point of his chin with a tuft of longer hair. His cheekbones were high and prominent and his nose long and slim. He wore white baggy trousers and a long white tunic with gold embroidery around the neckline and a heavy gold bracelet. Lily had never seen a man dressed like that, when she had seen him on the first two occasions, he had been dressed like other men.

On the way home in the carriage, Lily realised her face was aching from constantly smiling. Her father quietly held her hand, and they remained lost in the silence of their own thoughts for the rest of the journey home.

Lily's happiness was contagious, and even John noticed a spring in his own step. He decided he would give Aziz Shadi Rashad Salamar Badr al din his blessing. He could no more deny her this man than deny her air to breathe. Even if it meant she went to China and never returned.

The messenger had become such a regular visitor, that he was now invited in to sit and take refreshment. John sent a message this time requesting a meeting with Aziz Shadi Rashad Salamar Badr al din. No sooner had he left, it seemed to John, that Aziz Shadi Rashad Salamar Badr al din was galloping into the yard on his black horse. Lily was out collecting plants.

'Mr John Martin, I came as soon as I received your welcome message.'

'I wanted to tell you that you have my permission to marry my daughter and my sincere blessing, please take good care of her............I'm sorry, I do not know how to address you.'

'As you are to be my father, you can call me son...or any one of my numerous names, that all have separate meanings, which I will tell you, Aziz means 'dear', Shadi is 'enchanter', Rashad means 'integrity', Salamar is 'safety' and Badr al din means 'full moon of the faith', and I should like very much to call you my father, and I promise you that I would lay down my life for Lily.'

'Shadi is tempting as you have certainly enchanted the pair of us, but I would be very proud to call you son, if you don't mind, less chance of forgetting that!' chuckled John.

'I would be honoured my father,'

Aziz Shadi Rashad Salamar Badr al din left, after rescuing his startled horse from a crowd of small boys, amidst the blatant gawping of everyone in the village who had found out he was there. Undaunted, he waved at them shouting.

'I have a most honourable father and you are all invited to the most splendid wedding!' whereupon the scandalised villagers abruptly disappeared.

Aziz Shadi Rashad Salamar Badr al din visited the vicarage to arrange the wedding. The pale, nervous vicar was concerned that he was not a Christian, but was persuaded by the knowledge that Jesus was recognised and venerated as a prophet by Muslims and even more persuaded by a generous donation to the church roof fund. The wedding date was set for early summer of the following year.

William and Isabel were initially aghast that John would let Lily marry a foreigner from unknown lands, but Isabel was soon reduced to a blushing heap by the charms of Aziz Shadi Rashad Salamar Badr al din, ensuring that William was even more adamant that the union was unthinkable.

It was a good summer, the weather warm and sunny, the sheep healthy, and the wool plentiful. Aziz Shadi Rashad Salamar Badr al din often visited in the afternoons, taking Lily out on the back of his horse. John found he trusted him more and more and became genuinely proud to call him son. Lily had never been happier and she became more beautiful than ever. His ship was due to sail in early autumn, destined for the Mediterranean Sea, visiting Morocco for hides and Turkey for spices and silks. He would return in spring in time for the wedding.

John's little house was bursting at the seams with the influx of gifts, the latest being a vast pile of silk cushions in all of the colours of the rainbow. Aziz Shadi Rashad Salamar Badr al din suggested he build a larger house for John. But John being a proud man declined, until Aziz Shadi Rashad Salamar Badr al din explained that his father would undoubtedly need a larger house to accommodate his son returning from sea and the children that would, God willing, arrive in the following years. John was so delighted when he realised that he was unlikely to lose his daughter completely, he agreed. True to his word, and with the usual punctuality of Aziz Shadi Rashad Salamar Badr al din, John's adjoining plot of land suddenly became a hive of activity, with piles of lumber and carpenters from the ship, swarming like ants. The house grew at an alarming rate and was completed a week before the ship was to sail. There was even a stable for Elija the black horse, who was to stay behind, Elija was greatly relieved, not being a good sailor.

John and Lily spent the last evening onboard with Aziz Shadi Rashad Slamar Badr al din, and said their goodbyes, and Lily went to the shore the next morning to watch him sail past, she could not bear to go to the dock. When the ship was level with her, Aziz Shadi Rashad Salamar Badr al din, set off three rockets into the air that exploded into a cloud of smoke and red stars. Lily waved and waved, hoping he could see her and watched the ship until it disappeared over the horizon.

As she walked home across the marshes she thought about the last remarkable four months and was unable to clearly recall what life had been like before. When she arrived home, her father was moving their belongings across the yard to their new house. It had two stories, with four large rooms on the top floor, a hallway in between. Downstairs, there was a kitchen and three other rooms. Two large stone chimneys supported the building and there was a large fireplace in each room. Their meagre belongings would easily fit into one of the rooms. Lily chose the bedroom with a view of the estuary, so she could watch for the ship. She set about arranging her bedroom, using the bright rugs and cushions. As she unrolled the rugs, she found a small parcel. It contained three thin glass vials of a clear liquid. When she removed a stopper, she was engulfed in the warm smell reminiscent of Aziz Shadi Rashad Salamar Badr al din, which she now knew to be oil of jasmine.

Over the following few days, various unexpected carts arrived at the Martin residence. One delivered sacks of flour, sugar and dried fruits. Another brought enough logwood for the winter fires. Yet another brought new pots and pans. New winter clothing arrived from the seamstress, dresses of soft wool in vibrant colours, silk nightdresses and undergarments. The last carts to arrive delivered a large table and twelve matching chairs, two of them with arms, a dresser, new beds and mattresses, closets, sofas, more rugs and a box of linens, sheets, curtains and tablecloths, all embroidered with exotic patterns of gold, purple and crimson. Lily and John stood and stared at each other, wondering what had happened to their simple little world. Other mothers in the village, originally staunchly opposed to the union, began ruthlessly nagging their daughters for their lamentable lack of foresight and failure to attract the attention of some foreign prince with money to throw around.

Aunt Isabel arrived to help organise the house. She clattered around in the kitchen finding places for the pots and pans. Isabel's boys carried the beds, trunks and closets up the stairs to the bedrooms while the women arranged the sofas and rugs.

Just before Christmas, two large crates arrived containing a goose, half of a side of beef, Christmas pudding and cakes, marmalade, jams and an extensive variety of cheeses, pickles, biscuits, a patterned tin containing tea and a box with a tall glass teapot and twelve blue glasses with gold edges. John and Lily invited William, Isabel and the boys for Christmas to help eat the feast, and ensure that Isabel would cook the Christmas dinner, which was far beyond the culinary capabilities of Lily. William was reluctant to attend, but outvoted. On Christmas day, John sat at one end of the table in his carver chair. William, Isabel, their 7 sons and Lily sat along the sides. They left an empty carver chair at the other end of the table out of respect for Aziz Shadi Rashad Saladar Badr al din. The house smelled of jasmine, and Lily, surrounded by his generosity, could almost feel his presence. They drank a toast to him with hot sweet tea, and wished him a safe voyage home. Grandfather William assured her he was safe and off the coast of Turkey.

Following Christmas and the New Year, life slowed down for Lily and she began to miss Aziz

Shadi Rashad Salamar Badr al din. She spent hours watching for ships from her bedroom window, even though he was not due home until the spring. Elija was a comfort to her, and she rode him around the countryside and they watched the estuary together. She busied herself with her remedies, which she now gave away to anyone who needed them. The lambing began early that year, and Lily was kept busy helping with the new lambs, several of them were orphans and huddled together in a box beside the roaring fire, bleating for milk. One morning towards the end of March, Elija became very restless, stamping and whinnying and kicking the sides of the stable. Lily tried to settle him, she checked his hooves and spoke to him gently, patting his neck and stroking his face. He continued to whinny as if in pain, eyes rolling, so Lily led him out of the stable to see if he was limping. Once outside Elija reared, wrenching the rope from her grasp and ran off up the lane. Lily called him and tried to chase him, knowing that it was useless, he was far too fast for her. She was angry with herself for letting him out, how could she explain to Aziz Shadi Rashad Salamar Badr al din that she had lost his precious horse, after all he had done for her and her father.

Two hours later, Elija returned with an innocent, yet triumphant, expression on his face and Aziz Shadi Rashad Salamar Badr al din on his back. His ship had arrived at night, and Elija knew where to find him. Lily did not know who to hug, the horse or the man. Aziz Shadi Rashad Salamar Badr al din jumped from Elija and hugged Lily. Elija nuzzled his shoulder. The three of them remained locked in that silent embrace until John arrived home with another rejected lamb. During the afternoon, Aziz Shadi Rashad Salamar Badr al din rode Elija back to the dock to collect the cart full of belongings he had intended to drive to the house before Elija rudely interrupted him earlier that morning. Unable to let him out of her sight, Lily accompanied him. They sat together on the cart on the way home, Elija trotting beside them. The cart contained a dozen lanterns from Morocco, made of ornate metal and patterned coloured glass, smaller glass lanterns on long chains from Turkey and a number of exquisite, thin embroidered rugs which, Aziz Shadi Rashad Salamar Badr al din assured her, were wall hangings. There was a large, intricately carved wooden box for keeping blankets in, which was full of a series of carved boxes getting smaller and smaller. He had acquired them from Turkey but he said they were carved in Northern India. Her favourite item was a vast bedspread, made from deep violet/blue silk, padded and thick and with thousands of tiny mirrors embroidered into the surface, which glittered like stars in the candlelight. It was to be saved for their wedding night. For John he had brought an emerald green silk padded dressing gown, the colour shimmered like new spring grass.

'For my father to wear on winter evenings beside

the fire.'

Chapter 4

The wedding severely disrupted the normal, quiet, humdrum village life for days on end. The ceremony itself was a private affair, with only a few very close relatives, but the rest of it was noisy, colourful and chaotic and lasted for days. There was singing, dancing and eating. A sudden firework display at midnight on the final evening startled the elderly and those who had retired to bed in an attempt to visibly boycott the whole affair.

Aziz Shadi Rashad Badr al din dealt with the pockets of stubborn animosity by ignoring them and banging on front doors, armed with dishes of food and a wide smile. The poor villagers were aghast and dreadfully embarrassed by his blatant lack of inhibitions. They thanked him for the food, shut the door and were then angry and frustrated with each other for accepting a gift from a foreigner with no respect for their privacy and the inability to notice their severe disapproval.

Most of the villagers enjoyed themselves, seduced by the joyful atmosphere. Lily was ecstatic and John was proud. Only Joseph was quiet and withdrawn. As the wedding had approached, he had been troubled with feelings of desolation and a dreadful sadness.

Aziz Shadi Rashad Salamar Badr al din's ship was due to sail at the end of that idyllic summer. John struggled with the news that Lily intended to sail away as well. If they were to raise a family, this may be her only chance to travel with her husband. The evening before departure, William, Isabel and sons attended for a family meal. Joseph did not accompany them, but sent a message saying he was unwell. In truth, he was unable to bear the happiness of others.

John accompanied the couple to the ship, unwilling to part from his daughter until the very last moment…in case it really was the last. The heartrending goodbye was thankfully interrupted by high tide and the need to sail. John rode Elijah home. They plodded slowly through the marshes, dolefully watching the ship disappear into the distance.

The village gradually returned to normal. John continued to teach his nephews, Thomas and Charles, the skill of shepherding. Edward and Henry followed their own father's footsteps and worked on the land. William worked with heavy horses and Ernest raised pigs. Joseph worked with the local undertaker, the solemnity of the work befitting his own somber mood. It was his mother who first recognised the source of his despair, long before he did, from the wretched, disconsolate look in his eyes each time his cousin Lily was mentioned. His deep love for her, from when they were small children, was so familiar to him that he had failed to notice it himself.

It was a harsh winter, the worst in living

memory, and the village was buried under a deep layer of snow and ice. John and his nephews built a high fence around their yard and drove the sheep up from the marshes to avoid them being frozen to death where they stood. The sheep huddled together in the shelter of the fence avoiding the worst of the raw, glacial wind. Elijah wore a thick blanket and had a lighted stove in his stable, causing the chickens to desert their chilly coop, currently festooned with icicles, and join him in the stable, laying their eggs in his hay trough.

Tempestuous blizzards blew for days on end and feeding the beleaguered animals in the yard required superhuman effort on the part of John and his nephews. The water pump froze and John relentlessly thawed out buckets of snow and ice. Everyone was busy keeping their animals alive, and their houses warm. Joseph was busy burying the dead, particularly the very old and very young, unable to withstand the bitter winter. When the soil froze in the graveyard, the frozen bodies were piled in the charnel house, situated at the far corner of the churchyard. In January, when everyone thought the winter would last forever, William and Isabel finally admitted defeat and, along with their sons, shut up their damp, draughty cottage and moved in with John. Isabel tirelessly kept all the fires alight, cooked large pots of stew, bread, cakes and puddings and forbade the numbing cold from entering. She cooked potatoes and bran for the chickens and fed it to them hot. At the end of the day she surveyed the family with pride, as the men and their dogs sat steaming and red faced in the heat of the roaring fire, stomachs full.

Inevitably, winter gradually released it's chilly hold, the snow subsided and the thaw began. Then the real devastation became evident. Stiffened corpses were found in the snowdrifts, curled up like newborn babies. Entire families had burnt their furniture, stick by stick in a futile attempt to avoid the inevitable, and were discovered huddled together in a solid heap like animals. Joseph, along with the others who dealt with the dead, had to wait for the piles to thaw before separating them and revealing generations of sadness when they found the tiniest bodies entombed in the centre. The surviving inhabitants wandered around in dismay, discovering the awful demise of their friends and relatives. The bodies in the charnel house thawed before the graveyard soil and the tormented survivors were choked by the suffocating stench of death. Even after the dead were buried, which took several weeks the melancholy odour of decomposition persisted for months.

The sheep, unmoved by the sadness in the village, gave birth and the yard rapidly filled with bleating lambs that invaded the house. William's sons Edward and Charles married their sweethearts and moved out to start families of their own.

John persuaded William and Isabel to remain living with him, and use the better weather to complete repairs on their cottage before returning. In truth he did not want them to go. Despite missing his daughter, sharing his home with his family over the winter had been a happy time for him, reminding him of his early childhood, before untimely death had become a regular visitor.

The early summer was as hot as the winter had been cold. John and his nephews were kept busy shearing their rapidly increasing flock. Other shepherds had lost sheep to the cold on the marshes. As the summer progressed, John began to wonder when his daughter was coming home. He knew it may be several more months, as Aziz Shadi Rashad Salamar Ben al din had told him they were going to North Africa and Turkey, then he hoped to travel overland in Persia, before sailing home. He wondered how Lily was coping, he hoped and prayed that she was happy and well. He was thankful that she had missed the misery of that winter.

Chapter 5

Lily adapted well to life at sea. She had watched the shore of her homeland disappear and wondered if she would ever see her father again. She soon discovered that her long skirts were not the most suitable attire for living aboard ship, so she cut the bottoms off several pairs of Aziz Shadi Rashad Salamar Badr al din's baggy trousers and wore them. The crew found this immensely amusing. She mastered the skill of sleeping sounding in a hammock. By the time the terrible winter hit the village, Lily had arrived in North Africa. The first few days she remained on the ship whilst her husband arranged their trip inland. He had told her that she must cover her hair at all times when off the ship. He showed her how to tie up her hair and cover it with a large silk scarf, which tied at the back of her neck. He advised her to continue to wear his trousers under a djellaba, a long hooded coat worn by local people. Despite being covered from head to foot, with only her face showing, Lily was stared at from the moment she set foot on land. Aziz Shadi Rashad Salamar Badr al din kept her close beside him at all times. She had assumed that they would travel by horse, or on a wagon, and was seriously disconcerted she first encountered a herd of very large hairy creatures. They had immense necks and long bony legs and huge feet and they grunted constantly and spat with uncanny accuracy. Bright striped blankets covered their lumpy backs. It would have been of no use for Aziz Shadi Rashad Salamar Badr al din to tell her they would be travelling by camel. Lily had never heard of, or seen a camel. He was unable to stop laughing at the look on her face when she realised she would have to ride on one.

A man dressed all in white flowing robes and scarves on his head came forward with a camel and spoke to Aziz Shadi Rashad Salamar Badr al din who was still laughing. The man turned to the camel.

'Ssshhhh.' he said to it.

The camel blinked its eyes slowly. Lily had never seen such long eyelashes on any creature. It sighed dejectedly and then began a laborious process of sitting down on the sand, its maneuvers resulting in its long legs becoming neatly folded up underneath it. The man in white pointed to the camel and said something to Lily. She looked at her husband, who was unsuccessfully suppressing his amusement.

'Get on the camel Lily.' he said.

She hesitated, unsure of quite where to sit, wondering if it would bite and whether it dribbled like that all of the time. The camel surveyed her with cool distain. Eventually Aziz Shadi Rashad Salamar Badr al din managed to get her settled on the camel's back, showed her how to hold on and stood back. Lily suddenly realised that the beast would now have to get up again this time with her on it!

'Which end comes up first?' she shouted to

Aziz Shadi Rashad Salamar Badr al din in abject panic. He fell to his knees, entirely destroyed by laughter and was no help at all.

The man in white, shaking his head, stood in front of the camel and repeated.

'SShhhh.'

Lily, eyes wide with terror, held on as tightly as she could. After an initial shudder, the camel rose up a short distance at the back end, followed immediately by a colossal ascent at the front end and a final jolt from the back as the rear end caught up. Lily was thrown back and forth but miraculously remained aloft. Her husband took a long time to stop laughing. She took a long time to stop trembling. Due to her novice status as a camel rider, her camel was attached to her husbands mount with a length of rope and when she finally settled into the motion of it, she began to look around her. There were mountains in the distance, their tops covered in snow. Desert stretched on for miles, dotted with stunted trees and bushes. Sometimes there were clusters of palm trees. They rode on for hours with little change of scenery. Lily had never seen anything so vast, except the sea. The sun shone mercilessly throughout its journey across the vast sky. Their journey lasted several days. They stopped in the evening and the men built a fire and made strong sweet tea, Lily discovered why there were a few goats accompanying them, attached to the camels with a rope. They were dinner. At night when it grew cold, she slept beside the fire, curled up in the warm curve of her husband's body wondering who she had become.

On the fourth day they approached a town, surrounded by high terracotta walls, with turrets at regular intervals. They passed through a huge arched gate, decorated with elaborate patterns. The town inside was a surprise to Lily. There were tall buildings, houses, mosques with tall elegant minaret towers, trees, gardens of brilliant flowers and long pools of clear, sparkling water. They dismounted from their camels, which she still found disconcerting, outside of a large house and they entered through a tall arched gate. A number of men rushed out and greeted Aziz Shadi Rashad Salamar Badr al din with great warmth. He introduced Lily. The men bowed shyly.

'As-salaam alaikum.' they said.

'Wa-alaikum as-salam.' answered Lily, hoping she had remembered correctly.

The men escorted them inside and Lily was handed over to the females of the house, who fussed around her in great excitement and led her off to a large room with a deep pool of water. They chattered to her and waved their arms about and pointed, she eventually realised they meant she was to get into the pool of water to wash, which after four days on a camel was a very tempting idea. She was unused to taking her clothes off in front of others, but her husband had prepared her for this eventuality. The women helped her undress and led her to the bath. They washed her with soap that smelled exquisite and lathered her long hair. Then refreshments arrived, glasses of tea, fruit juices and plates of sweets and biscuits. After she had eaten, they helped her out of the water and doused her with bowls of clean warm water, rinsing her hair until it squeaked. They dried her with towels and gave her clean clothes. The outfit consisted of ivory silk baggy trousers, a long ivory silk tunic with silver and white embroidery around the neck and cuffs, and a long scarf to cover her hair.

The men ate their meal together, seated on the floor. Lily ate with the women in another room. She had no idea what she was eating, and no one to ask. She didn't see Aziz Shadi Rashad Salamar Badr al din until he joined her in a sumptuous room at bedtime. He was meeting his business suppliers the following day and had arranged for Lily to go to the souk, the market in the centre of town, with two of the women. He gave her money to buy anything she liked but advised her to let the local women barter the price for her.

Breakfast arrived on a tray in their room, spicy pancakes, fruit juice and tea. The sun streamed through the curtains as her husband dressed. He kissed her goodbye and left the room. Lily sat in bed and listened to the call for prayer, from a couple in nearby mosques and some far away. She thought about her father and wished he could see where she was now. The village seemed a lifetime away. Even Grandfather William's voice was difficult to hear. He said her father was well but the village was going through a difficult time. She became acutely aware of her vulnerability. If her husband failed to return, she would never get home again.

Khadija and her daughter Sameh arrived to take Lily to the souk and helped her to dress. The souk was in the centre of the town, lots of narrow alleys packed with clothing, pots and pans, pottery, jewellery, leather goods, spices and food. This permanent area surrounded a huge square, where nomadic tribes visited and set up their stalls. Lily saw long, brightly coloured snakes and little monkeys dressed in clothes. The crowd that began to follow them alarmed Khadija, trying to get a closer look at Lily's white face. She purchased a garment that covered Lily's head completely, with tiny embroidered holes so she could see out, but others could not see in. Her beautiful white face was covered, which enabled them to peruse the souk in relative peace. She bought long ivory coloured necklaces, carved from camel bones, or rather Khadija did. The process required sitting on the floor drinking green tea with the vendor and half an hour of enthusiastic haggling.

Aziz Shadi Rashad Salamar Badr al din returned late in the evening. He had bought a large consignment of high quality leather hides, destined for London. He had also bought Lily a present, and exquisite pale cream leather bag from a Bedouin tribesman. The entire surface was decorated with an embossed pattern of flowing shapes and it had a long strap to go over her shoulder.

The following day the bales of leather hides were tied to the camels and they set off back to the coast. The journey was arduous and Lily quickly mastered the art of falling asleep to the rhythmic rocking of her camel without falling off. Boarding the ship was almost like getting home, Lily discarded her travelling clothes and put on the old pair of her husbands trousers and a shirt, uncovered and plaited her long hair and went on deck to watch the loading. Dozens of men scurried like ants, with huge bundles of leather hides on their shoulders, up the long steep gangplank and deposited them of the deck. The crew passed them down into the hold and tied them in place.

They set sail in an easterly direction heading for Turkey. The weather was warm and the sea calm. The shipped sailed within sight of the shoreline and Lily spent the day on deck, watching the changing coastline pass slowly by and listening to the soft flapping of the sails.

Chapter 6

It was a sad summer that year in the village. Each day brought news from the surrounding villages, reporting the deaths of more relatives and friends. Isabel's sister, her husband and their four children had perished, frozen in their bed. Joseph arrived home at night, exhausted and downcast from so much death. Many of the surviving families were struggling to cope with the loss of livestock. John, with his healthy flock of sheep, the value of which had doubled, and his own family's survival, felt very fortunate. He was aware that the extraordinary generosity of Aziz Shadi Rashad Salamar Badr al din had enabled the family to survive and prosper. He remembered the day Lily was born, such a tiny, fragile scrap of life. Yet she had changed the fate of his family.

John and Elijah developed a close bond. He would frequently leave the sheep with his nephews and ride out on Elijah as his daughter had done in the past. Elijah was grateful and listened intently to John, who found it easier to talk of important matters to a horse rather than another person. John convinced himself that Elijah knew how his daughter and her husband were faring on their journey, so all the time Elijah was in good spirits, he was happy. He was able to sell the fleeces for a high price and used some of the money to replenish the stocks of flour used during the winter, kept enough for his needs and distributed the rest to the hardest hit families in the village. He also gave half a dozen lambs to each of the shepherds who had lost their flocks. He gave Edward some money as he and his new wife Mary were expecting their first child in a few months. To his other married nephew Charles, he gave half of the flock of sheep. Ernest was planning to marry in the autumn and John persuaded his brother William to let him have the old cottage for him and his wife, ensuring that William and Isabel and their four unmarried sons would spend another winter with him. With Lily away, Isabel had become the heart of the home, filling it with laughter and good food.

Next to his rides on Elijah, John's favourite times of the day were meals. The whole family sat around the large table, Isabel would clatter in with dishes of steaming food and hand out the warm plates. The family would talk of old times, plans for the future and exchange news from their day. They always finished the meal with tea, as Aziz Shadi Rashad Salamar Badr al din had done. Then even managed to briefly lift the spirits of the disconsolate Joseph, brought down by the absence of Lily and the constant pestilential vapour of death.

Towards the end of summer, John and his nephews, driven by the fear of another harsh winter, felled two large trees. They dismembered them and transported them home. After replenishing their own woodpile, John, with the assistance of Elijah, delivered sacks of wood to the old people so they could keep warm without resorting to burning their furniture.

In the autumn Edward and Mary moved into one of the downstairs rooms in the house, as she was approaching the birth of their child. Their cottage was outside of the village. The close proximity of Isabel, well practiced in childbirth, and Mary's mother who lived nearby, was deemed a sensible precaution. Mary was a plump, cheerful young woman, with an unruly mass of chestnut curls, and bright blue eyes not unlike her mother-in-law, and they got on well. Despite being heavily pregnant, Mary insisted in helping Isabel with the chores. The kitchen turned into a haven for sudden bouts of uproarious laughter. John wondered what the two women could possibly find to laugh about quite so much. Mary laughed at just about anything and Isabel could not help joining in. Sometimes they themselves did not know why they were laughing.

Being a stoic individual, Mary failed to tell anyone when her pains began. She continued with her usual chores and as the pains increased, she just leant against something sturdy until they passed. When Isabel became alerted by the absence of her daughters-in-law's chattering, she went into the yard to look for her and found her stuck fast in the chicken coup, paralysed by a particularly strong pain. She summoned a neighbour and they managed to extricate her form the chicken coop, watched closely by the startled chickens that clucked in morose unison. Mary refused to take to her bed and sat in a low chair in the kitchen and began peeling the vegetables for the meal.

Isabel watched her from the corner of her eye and silently admired the young woman's strength. During a pain, Mary merely bowed her head and held onto the chair arms, her knuckles white. Isabel could hear her heavy breathing. It was the only sound she made. Then she resumed her peeling. The men of the house began arriving from their work, washed and took their places around the table. Isabel quietly told them that it was Mary's time, but to behave normally, the child would probably be born sometime that night. She instructed Edward to send word to Mary's mother after the meal. The men took the news in several different ways. Edward fidgeted in panic, his brothers grinned with excitement and John waited for the hideous, distressing screaming to begin. Isabel served the food and explained that she would eat in the kitchen to be with Mary. No one, not even Mary, was prepared for the next few moments. As Isabel returned to the kitchen, Mary had flooded the floor with her waters and was on all fours in front of the fire. Isabel slammed the kitchen door and ran across the room just in time to catch her first granddaughter before she landed on the rug amongst the bemused sheepdogs. The big, pink, healthy child yelled instantly, causing a stampede of men from the dining room. Isabel shooed them back, cut the cord, rolled the child in a clean towel and passed her to her joyful father.

Isabel helped Mary back to the low chair and covered her with a blanket. Mary was smiling and all she wanted was a cup of sweet tea. Tea served, Isabel went to get the bucket and mop. When she returned, Mary was drinking her tea, happily watching the dogs devour the afterbirth. Horrified, Isabel averted her eyes and busied herself with mopping up the flood that had collected at the other end of the kitchen. Edward was sent off to fetch Mary's mother and the baby was passed to John. He sat beside the fire pondering, aghast at the unimaginably wide variety that is womenfolk.

By the time Edward returned with Mary's thrilled mother, Isabel had finally managed to get the imperturbable, smiling Mary to bed in a clean nightdress and she was sitting up proudly feeding her daughter, her blue eyes shining. They called her Ellen Lily, after Edward's grandmother and his absent cousin. The joy in the house was infectious and even Joseph found himself smiling. Isabel had a good cry that night, but it was a happy cry. William, unsure how to respond, patted her on the head, which made her laugh. This inadvertently convinced him he had done the right thing and he pottered off happily to have a smoke on the veranda and watch the stars with his brother.

Chapter 7

By the time Ellen Lily was born, Lily had
briefly visited Italy, Crete and a Greek island for
fresh supplies, sailed through the Sea of
Marmara and arrived in Turkey. In
Constantinople Aziz Shadi Rashad Salamar Badr
al din took Lily to visit the hamam, a bathhouse
built by the sultan for the use of his people. Lily
went in one side of the baths, her husband in
another. She was ushered into a small room,
given a towel and wooden soled shoes. She
undressed, wrapped herself in the towel and
emerged. She was then taken to a huge domed
room, made entirely of the palest grey marble.
The room was circular, hot and steamy. Around
the edges were marble benches to sit on and
marble sinks shaped like shells. Taps constantly
filled the sinks with hot water and there was a
bowl with which she could douse herself with
the hot water. In the centre of the room, directly
below the huge dome, built of marble and glass,
was a round marble plinth about twenty feet in
diameter.

After almost an hour of dousing, Lily was
invited to lie down on the marble plinth, which
was surprisingly warm. She was given a small
leather cushion to put under her head. Lily lay
looking up into the vast marble and glass dome
directly above her head, she felt completely
relaxed until a sudden unexpected drip of

condensation landed directly in her eye. The female attendant then put on a white mitten, made of some sort of linen or cotton and began to firmly stroke Lily's body, starting on her stomach. Lily was astonished to see the layers of grey dead skin peeling off. The attendant stroked and scrubbed every area of her body until the skin coming off was pure white. Then she covered Lily with bubbles and massaged every inch of her until she felt as if she was almost flat. Then the attendant rinsed her thoroughly with numerous bowls of hot, steaming water. Lily was then sat on the floor, grasped firmly between the knees of the attendant, who began dousing her head. She then washed her hair vigorously, kneading her scalp with her strong fingers, doused again and added a slippery substance that she carefully combed through her hair, removing every tangle. Then more rinsing and Lily was reduced to feeling like a two year old child. She was finally rolled in a number of hot towels and left to recover. By the time she got dressed and found the tearoom, her husband was waiting for her. She had never felt so clean in her entire life.

During the following couple of days, Aziz Shadi Rashad Salamar Badr al din took Lily to see Hagia Sophia, as he believed it to be the most beautiful mosque in the world. Hagia Sophia had originally been built by Christians, which accounted for the incredible mosaics depicting the Virgin Mary and Jesus. After the Islamisation of Turkey, it became a mosque. Lily had never seen anything so large. The massive dome was so heavy, the sides of the building had to have extra ramparts to support it. Many of the mosaics had backgrounds of pure gold that remained as bright as in the days when they were constructed. They visited the blue mosque, named due to the entire internal surfaces being covered with blue and white tiles in a variety of designs. She saw the Sultan's palace, which was the size of a village. At the markets Lily saw the same type of lanterns that her husband had given her and discovered a delightful delicacy known as Turkish Delight.

At night they returned to the ship. This was the only place that Aziz Shadi Rashad Salamar Badr al din felt safe. Although he insisted that Lily be well covered whenever they went out, he soon become aware that she had been noticed, due to her visit to the hamam. People were talking about the young woman with skin as white as the clouds, hair like coiled silk and eyes the colour of amethyst jewels. He feared that news of her beauty would reach the Sultan, who may insist on buying her for his harem. He could not take her with him whilst doing business and it would be improper to leave her alone on board with an all male crew. For the first time, he regretted bringing her and putting her at such risk. Aziz Shadi Rashad Salamar Badr al din made the decision to leave and sail northeast, through the Bosphorus and into the Black Sea port of Batumi in Georgia, then travel overland to Persia, his homeland.

Lily sat on deck as they sailed through the

narrow stretch of water dividing the east and west of Turkey oblivious as to why they had left so suddenly. The ship hugged the coast of the northeast of Turkey and headed for Batumi. In Batumi, Aziz Shadi Rashad Salamar Badr al din hired a large number horses and riders to begin the journey to Persia. Lily knew that her husband's parents were dead, and that he had many other relatives in Persia. Many of them were merchants, travelling the Silk Road, bringing silks and porcelain from China. Aziz Shadi Rashad Salamar Badr al din was the only one that sailed the sea, vastly increasing the markets they could reach. Lily was delighted that she would meet his family soon. The climate was cooler, much more like her home and she was grateful for the layers of clothing that her husband had provided. He had sent riders ahead into Persia to herald his arrival. Their own journey would be slower and expected to take months. Lily was relieved that she was given a horse rather than a camel. The countryside was mountainous, with green fertile valleys, reminding her of home. As they journeyed south, into Persia the mountains were bigger and the area less populated. They rode through vast forests that took weeks to traverse. The temperature gradually began to rise when they reached a huge plateau that stretched as far as the eye could see, and after a few more weeks they were in desert and it was time to change the horses for camels. Aziz Shadi Rashad Salamar Badr al din's family lived in several large houses on the edge of a small town. The welcome they received was lavish and chaotic. Lily lost count of his cousins and uncles and was relieved to be shown her room, where she slept for hours. To her great relief this was to be their base for many weeks, enough time to rebuild her energy for the return journey. The family had erected large tents to house the crates of porcelain, tea and parcels of silk that had arrived from China and bags of spices from India along the Silk Road. More crates and parcels arrived on almost a daily basis. Aziz Shadi Rashad Salamar and his family hired drivers and animals that left every week on the long journey back to the ship. The family was very kind to Lily and she had mastered enough of the language to communicate a little, but for the first time since she left her home she was dreadfully homesick.

Chapter 8

Little Ellen Lily thrived well and after a few weeks, Edward and Mary returned to their cottage, promising John they would return if the winter proved to be harsh. The house was very quiet after they left. Isabel missed the laughter and companionship of another woman. John missed little Ellen Lily, who had just begun to smile at him. Even the dogs sunk into a miserable lethargy. Then Edward arrived one evening, asking it they could return for a while as Mary missed everyone so much. Their return lifted everyone's spirits, Mary resumed her place in the kitchen with Isabel, Ellen Lily slung across her back in a shawl. Each day she would trot along the dirt track to Charles and Ivy's home as Ivy was now with child. Ivy was a quiet, unassuming young woman. She had been the overlooked, uncomplaining little girl amongst a number of noisy brothers. She had quietly idolised her father, who never noticed her. She grew into a frail young woman with few expectations and dreams, expecting no more from anyone than she had received from her father. Mary initially startled Ivy, unfamiliar with her boisterous, unrestrained affection. Her warm impromptu hugs, the first Ivy had ever experienced, brought tears to her eyes. Mary was unaware of her discomfort, and eventually Ivy's inhibitions were soundly breached and she was able to hug her back. Mary was the only friend that Ivy had ever had.

Mary prized Ivy out of her little cottage, and out of her solitary existence, introducing her to her husband's family and John. Isabel and Mary fussed around her during the last few weeks of her pregnancy and insisted that the baby should be born in the big warm house. Her confinement was unlike Mary's. It was slow to start, long and utterly exhausting. Poor little Ivy lay in bed, as white as the sheets, bathed in cold sweat and visibly began to shrink. Mary stayed with her throughout, soothing and encouraging her. By the time her little son was delivered, Ivy fell into a deep sleep and Isabel feared for her life. The indomitable Mary took charge of the situation. She breast fed the child and remained in the same room as Ivy for over a week. Isabel made nourishing soup that they managed to get her to take during her brief spells of consciousness. As the days passed, Ivy gradually regained some strength and Mary carried her to the kitchen and sat her beside the fire, believing this would do her good. Within a month, Ivy was much stronger and able to feed her son that Charles had named William John, but was always known as Jack, when he first saw him.

The winter was a mild one, with only a light dusting of snow. The sheep stayed out in the fields. Christmas was a happy time, with good food, laughter and two new lives to celebrate. It was the second Christmas with no Lily and John missed her desperately.

Ellen Lily proved a great comfort. She was crawling by Christmas and loved her great-uncle John with a passion, clambering onto his lap at every opportunity. Mary was a relaxed generous mother, undaunted when John began to leave the house for hours, with Ellen Lily perched on this shoulder.

Joseph continued to bury the dead. It was not unusual event to bury a baby within a few days of its Christening, often followed by the mother. He buried a dozen or so bodies most months, over half of whom were under a year old. Many died of sheer poverty and desolation. The numerous corpses of the itinerant workers were listed as 'Irishman, unknown' and 'Female pauper and bastard child', in the Church records. He would trudge home from work in the evenings, weighed down by sadness, acutely aware of the amount of pain and grief life frequently provided. The pointlessness overpowered him and he doubted the existence of God. As he stepped into the kitchen his world was transformed. There was his mother and sister-in-law laughing and singing whilst preparing the meal, undaunted by life. It seemed to him that Mary possessed the ability to ward off death and misery with the same ease that she evicted unwelcome insects, completely unaware that her happy disposition and boundless energy protected the entire family from depression.

Chapter 9

The bulk of the crates and packages had left Aziz Shadi Rashad Salamar Badr al din's family home and were on route to the ship. Arrangements were made for him and Lily to follow. He had sensed that she needed to go home, although she had not complained. The farewell celebrations were lavish and the family presented her with a purple outfit embroidered with pure gold thread. As she was about to leave she allowed herself to think about home. She wondered how her poor father had coped alone in the big house, whether he was well, whether he was still alive. She felt so very far away and knew it would take many months to reach him, but each step was a step closer.

Aziz Shadi Rashad Salamar Badr al din was relieved to see the brightness returning to his wife's eyes during the journey. She began to talk about her father again and was happy to ride all day, only stopping when it was too dark to see. Lily measured their journey by the changes in the terrain, desert, plateau, mountains, and valleys. By the time they arrived at the ship she knew she was with child.

The crew, who had loaded the ship with the crates and packages, that had arrived over the preceding weeks gave them a warm welcome and set about preparing the ship for sailing the following day. Lily was ecstatic, by the time they would arrive in England she would have been away for almost two years. She had learned to read and write, thanks to her husband, and could even hold a limited conversation in his native tongue.

Lily spent much of her time, wrapped up warmly in a hammock on the deck, watching the crew tend to the sails. It was a relief to do nothing for a while. It would be spring in the village and if all went well they would arrive home in summer. She did not tell her husband about the baby as he had enough to think about. She had no idea when it had been conceived, whether it was at his home or on the journey. She just hoped she would be home before it arrived, there being no women on the ship to help her. The weather grew warmer by the day and apart from brief stops to replenish the fresh water and food, they made steady progress. Aziz Shadi Rashad Salamar Badr al din noticed his wife's condition without being told. She was sitting in her hammock on deck during a warm evening. He approached her and placed his hands on her belly and smiled into her eyes. There was no need for words. From then on the ship made the most of any breath of wind, but it was early summer and they were often becalmed for days at a time. Lily remained calm and serene but was aware of her husband constantly watching the sky. After several weeks of peaceful sailing close to North Africa, they rounded the bottom of the Iberian peninsular and sailed into the Atlantic. The weather changed and the sea became rougher, the sky darkened and Aziz Shadi Rashad Salamar Badr al din, knowing a storm was approaching, insisted that Lily get below in a hammock. He bound her in with blankets, explaining that it was the safest place and returned to deck with the crew. She could hear the thunder and the ship pitched and lurched and her hammock swung violently. The cook Mustapha struggled in with a drink of hot tea and stayed with her, trying to mimimise the violent swinging of the hammock. Lily was more concerned about her husband being swept over the side of the ship. Mustapha, the resourceful cook, capable of a meal in any conditions, assured her that the men on deck would all be secured by a sturdy rope around their waists and would be hauled back on deck should they go over. The storm raged for hours. Despite the noise and the savage swinging, Lily fell asleep. When she awoke, Mustapha had gone and her husband was lying, wet and bedraggled, fast asleep in his hammock. The ship had stopped pitching and was rocking gently. Lily disengaged herself from her hammock and went off in search of tea. She found the galley in a mess, pots and pans had fallen and Mustapha was fast asleep at a table. She helped herself to tea, from a pot that was still warm and climbed up onto deck. A few crew members were tidying up the chaos left by the storm, they looked exhausted. She carried the big warm pot of tea up onto deck, found some cups and served tea for the crew. That was how Aziz Shadi Rashad Salamar Badr al din found her when he awoke, sitting cross-legged on the deck, heavy with his child, serving tea to the tired men. He loved her then, more than he thought was possible.

They had been blown off course and all land was out of sight. That night, by the stars, the crew navigated their way back and headed for the coast of England. In that last couple of weeks, Lily could not contain her mounting excitement, she was unable to keep still. Aziz Shadi Rashad Salamar Badr al din gave up trying to make her rest.

Chapter 10

John, desperate for the return of his daughter, had taken to riding Elijah along the sea wall every day, often with Ellen Lily. The three of them would stand and scan the horizon, hoping for the appearance of the ship.

One morning, at the height of summer Elijah woke the household, kicking the sides of the stable and neighing loudly. John was unable to subdue him. He remembered the time when Elijah had ran off to find Aziz Shadi Rashad Salmar Badr al din and dared not allow himself to hope that the ship was arriving. He saddled the excited horse and the moment he mounted Elijah was off, not towards the dock, but headed for the shoreline, where they had been watching for weeks. John was aghast to see the masts of a ship, rounding the bend in the estuary. Elijah was stamping and whinnying, John strained to see as the ship approached, afraid to believe it was the return of his daughter, praying that she had survived. As the ship drew level with him a bright purple flag unfurled at the top of the mast and he knew she was well. Elijah trotted along, keeping pace with the ship, trembling with excitement. John just cried.

Lily had seen Elijah and her father from the ship and was beside herself, running to and fro the length of the deck waving wildly. Her husband, fearing she would do herself an injury, held her fast against the side of the ship until they had docked and the gangplank was tied in position, then he let her go. He gave father and daughter time alone whilst the ship was being tied up. It was John who came aboard, leaving Lily hugging Elijah, and hugged Aziz Shadi Rashad Salamar Badr al din. Neither of them spoke, both of them knew what the other was feeling. Tea was served on deck and when everyone had calmed down enough to speak, John felt he should warn them, and apologise for the house being full of relatives, and explain that arrangements would be made to move them out directly. Aziz Shadi Rashad Salamar Badr al din disagreed, believing that a home was vastly improved by being crammed with loved ones and he could not wait to meet them again.

John and Lily were sent home by horse and cart, crammed full of provisions from the ship and Elijah waited for his master who would follow them later. The men were all at work and Lily entered the kitchen surprising her Aunt Isabel, who stared at her as if she were an apparition. Mary realised who she was and put the kettle on to boil for tea, shoved the silent Isabel into a chair and with a huge smile, pulled up a chair for Lily. Little Ellen Lily wandered in from the yard. She was the image of her mother, with a mop of chestnut curls and bright blue eyes. Like her mother, she was undaunted by a stranger and climbed onto Lily's lap for a better view of her. Mary, taking charge as usual, sent the grinning John up the lane with orders to return with Ivy and Jack. When John returned, the women had moved to the big table and Ivy took Jack in to meet them. John stood at the kitchen door watching the four women and their children, his own daughter soon to have his first grandchild. He believed he was the most fortunate man alive and went into the yard, perched himself on the edge of the chicken coop and wanted for nothing more. Mary took him a mug of tea, kissed him on the cheek and returned indoors. Then she gave a penny to a neighbour's lad to run and tell Jane that she and Ernest were expected for dinner.

After an hour of tea drinking and chattering, Isabel, Mary and Ivy set about producing an evening meal. Lily refused to go to bed and rest and sat in the kitchen watching them bustling about. It was necessary to find a plank of wood to put across the chairs to enable everyone to sit at the big table. Joseph was overcome with emotion when he arrived home to discover Lily in the kitchen. Aziz Shadi Rashad Salamar Badr al din arrived in time for the meal, Elijah laden with packages. He was visibly moved to discover that his place at the head of the table had been reserved for him for almost two years.

As the evening progressed, Lily went to bed, exhausted by excitement. Charles and Ernest took their wives home, Isabel and Mary attacked the chaos in the kitchen and the seven men sat on the sofas and caught up with each other's news. When Aziz Shadi Rashad Salamar Badr al din finally went to bed, Lily was asleep under the blue quilt of stars with a smile on her face.

.

Chapter 11

Lily had no idea when her child was due. Isabel and Mary investigated her belly and asked a lot of questions. They told her she had a few more weeks, but in truth they were undecided. John fussed around his daughter, plagued by the harrowing memories of her own birth. Mary sensed his helpless agony.

Aziz Shadi Rashad Salamar Badr al din was kept busy, travelling to and from London delivering goods. Mustapha the cook joined Isabel and Mary in the kitchen, passing on his vast knowledge in the use of the numerous spices that had been delivered, now arranged in jars on the kitchen shelves. They produced dishes of incredibly tasty tender lamb that was gently cooked for so long Isabel was convinced it would be ruined. He taught them to make sauces that burned the tongue and made eyes water, but were delicious with chicken. He made sweet puddings full of strange fruits and nuts, with such an exquisite flavour that they almost caused a riot at the dinner table. Isabel and Mary were initially bewildered by the presence of a man in their kitchen, but he soon became essential and Mary insisted he moved in until she and Isabel had completely mastered his remarkable skills. Mustapha, a slight man of uncertain age, his head invariably swathed in twisted white scarves, with a long black beard speckled with grey, surprised everyone by falling incurably in love with the dark eyed widow next door whilst visiting the chicken coop. He began making little parcels of delicacies and leaving them on her doorstep in an attempt to gain her attention. Distracted, he watched her house, praying for a glimpse of her in the garden. Mary, frustrated by his pathetic hesitancy, marched him next door and introduced him to the widow Munn, and to his abject, cringing embarrassment, announced his feelings for her. The widow Munn blushed profusely, and to Mary's profound satisfaction and Mustapha's gleeful astonishment, she agreed for him to call on her whenever he was free. He sang tunelessly all afternoon, banished the women from the kitchen and proudly presented the family with an exquisite meal.

Lily's child showed no sign of being born. She was fit and well and regularly walked the countryside collecting herbs, having been forbidden by her husband from riding Elijah at present. Mary joined Lily on the walks, pretending she wanted to learn about the plants she collected, in truth she felt the birth would be soon, due to the now alarming size of Lily's belly that was beginning to impede her usual walking speed.

It was on a sunny, crisp day in early autumn on the marshes when Lily confided in Mary that her back was aching. They turned towards home and Lily plodded slowly, leaning on Mary's arm. Their progress was slow, Mary could see the pain on Lily's face and ignoring her protests, picked her up like a baby and carried her for the final half mile to the house. She sat Lily beside the fire in the armchair and made some tea. Apart from her back aching, Lily had no other pains, but Mary knew her time had come. So did Isabel, who, from personal experience knew that severe backache often heralded the beginning of labour. The intuitive Mustapha refused to leave the kitchen and busied himself crushing seeds in a mortar, adding drips from a range of tiny glass bottles, stewing and straining the concoction, which he administered to Lily. It made her laugh, brought her Grandfather back to life, destroyed her sense of balance and obliterated the pains in her back. During their sea voyage, Mustapha had developed great respect and deep affection for Lily. He was not going to leave her now, despite the women's vehement protests that childbirth was women's business. He insisted on tying a rope around a beam directly above Lily, explaining to the startled women that it would help her in the last stage of her labour. Aziz Shadi Rashad Salamar Badr al din, accustomed to the extraordinary skills of Mustapha, gladly placed his unmitigated trust in him. John's uncontrollable panic was subdued by a timely dose of one of Mustapha's concoction. Unlike Lily, John did not laugh and see dead relatives, but fell into a deep, peaceful sleep on a sofa, much to everyone's relief.

Lily's waters flooded the kitchen following a second dose of Mustapha's mixture at midnight. When she became agitated and restless, he explained to Mary and Isabel that it was time for her to pull on the rope he had hung up and this would help her to deliver her child. Isabel was dubious, but Mary, having recently given birth in the kitchen was in agreement. Mustapha showed Lily how to pull on the rope and exert pressure to expel the child. He warned her that a first child would be slow to emerge and required significant effort. He then made up another preparation for Lily that would give her strength and endurance. Mary and Isabel began to wish they had had Mustapha at their own deliveries, even if he was a man. The baby's head emerged at a little after I o'clock, a mass of black curly hair, rapidly followed by the rest of him. Isabel wrapped him in a towel to pass him to his mother. Lily was reluctant to sit down and continued to cling to the rope and pull. It was Mustapha who first realised that there was another child on its way. Eight minutes later an identical child arrived. By then Mustapha had tied a string around the first one's little wrist, to ensure that they were not mixed up in the excitement. Lily sat down then and Mary tended to her needs, finally shoving Mustapha out of the kitchen with Isabel and the babies to meet their father.

Aziz Shadi Rashad Salamar Badr al din was astonished to have become a father of two sons instead of one. He shook John until he woke him, to show him his wonderful grandsons. Then Aziz Shadi Rashad Salamar Badr al din and Mustapha took the babies out into the yard, and under the stars they held them aloft, shouting to the heavens. The rest of the family watched, astonished. Mary cleaned Lily up and carried her from the kitchen and placed her on a sofa. John, who feared he was dreaming, carried the wooden crib secretly made by the ship's carpenters and furnished with blankets made by Isabel. Both babies fitted in, but they would need to make another. Aziz Shadi Rashad Salamar Badr al din sat on the floor beside his wife. John stared at the babies in the crib. Isabel and Mary made tea and Mustapha, the hero, stood at the kitchen door, thinking about the widow Munn.

Chapter 12

The firstborn was named Sameer Mustapha John, known as Sam. His brother was named Salamar Muhsin Amir, and known as Sal. The two little boys had dark curly hair and their eyes were dark brown, although in bright sunshine there was a hint of violet. By Christmas they were smiling and inseparable. The carpenters made another crib, but the babies refused to settle alone in a crib and continued to sleep in the same one. Christmas was a very happy one, with lavish food provided by Aziz Shadi Rashad Salamar Badr al din. Mustapha, Isabel and Mary cooked the meals. The widow Munn enjoyed her best ever Christmas, having spent many years alone.

The farmer that William had worked for since he was a boy died suddenly, leaving a childless widow. She sold the entire farm to Aziz Shadi Rashad Salamar Badr al din out of spite and a desire for vengeance, as she was aware that the wealthy landowner, with whom there was much rancour, had been waiting for the opportunity to enlarge his farm for many years. Aziz Shadi Rashad Salamar Badr al din knew nothing about farming. He installed Henry and his new wife Sarah in the farmhouse and handed the running of the farm over to John's brother William. He instructed William to restock the farm with chickens, cows, horses and sheep, but no pigs. He put his carpenters at William's disposal, with instructions to repair or replace the neglected buildings. Young William left the farm he worked on, moved in with Henry and Sarah and took control of the horses. Edward and Henry began planting the fields.

The villagers were perturbed, it was one thing having a foreigner marry a village girl, but it was unprecedented for a foreigner to own village land. Their consternation increased when Mustapha married the widow Munn, moved into her cottage and transformed her garden. He grew exotic plants and flowers of intense, vivid purples and pinks, which he used in his increasingly popular concoctions. He became known as Mustapha the Magician. He was treated with insatiable suspicion by the vicar, but welcomed with desperate enthusiasm by expectant mothers. Mustapha never charged for his remedies, believing them to be a gift from God, and therefore priceless.

The new farm prospered in the first summer and William and Isabel moved in at harvest time. Edward suggested he and Mary move as well, but Mary was adamant she was not leaving Lily and Mustapha. John was relieved, as he loved Mary almost as much as he loved his own daughter and he did not want to be separated from Ellen Lily.

Life in the village was good for the next few years and even Joseph's business was slow with very few deaths. He took on the task of teaching the children to read and write, a skill he had acquired from the elderly Harold who filled in the church record books. Ellen Lily was the brightest child and learned quickly. Jack, a quiet little boy, plodded methodically and the twins spoke a strange language that only they understood and were far more interested in chasing chickens and tormenting the dogs. Ida, formally the widow Munn, astounded everyone, including herself by producing her first child at the age of thirty-nine. Mustapha was thunderstruck, having attributed her tiredness and slight weight gain to her change of life. Mary took charge of the birth, administering the concoctions. Mustapha was reduced to uselessness by the shock of finally becoming a father. He named his precious little daughter Maria. Aziz Shadi Rashad Salamar Badr al din threw a huge party for Mustapha and his unexpected family.

In the same few years, Aziz Shadi Rashad Salamar Badr al din extended his stake in the village, buying land whenever it became available, as an insurance against poverty for his family. He had not wanted to be away from his little sons in the first few years and had limited his voyages. He was due for a longer visit to Turkey and wanted to ensure his family was well provided for in case of his failure to return. During those years he had gained the grudging respect of the other landowners. He had proved to be a fair man, honest in his dealings with others and respectful to all.

Aziz Shadi Rashad Salamar Badr al din set

sail when his boys were approaching their fifth year. Lily bid him a tearful goodbye, unaware that she was bearing another child. Mustapha refused to sail with him, unwilling to leave Maria and Ida. He had foreseen this eventuality and had taught the younger ship's cook the secrets of his concoctions and furnished him with a tin of supplies.

The autumn was wet, great sheets of rain blew in from the estuary, soaking everything. Fungi started to grow in the most extraordinary places. Mould attacked fabrics and discoloured the walls. Mustapha became distraught and worried at John and his nephews until they finally agreed to move their sheep from the marshes to higher fields on the farm. He insisted that the dairy herd be put in the new barn months earlier than usual. Everyone wondered if he was losing his mind, but due to the reputation of his wisdom and foresight, dared not ignore him. The rain continued relentlessly and the wind from the northeast steadily increased to gale force. The following day the flood came. The water in the estuary, swelled by the high tide, that was forced higher than usual by the unremitting wind blowing up river, burst over the sea wall in great surges of swirling water and drowned the marshes and any unfortunate animals in its path. The jetties were smashed and the vessels blown onto rocks. The water level in the river continued to rise and the floods reached as far as London.

Cottages on the marshes were swamped and any inhabitants that had ignored Mustapha's ravings were drowned. During the following weeks bloated bodies, swollen by immersion in the water, were delivered to Joseph. Some of them disintegrated as they were lifted into coffins. The stagnant reek of death once again enveloped the village.

Mary and Lily kept the fires burning to deter the mould. They tied a gate at the kitchen door in an attempt to limit the mud to the kitchen floor. They banned the children from going out into the boggy yard and moved the beleaguered chickens from their rotting coup into the stable with Elijah.

The marshes continued to flood at high tide even after the water level fell, due to the damage to the sea wall. Repairs were impossible until the ground was hard enough to support a horse and cart. Everyone welcomed the first frosts of the winter that year, as it made getting about less hazardous. The mud finally froze solid enabling horses and carts to travel about again without sinking. When the winter snow melted in early spring the whole village became a quagmire. The animals that had survived the flood developed a stinking foot rot, which caused the death of many. Only John's sheep had survived unscathed, most shepherds had lost a significant amount of their flocks. The cattle had suffered the worst consequences. The ones that had survived the flood had become firmly stuck in the mud and died slowly of starvation. The farm that William and his sons lived on thrived well, their dairy herd all survived and produced a record amount of calves in the spring.

William senior became ill in early spring. His decline was sudden. John, who had not seen him for a matter of weeks, was horrified by the change in his appearance. William was tortured with an unrelenting agonising pain in his belly and an insatiable thirst. Mustapha was summoned and knew immediately that he was dying. His eyes were dull and sunken, and they pleaded silently for an end to the pain. Mustapha's drinks gave him several days in which he slipped in and out of a painless consciousness, surrounded by his family. He died in his sleep beside Isabel. William was buried beside his parents on a warm spring day. Isabel moved back to be with Mary and Lily, who was close to giving birth.

Rose was born on a stormy night in early June, with the help of Mustapha, his concoctions and his rope. The event lifted the mood of everyone. Rose was the name that William had chosen.

Chapter 13

A stranger, a man in his thirty's, arrived in the village in July and began making enquiries about the Martin family. He was directed to John's house. He arrived when the men were out working, Mary saw him approaching when she was in the yard hanging washing on the line. His clothing was good quality, but he was unshaven and filthy and she initially thought him to be a tramp begging for food. He threw down his bag, ignoring Mary and knocked on the door. Ellen Lily opened the door.

'I wish to see John Martin.'

Ellen Lily looked at her mother. Mary approached and asked his business with John. The stranger looked her up and down with a supercilious smile on his thin lips.

'My business is with John Martin, not with you!' He replied arrogantly.

'Mr Martin is not here at present, come back this evening.' She pushed past him with the washing basket and slammed the door in his face.

She assumed the stranger had left, but the children found him asleep in the yard, his head resting on his bag. He was still there when John returned. Mary explained that a rude man was waiting to see him and John woke him with the toe of his boot.

'How dare you!' Exclaimed the stranger.

'I most certainly do dare, this is my property, and you are uninvited!'

'You are, I believe, an Uncle on my mother's side of the family, my name is Jacob Wesley.' He announced, as if expecting a round of applause.

'So, what is your business with me?'

The stranger hesitated, unsure of what to say, he had expected a warmer welcome.

'Well, I. erm, my parents are both dead now, I, er thought you may wish to know.'

'My sister left here over thirty years ago, she never contacted her family again, of what interest is it to me?'

'I have travelled a considerable distance to inform you of this!'

'No one asked you to!'

'Well, er, my mother often spoke of her family fondly, and I thought I should like to meet with them.'

Curiosity got the better of John and he invited Jacob into the kitchen for refreshments. Jacob's eyes widened, the house was not what he had expected. His mother had said that John was a shepherd. The opulence of the furnishings in this large house denoted an unusually wealthy shepherd. John introduced him to Isabel, Mary and Lily. When he saw Lily, he wished he had visited long ago. She resembled his mother, but was even more beautiful. His disappointment was obvious, when she introduced her three children and explained that her husband was currently at sea. He explained to John that his father had recently died, that his two younger sisters were married and that he was the sole heir of the family estate. He added that he would quite like to remain in the village for a week or so. John recommended the Inn beside the church a suitable place for a gentleman to stay. Jacob became uncomfortable and was forced to explain that as yet his inheritance money was still in the hands of his lawyers.

'You'll be looking for work then, to tide you over?' asked John.

Jacob had never worked a day in his life and had no intention of doing so if he could avoid it.

'Unfortunately.' He sneered. 'I know little about farming.'

'No matter,' answered John, 'mucking out cows is soon learned!'

John walked to the new farm with Jacob and introduced him to William, Henry and Sarah, explaining that he would work for his keep until his 'fortune' materialized. John had no intention of allowing him to stay anywhere near Lily when Aziz Shadi Rashad Salamar Badr al din was away.

Jacob succeeded in blinding William and Henry with extravagant lies about his vast estate in the Midlands, where one could walk all day and never reach the boundary. He promised to repay them handsomely in the future if they put at his disposal a decent horse so that he could explore the area. He visited the larger farms and introduced himself as Jacob Wesley, heir to the Wesley estate, and nephew of John Martin. He was made welcome at several farms, particularly the ones with marriageable daughters and no suitors.

John received news of his exploits and decided to give him enough rope to hang himself. He had his doubts about the 'fortune'. He was right. Jacob's father had inherited a healthy estate and a great deal of money, but he was a gambler and a womanizer, with an appetite for alcohol. He became violent when drinking and he had beaten his wife and been involved in many brawls. The money ran low and after his death, Jacob discovered that as well as there being no money, there were extensive debts and the bank owned the estate. Destitute, he had initially tried to gain support from his sisters husbands. When this venture proved unsuccessful Jacob decided that his only choice would be to marry into money. Hoodwinking some dim shepherds had been his first move in his long-term plan.

Jacob began courting Emily, one of four daughters of Farmer Paine, whose farm was just outside the village. She was a plain, clumsy girl and besotted with him, having become resigned to spinsterhood at the age of twenty-five. Her mother encouraged her daughter to marry him as quickly as possible, in case he had a change of mind. Her husband erred on the side of caution, suggesting it would be best to wait until Jacob's finances were settled. The five women that dominated his existence ruthlessly rejected Farmer Paine's concerns. Emily declared that she would drown herself. As usual he was relentlessly nagged into silent submission. The couple married in a quiet ceremony at the local church. Emily was delighted, her sisters jealous, her mother relieved, her father tormented with misgivings and Jacob home and dry. Her dowry was substantial and Jacob began spending it on fictitious visits to his lawyers in the Midlands. In reality he was in a whorehouse some thirty miles away.

Chapter 14

Lily saw the ship arriving as she was riding Elijah along the shore, almost exactly a year after its departure. She was standing on the new jetty as the ship docked and Aziz Shadi Rashad Salamar Badr al din jumped ashore before the ship's gangplank was tied in place. They had tea on the ship and shared their news. He was distressed to hear about the floods and the death of William. Lily struggled to keep secret the birth of his daughter. She wanted to surprise him at home. They rode home on Elijah. John had seen the ship arriving and Mary, Mustapha and Isabel had sprung into action. Mary and Mustapha prepared the meal and Isabel quickly bathed Rose and dressed her in her best clothes of lavender silk ready to meet her father. When the initial round of hugs in the kitchen had slowed down, Lily told Aziz Shadi Rashad Salamar Badr al din that there was a surprise for him in the dining room. Mustapha was hopping from foot to foot with badly concealed excitement.

Aziz Shadi Rashad Salamar Badr al din entered the room and looked around. Rose was kicking her legs in her crib. He stared at her in disbelief and she smiled directly at him, her violet eyes shining. He picked her up and ran into the yard, he held her above his head and chanted something unintelligible into the sky.

Mustapha joined in and they stood together shouting, the startled little girl held aloft, fluttering like a lavender bird in the breeze. Isabel broke down and cried and John comforted her.

'Father, I too am now the most fortunate father of the most beautiful daughter!' Aziz Shadi Rashed Salamar Badr al din shouted to John.

Aziz Shadi Rashad Salamar Badr al din had returned home with his usual mountain of gifts for everyone, but the biggest surprise this time was the two disgruntled, disorientated young camels he had brought back for the twins. Elijah was disgusted. He refused to share his stable with them, necessitating an urgent construction of another stable for the camels before the colder weather set in. Sam and Sal, delighted with them, named them Lumpy and Humpy.

Mary gave birth to her second child, Robert John, resulting in the inhabitants of the house numbering twelve, so Aziz Shadi Rashad Salamar Badr al din decided it was time to enlarge the house. He had four extra room built on the back, plus a large one story room for the children to study and play in during the winter. He purchased a large area of woodland to the West of the farm and had plans made for a new house, this time made of bricks, mortar and tiles rather than wood, to better withstand the damp, cold winters. The new house took almost two years to build, with tall ornately built brick chimneys. The family moved in during the autumn, just after Rose had reached her second birthday. The house had a large kitchen at the rear and the rest of the house was roughly divided into three adjoining sections. Lily, Aziz Shadi Rashad Salamar Badr al din, Sam, Sal and Rose lived at one end, Edward, Mary, Ellen Lily and Robert at the other and John, Isabel and Joseph shared the middle section. The large dining room and reception rooms were communal. Stables were built behind the house and occupied by a growing menagerie of animals. The windows at the front of the house overlooked the fields and in the distance, the marshes. The back of the house was sheltered from wind by the large area of woodland that rose steadily up the hill behind. The wood was a beautiful area, with oak, chestnut, ash and hawthorn. The first flowers in spring were the delicate white wood anemone and snowdrop. These were followed by the appearance of the pale yellow primrose and bright yellow celandines. All of these were paled into insignificance by the dramatic carpet of the bluebells and orchids. It was the most wonderful garden in the world and needed little maintenance. Edward helped the twins build a tree house in the massive old oak tree behind the stables. They made a ladder of rope and sturdy planks of wood that could be pulled up behind them. Mustapha added a pulley system that allowed the boys to haul up the refreshments.

Isabel and Mary continued to cook the meals. Aziz Shadi Rashad Salamar Badr al din employed three young village girls to help with the housework. John, having handed over all the sheep to his nephews, tended to Elijah, the camels and the chickens. Lily was eternally grateful to Mary and Isabel for managing the kitchen, as she had never managed to generate an interest in cookery. She joined forces with Ivy, Charles's wife, who possessed remarkable skills as a seamstress. Using the beautiful materials that arrived at the end of each voyage, Lily designed dresses, shirts, nightwear and undergarments and Ivy worked out how to construct them.

Joseph continued to bury the dead. This depressing task was balanced with educating the children. San and Sal had eventually settled down and were able to read and write well. Their father and Mustapha taught them to read and write Arabic in preparation for them to continue in the business. Ellen Lily wanted to be a teacher, and at ten was already teaching the younger children their alphabet. She had her mother's tireless energy and cheerful disposition. She and John remained very close.

Lily loved her children very much, and when Aziz Shadi Rashad Salamar Badr al din announced that the boys were old enough for their first voyage with him, she was speechless. To her they were still little boys, her precious firstborn sons. To their father they were almost young men and needed the experience and discipline of life at sea. He himself had gone to sea at the age of ten. The boys were ecstatic and wanted to leave at once. The ship was due to sail in late summer and Lily spent the next few months pleading with Aziz Shadi Rashad Salamar Badr al din to reconsider. She enlisted the support of Mary and Isabel. The men refused to take sides. Her husband just laughed, reminding her that she had coped at sea and did she not trust him to protect his own treasured sons?

When Sam broke his leg falling from his camel during a race with his brother, Lily rejoiced, believing that he would be unable to go on the voyage. Mustapha was sent for. He administered his potion and attempted to pull Sam's leg back into shape. He was then forced to administer the same potion to Sal, who screamed with pain, even though Sam was unable to feel anything. The bone healed quickly and within a few short weeks, the splint was off and Sam fully recovered. Aziz Shadi Rashad Salamar Badr al din spent much of the last few weeks with Rose, riding the countryside on Elijah. He could understand why Mustapha had refused to leave his little daughter. Rose was a beautiful, slight child with thick black curly hair and her mother's violet eyes. She laughed from when she woke in the morning, until she went to bed. She loved playing with Maria, who was a year older and just as beautiful with her deep brown eyes. Both fathers secretly dreaded them becoming young women.

The ship sailed on the evening tide in early autumn, complete with Sam and Sal. Lily thought her heart would break. Mary went to the dock with her and supported her as she waved goodbye to her beloved husband and sons, praying that she would see them again. Joseph sat at home, tortured with guilt as part of him hoped that she never would. Rose ran around crying for her father for two days. Mustapha took her home with him to stay with Maria for a few days, which finally returned the familiar smile to her little face.

The house settled into a dreary depression, even the indomitable Mary struggled to lift the mood. Everyone was so melancholy that no one noticed that John was unwell. He was visibly slowing down. Elijah was the only one that noticed. It was Isabel that found him collapsed in the stable struggling for breath. Mary carried him to his bed and sent Ellen Lily to fetch Mustapha. Mustapha diagnosed a congestion of the chest and boiled saucepans on the fire in John's room, dampening the air to ease the passage of his breathing. He burned oils that gave off minty, sharp vapours and prepared poultices that made John's eyes and nose stream. Expecting the worst, the family clamoured into his room. Mustapha shut them out, insisting he needed to rest. John slept for long periods, interrupted by vivid memories of his childhood. He became trapped in a web of nostalgia and remembered sitting on his mother's knee beside the fire. He remembered searching for bird's eggs with his brothers and trapping rabbits for the delicious stew his mother made. He remembered his father carving animals out of firewood, his boots covered with tiny slivers of wood. For the first time in years he could clearly recall their faces and hear their voices. He could hear his sister laughing when her brother fell in the pond. He recalled the smell of the prickly blankets on the bed the boys shared. He spent so long in his reminiscences that he began to think he was a child again, being nursed by his mother. Isabel was the first one to become permanently implanted in his past when he began to believe she was his beloved mother. Then he thought that Lily was his sister. Isabel's sons became his brothers. Then he fell in love with Mary and thought she was his wife and the numerous small children became the large family he had always hoped to have. Ellen Lily read to him for hours, fantastic stories that further eroded his feeble, fleeting grasp on reality. He thought she was his daughter and that little Rose was Lily. The family was confounded by his confusion but Mustapha believed it best to join in the façade, John was in no pain and happier than ever in his imaginary world.

Jacob, having heard that his Uncle was ill took the opportunity to visit, hoping to be remembered in his will. John thought he was the man that stole his sister Lily from her family and had to be restrained by Mustapha. John had regained much of his physical strength and by Christmas was allowed out of bed. Everyone hoped that his mental disarray would also improve. It did not and Christmas was chaotic, when the family members struggled to remember who John thought they were. The children coped best as Mary had explained it was all a game of pretend. It was on Christmas day that John decided that Mustapha was the Lord Jesus, restoring his belief in religion. The sudden realisation that logically followed this discovery in John's disorientated brain, was that he was, in fact, dead. This was indeed Heaven, where he lived with Jesus and all of the people he loved, consistent with the stories he had been told as a child. Mustapha tried to restore John's memory with a variety of potions. Some made him fall sleep whilst continuing to talk, one made him so full of energy that Mustapha had to run to keep pace with him in the woods. One caused him to believe that he was capable of levitating and floating around the house. None of them restored his brain.

John remained dead for the rest of his life. The family kept a vigil of supervision. He could not be left alone. Mustapha, Ida and Maria moved in, as the Lord Jesus was the only one able to deter John from his more extreme ideas. Being dead had robbed John of his ability to assess risk and danger. Being already dead had robbed him of the fear of dying, as he now believed he had achieved immortality.

John had lost all memory of Aziz Shadi Rashad Salamar Badr al din, the twins and the ship. The last ten years or so had been permanently lost in the mysterious recesses of his disordered brain. The vicar was scandalised when he discovered that John thought Mustapha was the Lord Jesus and recommended an exorcism. The family, staunchly opposed, declined.

William and Henry were forced to hire extra workers on the farm. Ernest finally gave up working with pigs and joined his brothers on the new farm working as a shepherd. Henry's wife, about to give birth, joined Mary and Isabel at the big house in preparation for her confinement. There was much excitement as this was to be the first birth in the new house. With the assistance of Mustapha's rope and potions, Sarah gave birth to her first son and named him Thomas William. John became very distressed and cried all night, convinced that for a new baby and his mother to arrive in Heaven, they must have died on earth. He cried for the family on earth that had tragically lost them. Sarah and little Thomas returned to the farm a few weeks later and John quickly forgot all about them.

During the summer, John began to forget the names of familiar objects. He was not upset by this development. On the contrary, he found it exceedingly amusing. Explosive laughter rang out in the kitchen every day as he failed to identify more and more objects. Mary, unable to help herself, laughed with him. That was how he finally died, eleven months after he thought he had, laughing with the wonderful woman he believed to be his wife, because he was unable to remember what an egg was called.

John was buried on a cold, but sunny,

November morning. The entire village turned out to pay their respect and to witness the burial of the only man they ever knew who had died twice. Lily, who felt that she had lost her dear father the first time he died almost a year ago, was finally able to mourn him. Joseph took the opportunity to comfort her.

Christmas was a quiet affair that year. Everyone had been kept so busy looking after John for the last year and they were unable to remember what life had been like before he became ill. Lily had expected her husband and sons to return home in the autumn and she began to worry that she would never see them again. The snow was heavy that year, but the house was sheltered by the woods at the back and much easier to keep warm. Mary managed the kitchen and began to teach Ellen Lily to cook. In turn Ellen Lily taught the little ones to make biscuits and tiny cakes that they proudly presented to the rest of the family.

Old Farmer Paine died of malevolent venom, he had suffered from sustained, clamorous nagging throughout his thirty-five tears of marriage, that had became increasingly deafening due to the birth of his four daughters, who learned the skill from their mother. He finally accepted that he had been duped by his deceptive son-in-law those fortunes had failed to materialise. Jacob inherited the farm, the house, the livestock and five dependent ill-tempered women. Joseph arranged the funeral amidst the hoard of wailing women, who demanded the best for their dear father. Jacob chose the cheapest, while constantly questioning Joseph about his cousin Lily, virtually a widow since her husband had failed to return. If anything untoward should happen to Emily, who had failed to provide him with an heir, his intention was to propose marriage to his cousin. Joseph was outraged, he had suffered years of torment and anguish since she had married her husband, but at least Aziz Shadi Rashad Salamar Badr al din was an honourable, loving, generous man. If anything happened to him, if he failed to return home, Joseph was determined to take care of Lily, even if she refused to marry him. He would kill Jacob if necessary to prevent him from taking Lily.

Jacob made sweeping changes to his household. He sacked the servants and sold the livestock, except for his horse and the chickens. He let several farmworkers go, just keeping enough to tend the fields. He ordered the women to take on the household chores. The women mounted a vicious verbal attack that was silenced by Jacob and his fists. He was a different breed from their poor subservient father. With the aid of a horsewhip he achieved submission. The traumatized women, bearing black eyes and welts from the whip, cleaned, cooked, chopped wood and lit the fire. The villagers began gossiping, but due to the women not being well liked in the past, no one did anything.

Chapter 15

Sam and Sal took to the sea like ducks to water and their father began the task of teaching them to read the navigational charts. Their first destination was North Africa, where Sam and Sal demonstrated their skills as camel riders, learned aboard Lumpy and Humpy. They rode far into the desert and learned the sacred art of the tea ceremony, carried out by men in much of Africa. The long ceremony fascinated the twins, who remarked later that it was not for the thirsty. The ceremony began with the teapot, carried on the men's belts, being packed with tealeaves, water and several large spoonsful of sugar. The pot was then placed on the fire to boil. When the pot was removed, the boys expected a cup of tea. Little tall glasses were made ready, but a man began to pour the tea, from a great height, into a glass, and then tipped the liquid back into the pot. The tea was poured to and fro countless times, the liquid becoming darker and darker. The boys wondered how the men could pour from such a great height and not spill a drop. The teapot was returned to the fire and boiled again, then poured again and again. Finally, it was served. The result was a very strong, yet not bitter, glass of extremely sweet tea that caused the boys to feel giddy for some considerable time.

Aziz Shadi Rashad Salamar Badr al din was very proud to present his sons to his friends that first met Lily almost thirteen years ago. He took them to the tanneries and they watched him barter for bales of leather hides. They were impressed by the welcome their father received wherever they went.

By the time that John decided he was dead, Aziz Shadi Rashad Salamar Badr al din and his sons had left North Africa. He had decided to sail to Persia, India and China. He set a course along the western side of Africa, heading south, and rounded the Cape of Good Hope. The twins, familiar with the grey estuary and the grey, often angry, turbulent Atlantic Ocean, were aghast to see the emerald waters of the Indian Ocean. They saw vast whales, blowing foaming water into the sky, the water was so clear they could see fantastic fish swimming below the surface. The ship dropped anchor off the east coast several times. They visited Mombasa to purchase spices and gold. The twins saw men so dark skinned that they were almost blue, who climbed the tall trunks of palm trees and cut down brilliant green coconuts. They caught fresh fish everyday, and they ate them with rice and fresh fruit. The Indian Ocean was dotted with tiny islands, green mounds covered in palm trees, bordered by white sand and transparent green water. The sun shone constantly and Sal and Sam's skins turned the colour of mahogany. By the time they reached the turquoise water of the northern part of the Indian Ocean, the boys had almost forgotten the village and it's people, their previous life seemed like a distant, half remembered dream. They docked in Southern Iran, known as Persia by Europeans, and journeyed inland on camels to the village where Aziz Shadi Rashad Salamar Badr al din's extended family lived. It was the village where the boys were probably conceived. The family welcomed them warmly and organized lavish celebrations. Sam and Sal met cousins, uncles and aunts. They stayed for several months and travelled around to meet other members of the vast family. The country was undergoing a period of instability, with different factions vying for position, so they resumed their journey. They sailed east and headed for the Indian continent.

They docked at a busy port on the western coast of India and went ashore in search of spices. Aziz Shadi Rashad Salamar Badr al din, declined the spices at the docks, and he and his sons travelled inland to villages, where he believed the spices to be fresher and of a higher quality. Some of the villagers remembered him from almost two decades ago. Although they had little common language, everyone knew what he wanted. They stayed at one village for several weeks, enjoying the hospitality, whilst the locals organized the harvesting and collection of sacks of spices available in the area. The women showed them how to mix the spices to produce extraordinary flavours and served them with delicious food.

A young woman, not much older than Sal and Sam, named Shanti, showed them that ginger and turmeric grew under the soil in knobbly lumps. Pepper grew on long graceful vines that twisted up the tall coconut trees. Chillies grew on bright green bushes and saffron came from the middle of a flower. They were entranced, not by the spices, but by the beautiful Indian woman, dressed in a bright green sari that matched her exquisite eyes.

The sacks of spices, Aziz Shadi Rashad Salamar Badr al din and his sons were loaded onto two donkey carts and driven to the docks. It took weeks for Sam and Sal to recover from their first infatuation, as they sailed east across the Bay of Bengal. By that time they were in China loading bales of silk, boxes of crockery and chests of tea. The boys were shocked by the food eaten by the local people, insects, lizard, snakes and other unidentifiable creatures, all picked up with sticks. They soon learned that it was best not to know what they were eating. Chinese New Year was approaching and Aziz Shadi Rashad Salamar Badr al din decided to remain in China for the occasion. Sam and Sal were fascinated by the tumultuous celebrations, deafened by the firecrackers, and startled by the rampaging dragons. Their father, who had not forgotten the village, purchased a number of silk hanfus for the women there and smaller ones for the little girls. He missed his wife and daughter with a passion and was delighted to embark on the long journey home. Sam and Sal, who had never travelled more than five miles from the village before, were staggered and overwhelmed by the sheer size of the world, in which journeys were not measured by distance but by time, by weeks, months and even years. It fostered in them a love of the sea and strange, bewilderingly exotic countries that would keep them moving relentlessly for the rest of their lives. The journey home was slow, with frequent stops for fresh supplies and because Aziz Shadi Rashad Salamar Badr al din had no wish to navigate the Atlantic until the spring when the risk of storms would be reduced.

Sam and Sal decided that the Indian Ocean, just off the coast of East Africa was their favourite piece of the world. They loved the miniature islands and the glittering, crystal clear emerald water. They saw immense shoals of sardines being pursued by fast moving dolphins and large slow whales. Sometimes the dolphins swam along beside the ship and somersaulted into the air. At night the sea was filled with the doleful, eerie music of the whales. The boys spent their time between chores on deck together, swinging gently in a hammock slung between the masts, as their mother had done not long before they were born. During the two and a half years they had been at sea, they had grown significantly taller and the hard work had rebuilt their bodies. They were almost the same size of their father.

The ship rounded the Cape of Good Hope in good weather in the early spring. They saw a great deal of large ships sailing to and from the West African coast. Aziz Shadi Rashad Salamar Badr al din informed his sons that they were slave ships that purchased men and women from Africa and sold them to farmers in the West Indies and the Americas. As a merchant, he bought and sold a variety of commodities but was vehemently opposed to trading in human beings.

Chapter 16

Lily had almost resigned herself to the loss of her husband and sons by that spring. Mustapha, Ida and Maria had moved in permanently as Mustapha believed it was his duty after the death of her father and the absence of her husband. Rose had almost forgotten her father and brothers. Lily and Mary spent their time learning the skills of Mustapha. His beard was now completely grey and no one knew how old he was, including him. After her father's death Lily harboured the fear that Mustapha would die taking the secret of his potions to the grave along with him, leaving the villagers vulnerable to painful childbirth and the agonizing deaths that had happened before he arrived. He taught them when to plant seeds, how to nurture them, harvest and prepare them. He showed them the different remedies for fever, pain and sleeplessness. He trained then to make ointments for stings and wounds, poultices for chests and boils and splints for broken bones.

When Lily turned to see who was entering the kitchen door, she initially failed to recognize the tall young man coming through the door. When another one, exactly the same as the first, appeared, she lost all control of her legs and fell backwards into a chair. Aziz Shadi Rashad Salamar Badr al din ran into the room laughing, swept her from the chair into his arms, and was somewhat disconcerted when he realized she was sobbing uncontrollably. It took her a considerable time to recover. Her sons had left as children and returned as young men and she had no idea who they were or which was which.

Aziz Shadi Rashad Salamar Badr al din was distressed to hear of John's death, which explained his wife's desolation. John had been told the intended route of the voyage and was well aware when they were due to return. Lily had been so distraught when they left, it was decided that John would give her three letters, one for each Christmas that they were away, enabling her to keep faith in their return. Sadly, John had been unable to fulfill the request, as when the first letter was due, he already thought he was dead. The letters were found in a drawer in John's room.

The entire family was overjoyed at the safe return of Aziz Shadi Rashad Salamar Badr al din and the boys. Joseph experienced mixed feelings, his chance to care for Lily was postponed but at least it would not be necessary to kill Jacob. Rose took a few days to remember her father. Sal and Sam brought their hammocks from the ship, unable to sleep soundly without them. They found it difficult to settle in the village and experienced an anxious impatience and dreamed about sailing again. They had been constantly fed with a marvelous variety of experiences and began to feel starved. To relieve the boredom, they travelled to London with their father, delivering goods and learning to be merchants.

At home they entertained the family with tales of their extraordinary travels, in order to convince themselves that it had all been real.

The farms were making a good profit, particularly the one worked by Henry and William. They employed a dozen farmworkers, including two cowmen to manage the large dairy herd. The farm supplied over half of the village with milk. Henry and William had worked hard. Aziz Shadi Rashad Salamar Badr al din was so impressed by their achievements, that he signed the deeds of the farm over to them. He had the old house repaired and turned into a school and Ellen Lily's dream of becoming a teacher became a reality. He was so thankful for the good fortune of the family that he threw a massive party in the field outside of his house. He hired cooks and maids for the occasion and banned the women of the house from the kitchen, determined that they should enjoy the festivities and none of the responsibility. He hired musicians to play in shifts throughout the afternoon and evening. Lambs were roasted on spits in the yard and the cooks were busy roasting potatoes and vegetables and baking fresh bread. Most of the villagers attended, some out of friendship, some out of sheer curiosity and others out of hunger. Even Jacob and Emily, the Widow Paine and her unmarried daughters attended. To Aziz Shadi Rashad Salamar Badr al din's consternation, Jacob approached him, greeted him with an uncomfortable familiarity and asked to borrow money.

'I do not mix pleasure with business matters!' he whispered curtly in response, believing the request to indicate unprecedented bad manners. 'Come and see me some other time, meanwhile, please enjoy the party.'

The weather was warm and fine, lanterns were lit as the sun went down and exhausted children fell asleep on the hay bales arranged around the field. Elizabeth, the youngest daughter of the Widow Paine, escaped her life of torment after talking to a young farmworker called Arthur, employed on Henry and William's farm and they were married a matter of weeks later. Lily watched the people enjoying themselves, resplendent in her purple silk dress and amethyst necklace, and her long dark curls hanging loose. She watched her handsome sons, relentlessly pursued by the giggling young village girls. Aziz Shadi Rashad Salamar Badr al din watched Lily. She was wearing the dress she wore on the night she agreed to be his wife. She was even more beautiful and he loved her more than ever. Joseph was also watching Lily.

Jacob went to see Aziz Shadi Rashad Salamar Badr al din several days later. He required an injection of cash as he maintained the farm had suffered neglect during the last few years. He also had the onorous responsibility to feed and clothe five women. He offered a generous interest rate on the loan, payable after a year. Aziz Shadi Rashad Salamar Badr al din thought he was a pompous idiot and not to be trusted. He agreed to a loan but declined his repayment plan that lacked any security. He would require the deeds of the farm, which would be returned on full repayment of the loan. Jacob was visibly disgruntled, and pointed out that families generally agree deals on a handshake.

'An English gentleman's word is his bond!' he reminded Aziz Shadi Rashad Salamar Badr al din arrogantly.

'And I am not an Englishman!' he smiled. 'Perhaps you would rather go elsewhere.'

Jacob fidgeted with discomfort as Lily entered the room with tea and warm biscuits, he hated this man with a fathomless, jealous ferocity, a damned Arab that owned half of the village, with a surfeit of money and power and married to this most exquisite woman.

'That will not be necessary, after all, we are family!'

'Very well.'

'How soon will the money be available? The need, as you can imagine, is fairly urgent.'

'The moment you furnish me with the deeds to your farm.' Answered Aziz Shadi Rashad Salamar Badr al din with a particularly charming smile that he reserved for pompous idiots.

Mary, who disliked Jacob intensely, felt obliged to warn Lily and her husband that she believed Jacob to be an untrustworthy, dishonest man.

'All the better!' laughed Aziz Shadi Rashad Salamar Badr al din as he hugged Mary.

'In a year his farm will belong to us!'

Jacob returned the following day and reluctantly handed over the deeds to the farm with a concentrated bitterness. His irritation increased when Aziz Shadi Rashad Salamar Badr al din produced papers for him to sign, agreeing to relinquish the farm and it's contents on failure to repay the debt. Mustapha was called upon to witness the signing. Jacob left with his money and a burning, compelling desire to kill Aziz Shadi Rashad Salamar Badr al din.

.

Chapter 17

Ellen Lily and Joseph knocked on doors in the village announcing to parents that the school would open shortly and that it would cost nothing to send their children there. They would be taught to read and write. Some parents were grateful and, others were suspicious, believing there was no need for them to learn letters to work on the land. Attendance was initially low, but once the harvesting was finished, more boys arrived. Some arrived with a chunk of bread wrapped in a cloth. Most did not. Many of the children were poorly nourished, so Ellen Lily enlisted the help of her mother Mary and sister-in-law Ivy. They arrived each day and provided a hot meal for the children. William delivered a churn of fresh milk daily.

Ellen Lily revisited the village homes with children, encouraging parents to send their girls as well as their boys. Some parents eventually agreed when they were assured that the girls would learn useful skills including cooking and sewing. When the girls were not cooking with Mary or sewing with Ivy, Ellen Lily taught them to read.

Aziz Shadi Rashad Salamar Badr al din obtained books in London. Daniel Defoe's Robinson Crusoe, the first adventure novel, was read aloud in the afternoons. The children were transfixed, they ran home and related the story, chapter by chapter to their parents. Sam and Sal made guest appearances, relating their adventures in far- flung countries. At Christmas they had a party, parents were invited and listened in awe to their children reading from the Bible and Encyclopedias.

It was a white Christmas that year. Aziz Shadi Rashad Salamar Badr al din loved the snow. He relished the challenge to keep his family warm and cosy during the winter. He liked the dramatic changes that the English climate provided. Coming from an arid area, he was particularly fond of the huge variety of greens that the seasons produced. In spring there was a vast variety, from pale yellowish greens to dark bluish greens. Summer turned the foliage a more uniform green and autumn burst into orange, yellow, brown and red. The one thing he missed was a decent bathhouse, so in the spring, with Mustapha's support, he set about building one. He hired stonemasons to build the structure at the back of the house, two large rooms joined by an arch, accessible from the kitchen via a short passageway. He installed a large round stove in each room with chimneys that poked through the ceiling and stood several feet tall on the roof. In one room he had the masons build four large marble troughs with a hole in the bottom that could be blocked with a wooden bung. Then he built a large water tank in the garden, which was filled with the aid of a length of lead pipe attached to the hand pump. A pipe from the tank led into the bathhouse through the wall, attached to a contraption that controlled the flow of water. Water was heated in large pans on the stoves. After a bath, the bung was removed, allowing the water to drain via a pipe into the garden. He lined the walls with wood and built benches and shelves in the adjoining room. The shelves held piles of towels and the benches provided somewhere to sit and get really hot before getting into the bath. Aziz Shadi Rashad Salamar Badr al din explained that this opened the pores of the skin, allowing impurities to pass out.

The bathhouse, completed by the autumn, proved a popular activity. Initially, Isabel, Mary and Ida, accustomed to a few inches of tepid water in a tin bath at the end of the kitchen every few weeks, thought that getting into water that deep and that hot would be dangerous. Lily encouraged them and once they conquered their modesty they were regular users. Isabel, who was now in her fifties, experienced a new lease of life as immersion in the hot water, perfumed by Mustapha's concoctions, miraculously alleviated her aches and pains. On cold winter evenings, it was not uncommon for all the women in the house, plus Ellen Lily, Rose and Maria to adjourn to the hot, candlelit bathhouse for hours, soaking in hot water perfumed with jasmine oil. They even succeeded in finally encouraging the blushing, embarrassed, giggling Ivy to join them. Aziz Shadi Rashad Salamar Badr al din, frustrated by the women's monopolization of the bathhouse, vowed to build another one for the men next year.

Elijah was twenty years old. The previous summer Aziz Shadi Rashad Salamar Badr al din had scoured the countryside in search of suitable mares. His own stable contained the short stocky ponies suitable for the children to ride. He found three, a tall elegant bad tempered black one, a gentle bay and a beautiful cream one with a mane and tail that was almost white. Elijah approved of them all and that summer three foals were born. The black mare produced a black filly, the bay had another black filly and the cream mare gave birth to a large, robust cream colt. Elijah was extremely proud.

In late summer Jacob arrived requesting an extension to the loan repayment due to his poor harvest. In truth he had gambled much of the money. Aziz Shadi Rashad Salamar Badr al din agreed, he was due to go the sea in a few weeks and extended the loan until the following autumn to coincide with his return. Jacob fervently prayed for his death at sea.

Sam and Sal were keen to begin trading in America, which had become a very lucrative destination. Aziz Shadi Rashad Salamar Badr al din, had never travelled across the Atlantic, he was considering this when the protracted War of Independence broke out in the colony. Within a short time many European countries declared war on Britain. Spanish, Dutch and French gunships began blasting any vessel flying the British flag out of the water. Fortunately, Aziz Shadi Rashad Salamar Badr al din's ship flew the Iranian flag and was largely ignored. During the following few years, he limited his voyages to North Africa and Turkey. Due to the unrest, the prices of goods more than doubled. Many merchants had been ruined by the trade embargo with America and were owed fortunes. Many more were sunk. This proved to be a very profitable time for him and his sons.

Aziz Shadi Rashad Salamar Badr al din and his sons were busy making the ship ready for sail, when he noticed a dock labourer standing beside Elijah. He appeared to be talking quietly to the animal whilst stroking his face and neck. Elijah was nodding happily. As the young man turned to resume moving sacks, Elijah followed him and nuzzled his back. The young man laughed and resumed stroking him. The man moved aside, bowed his head and apologized as Aziz Shadi Rashad Salamar Badr al din approached.

'He seems to like you.'

'He is a beautiful horse, Sir, I meant no harm.'

'I am aware of that, his name is Elijah and he is fussy about who he makes friends with.'

'I was reared with horses, Sir'

'Where are you from?'

'Form Ireland, Sir, my family bred horses.'

'Then why are you working here?'

'It is the only work I have found, Sir'

'Would you be interested in working with horses?'

'I would, Sir, indeed I would.'

'Where do you live?'

The young Irishman bowed his head and pointed to a bedroll beside a shed.

'There, Sir.'

'Come with me.' Aziz Shadi Rashad Salamar Badr al din said, mounting Elijah and pulling the young man up behind him.

At home he showed the young man the contents of his stables, even the bad tempered mare allowed him to stroke her foal. When he saw the pale colt, he shook his head.

'Sir, you have a rare winner there!'

Aziz Shadi Rashad Salamar Badr al din took the young man, whose name was Gabriel O'Malley, inside to meet the family and offered him the job of caring for the horses. Gabriel was speechless. Mary showed him around the house and allotted him a room next to Joseph's, overlooking the stables. She was adamant he would not sleep in the stable with the horses as he had expected to do. He stared in abject disbelief at the bathhouses and when he saw the camels he knew he must be dreaming.

Gabriel was a happy young man. He had his own room with a real bed for the first time in his life and was expected to eat his meals with the family. He rewarded Aziz Shadi Rashad Salamar Badr al din and his family with dedication and loyalty for the rest of his life. He and William formed a strong bond, based on their mutual love of horses and he often helped out with the horses at William, Edward and Henry's farm. He worked tirelessly and had to be bullied by Mary and Lily to take time off occasionally. He felt truly honoured to be free to ride the beautiful Elijah around the countryside.

Gabriel modified the horses' food intake, increased their exercise, clad them in warm blankets on cold days and kept their fires alight in the snow. He groomed them constantly until their coats shone like silk, he combed and braided their tails and manes and they followed him everywhere as soon as he opened the stable doors. He taught the younger children to ride properly and trained the ponies to jump. He joined forces with Mustapha and together they made remedies for common horse ailments. He even improved his skills, with the help of Mustapha, with the camels. In the summer he took the ponies to the school once a week and patiently taught the children how to care for them. By the autumn, when Aziz Shadi Rashad Salamar Badr al din and his sons returned, Gabriel had transformed the lives of the horses and fallen irredeemably in love with Ellen Lily.

Aziz Shadi Rashad Salamar Badr al din was so impressed with the condition of the horses and the news that all three mares were due to foal again next spring, that he presented the bad-tempered black mare to Gabriel as a gift. Gabriel, like John before him, thought he had died and gone to heaven. He named the mare Bess.

Jacob failed to repay his loan and Aziz Shadi Rashad Salamar Badr al din gave him six months to vacate the farm, which bordered the far side of the woods at the back of the house.

Lily and Mary were aware of Gabriel's love for Ellen Lily. He had never mentioned it, but they knew. Mary also knew that Ellen Lily loved him as they had already discussed it. Gabriel was unaware of any of this and was not about to jeopardise his employment. This was a very rich family of merchants and landowners who would no doubt find a suitable wealthy suitor for one of their extraordinarily beautiful daughters.

The family waited impatiently for Gabriel to declare his feelings for Ellen Lily. They even encouraged him to take her riding on the pale mare, believing that the sight of her on a horse with her unruly brown curls and vivid blue eyes may loosen his tongue. Aziz Shadi Rashad Salamar Badr al din became so frustrated with his unconquerable shyness that, on Christmas morning, he pushed the giggling Ellen Lily into a large tea chest, clutching a sign asking 'Will You Marry Me?' and presented the chest to Gabriel. The family clapped and cheered as Ellen Lily emerged with the sign. Gabriel stared in confusion. Then someone realized he was unable to read and read the sign to him. He had such an attack of the vapours that Mustapha resorted to a remedy to calm him. It was one of the most joyous Christmases the family had experienced for years. In the evening Gabriel formally asked Edward for his daughter's hand in marriage. Edward, a man of few words, answered him with a broad smile.

'Son, you are very welcome to her, I've

lived with her mother for twenty years and her for almost as long and they are more stubborn than any blessed horse!'

Aziz Shadi Rashad Salamar Badr al din, in his element, began preparing for the most spectacular wedding since his and Lily's twenty years ago. Rose and Maria were beautiful as bridesmaids, resplendent in silver-grey silk, their dark curls piled high on their lovely heads, studded with red rose buds, Gabriel felt like a real gentleman in his cream silk clothes and looked handsome, his pale skin contrasting with his dark curls and green eyes. Ellen Lily had never looked so captivating, dressed in ivory silk, her hair dressed like her bridesmaids and a bouquet of forget-me-nots. Gabriel and Ellen Lily rode home on Bess and the pale mare that she had named Molly. The family and villagers arrived on carts, on horses and on foot. The celebrations lasted for days, with lavish food and fireworks. Gabriel, accustomed to a hard life with little joy, broke down and cried. Mary found him sobbing in the stables and enveloped him with one of her hugs reserved for the very distressed, and rocked him like a baby.

After twenty years, most of the inhabitants had become accustomed to sharing their village with the foreigners. The most intransigent souls had either died or been gradually seduced by the parties, the free school and Aziz Shadi Rashad Salamar Badr al din's generous donations to the Parish Relief Fund. Almost every family in the village had benefitted from Mustapha's potions in times of pain and death and he was well respected by everyone.

.

Chapter 18

Jack, the only son of Charles and Ivy, became a shepherd and worked alongside his father and Uncle Thomas. He was a quite, gentle young man, with fair hair and hazel eyes and a fondness for reading. Ever since the flood, from which the marshes had not yet recovered, the sheep filled the numerous fields surrounding the farm where his three uncles lived. They had so many sheep that if took them all of them almost two weeks to shear them all. It fell to Jack and his dogs Shep and Sally to take some of them to the market that was held on a Friday in the town. The journey took all day. Jack set off between five and six in the morning with twenty-five sheep, the dogs keeping them moving steadily, arriving at market around ten o'clock. The farmers spent the morning assessing the animals and deciding what to bid for. The auction began in the early afternoon. Jack's sheep sold quickly and he and his dogs set off toward home. He stopped for refreshments and water for this dogs at an Inn and sat outside with the dogs, watching the constantly moving throng of people that live in towns. It was then that he saw Jacob walking across the road with a strange woman on his arm and entering a house opposite the Inn.

Jack told Arthur, who worked on his uncles' farm, and his wife Elizabeth, Emily's sister, that he had seen Jacob. Elizabeth was dismayed, as her sister had told her that Jacob had obtained employment with a firm of eminent lawyers in London. He had been sending a meager allowance once a month, which paid the two farmworkers and provided just enough provisions for the women to keep body and soul together. Emily's mother and sisters had no idea that Jacob had lost the farm and that it was now legally owned by Aziz Shadi Rashad Salamar Badr al din. They were just grateful that Jacob had left them in peace.

Jack went to inform Aziz Shadi Rashad Salamar Badr al din that he had seen Jacob in town with a woman. Jack was surprised to discover that he now owned the farm, due to Jacob's failure to repay the loan and was certain that the Widow Paine and her daughters were unaware of the fact. The following day, Aziz Shadi Rashad Salamar Badr al din and Jack rode into town and visited the Inn opposite where Jacob had entered a house to make enquiries. The innkeeper was very helpful. The gentleman in question was apparently a lawyer named Jacob Reynolds from the North. He had recently married a wealthy widow whose husband had made his fortune in cotton. Mr Reynolds was currently arranging for people to invest their money in the first mechanized cotton mills in the North. He had assured the investors that there was negligible risk and promised vast profits. The innkeeper had invested his own savings.

Aziz Shadi Rashad Salamar Badr al din was outraged, but not greatly surprised, by the information. He and Jack returned home and discussed their findings with Mustapha, Mary, Lily and Isabel. Everyone agreed that the Widow Paine and Emily needed to be informed of Jacob's current activities and of the fact that he had lost the farm by default. Widow Paine was so distraught she fainted away and later that evening disappeared. Her daughters found her in the woods, prostrate and vomiting after ingesting a quantity of deadly nightshade. Mustapha nursed her for two days. He purged her with emetics and administered potions to counteract the poison. She survived but was so hysterical at the loss of her security and the scandalous behavior of her son-in-law, that Mustapha was forced to sedate her for several days. Emily and her sisters were built of stronger stuff and their only concern was that Jacob would return. Aziz Shadi Rashad Salamar Badr al din was horrified to discover how the women had been treated, that they had been whipped and punched. His initial reaction was to find Jacob and strangle him with his bare hands. Instead, he arranged for the Widow Paine and her daughters to move to a house in a nearby village where they would be relatively unknown. He provided a monthly sum of money for them to live on and assured them that he would deal with Jacob.

Jacob had never met Gabriel, so it fell to him to dress up like a gentleman of means, looking for somewhere to invest his money. Gabriel rode Elijah into the town, as Bess was due to foal soon. He knocked on the door opposite the inn and asked to speak to Jacob Reynolds. He was shown into an office where Jacob sat at his imposing desk. Gabriel explained the reason for his visit. Jacob's interest was evident once Gabriel mentioned investing a considerable amount of money. He explained that the investments were in the new cotton mills being built by Thomas Arkwright in Lancashire. The profits, he assured Gabriel, would be generous. Gabriel expressed an interest in visiting the area and meeting this Thomas Arkwright. Jacob assured him that this would not be necessary and that Mr Arkwright was a very busy man. He was his contact in the South and he would deal directly with the mill owner. Gabriel arranged to return in a couple of weeks with money to invest.

Aziz Shadi Rashad Salamar Badr al din, Sal and Sam and Gabriel decided to travel to Lancashire to investigate the emerging cotton mills. Charles was borrowed from his farm to help Mustapha, who had a deep distrust of large animals, and the women look after the horses. They travelled by coach during the day and stayed at Inns overnight. Gabriel got used to being a gentleman of means. It took the best part of a week to reach Lancashire, where they hired horses and set off searching for cotton mills. It did not take them long. The cotton mills were not popular with many local people, who believed that the advent of machinery would rob them of their livelihoods. Mr Thomas Arkwright was indeed a busy man. They found him in a noisy building, surrounded by clanking machinery, his clothes covered in cotton fluff. He was disturbed to hear that a man in the South was said to be investing money in his developing mills. Not only had he never heard of Jacob Reynolds the lawyer, he had enough investors here in the North. He was an arrogant man and dismissed them rudely.

Their return home coincided with the births of Elijah's new offspring. Molly and the bay named Lady produced fillies and Bess had a colt. Gabriel advised that the mares be mated with a different stallion to avoid interbreeding in the future. Aziz Shadi Rashad Salamar Badr al din sent him off with the money to find one.

They family debated what to do about Jacob. Mary suggested killing him and burying him in the marshes. Mustapha preferred drowning him. Aziz Shadi Rashad Salamar Badr al din and the twins advocated kidnapping him and taking him on their next voyage and leaving him somewhere. Isabel thought that arming the Widow Paine and her daughters with whips and locking Jacob in a room with them would be justice. Joseph wanted to bury him alive with an adder. Lily thought his new wife should decide what to do with him. Edward decided they could feed him to pigs. The debate disintegrated into laughter as the suggestions became more imaginative. Tying him to a tree containing a hornets' nest and burying him up to the neck on the shore at low tide, facing the incoming tide causing the most hilarity. The family eventually settled down and decided that Jacob should be confronted.

Gabriel and Aziz Shadi Rashad Salamar Badr al din visited him the following day. His discomfort was obvious as soon they entered the room. He left the room to order refreshments and never returned. He grabbed a small bag full of money from his bedroom and to the consternation of his wife, ran out of the back door through the garden and disappeared. He was later robbed on the docks in London and pressganged on to a warship sailing to the war in America, where he was suspected of spying for England, scalped by a Mohawk and eaten by wolves.

Nobody in the village had any idea what had happened to him. His new wife was stunned and disgusted when Aziz Shadi Rashad Salamar Badr al din informed her that her husband had a wife in the village, no estate in the Midlands and was unheard of in the Northern cotton mills. The widow that he had married had a considerable fortune of her own and she repaid as many of Jacob's unfortunate investors as she could find, then she moved away. The Widow Paine and her daughters, terrified that Jacob would find them, lived like introverted nuns in a convent. Their only callers were the local tradesmen. The women did not go out and the curtains remained closed. They even stopped answering the door to Elizabeth as she brought memories of the outside world inside the house. After seven years, Jacob was declared dead, leaving Emily free to marry again, but the women had been in isolation for so long that they had developed a collective obstinate agoraphobia, and had no desire to venture out.

Chapter 19

Aziz Shadi Rashad Salamar Badr al din had the house on Farmer Paine's old farm demolished and built a new one. He had extensive stables built. Gabriel and Ellen Lily moved into the new house and most of the horses were moved into the new stables. Elijah, the ponies and the camels remained in their old home. Gabriel had purchased a new deep chocolate brown stallion to father the next generation of foals. He also began breeding and training heavy horses for use on the farms. His horses were in demand and brought a high price. Robert, Ellen Lily's brother, had become an exceptional horseman and worked at the stables with Gabriel.

Sam and Sal inherited their father's captaincy of the ship. Aziz Shadi Rashad Salamar Badr al din decided to remain at home and concentrate on increasing the market for the goods that his sons returned with. Gabriel proved to be an astute businessman and helped with managing the farms. Lily worried about her sons as she had worried about her husband during his voyages, but was grateful to have her husband beside her. Gabriel organized horse races during the summer months. The whole village arrived for the event, which was invariably followed by one of Aziz Shadi Rashad Salamar Badr al din's famous parties. More stables had to be built to accommodate the numerous horses that arrived from considerable distances in order to take part. Late summer was a busy time with harvesting and this often coincided with the return of the ship and numerous deliveries to London. The twins were rarely home and generally sailed away again after unloading the cargo. The winters were quieter. The entire family remained at home by the fire. Gabriel constantly replenished the woodpile with dead trees from the woodland behind the house. Mary, with her boundless energy, did most of the cooking, although Isabel still helped in the kitchen. She was getting smaller with age and suffered with stiffness in her joints that Mustapha relieved with one of his concoctions. Mustapha was also shrinking. His hair was pure white with a few streaks of black and his face a network of wrinkles, but his black eyes retained their sparkle and he was as fit as a flea. His wife Ida had fattened as she aged and his precious daughter had developed into a beautiful young woman. Maria and Rose had grown up together and remained inseparable. They had both received several proposals of marriage from men that did not inspire either of them to accept. They spent much of their time painting and drawing the surrounding countryside and each other. Ellen Lily had three children in the first three years of her marriage. The first, a daughter, was born easily in the kitchen with the help of Mustapha and Mary. The second, a son, arrived on the path in the woods, on route to the house. The shocked Gabriel carried both of them the rest of the way.

The third, another son, arrived without any warning, surprising the women by abruptly floating to the surface of the water in the bathhouse. Isabel remembered that Mary's grandmother had been the talk of the village in the past, famous for delivering many of her seventeen children in extraordinary places. One had landed in the milk bucket whilst she was milking the cow.

It was a warm spring morning. The bluebells had carpeted the woods. Elijah was galloping along the path when his old heart finally burst. He reared up and threw Aziz Shadi Rashad Salamar Badr al din against a tree, instantly snapping his neck. They were found some hours later by Rose and Maria during a sketching trip. Rose screamed so loud that the inhabitants of both houses on either side of the woods knew something unspeakably terrible had happened. Mary and Gabriel were first to arrive at the tragic scene. They had run from opposite directions, closely followed by Mustapha. Mustapha fell to his knees and wailed pitifully, he had known Aziz Shadi Rashad Salamar Badr al din since he was a baby and loved him as a son. Mary's heart felt like it was breaking as she clasped the thin old man in her arms and rocked him like a baby and stroked his hair until his sobs subsided. Then she gently carried the man she loved like a father back to the house and helped Ida put him to bed. They tried to stop Lily running through the woods to her husband, but she ran like someone possessed. She found her distraught daughter cradling her father's head on her lap. Maria was trying to comfort her. Gabriel stood mesmerized in dreadful disbelief. Mary ran into the village to tell Joseph, whose familiarity with death and grief enabled him to function in awful adversity. He took charge. He had the body moved to the house and arranged with Gabriel to bury Elijah in the woods. Gabriel was grateful for something to do. He spent the entire night digging a hole large enough for the horse. He refused all offers of help but was appreciative when Ellen Lily arrived with a jug of hot, sweet tea every few hours. Mary and Isabel helped Lily to wash her husband and dress him in his best pure white outfit with silver embroidery. Lily combed his long hair that was still jet black with a few strands of white around his temples. He was as beautiful as the day she had first seen him on the shore almost thirty years ago and she loved him more than ever. She had hoped to have him with her for the rest of her life. She massaged jasmine oil into his hair and tried unsuccessfully to shut his eyes. She put pennies on his eyelids, but they gradually opened again when she removed the pennies, so she left them. Lily sat with him all night. She talked to him, and then cried for him in equal quantities. Rose joined her for some of the night and they sat and sobbed together. Lily cut off a lock of her husband's hair, which she twisted with a lock of her of her own, she put half in the pocket of his white tunic and the other half she kept in a little cotton bag close to her breast for the rest of her days.

Aziz Shadi Rashad Salamar Badr al din was buried the following day on the insistence of Mustapha. The entire population of the village crammed itself into the churchyard to say goodbye to the unusual, outrageous, generous man with the unpronounceable name who, over the years had become accepted by almost everyone.

Gabriel needed help to push Elijah into his resting place. The earth would not fit back into the hole due to the displacement caused by the large stallion, so he shaped it into a mound that became the place of pilgrimage for everyone who had loved and respected Aziz Shadi Rashad Salamar Badr al din and Elijah. Family and persons unknown planted all manner of flowers on and around the mound and the little patch of the wood evolved into a fragrant colourful refuge. Lily spent considerable time sitting there, in all weathers, as it was where Aziz Shadi Rashad Salamar Badr al din and Elijah had both left her life, together, just as unexpectedly and dramatically as when they had first arrived.

Chapter 20

Joseph succumbed to a harrowing crisis of conscience. He was ashamed that he had wished for the death of Aziz Shadi Rashad Salamar Badr al din. Now he had actually died, Joseph would have gladly given his own life in return for having him back. He could not bear to see Lily so forlorn. In desperation he confided in his mother and admitted that he had wished for the death. Isabel understood, as she had known that he loved Lily long before he did. She advised him to be patient, to be supportive to Lily and give her time to grieve.

Joseph, with the help of Gabriel, took over managing the extensive management of the farms and import business. There was so much to do that Joseph temporarily gave up the business of the dead. Aziz Shadi Rashad Salamar Badr al din had kept extensive records of the incoming and outgoing money. Joseph was puzzled by the payments to storekeepers in another village. A monthly amount had been paid for many years. He and Gabriel visited the village and discovered that the money was payments for regular orders to a cottage on the outskirts of the village. The storekeepers left the provisions outside of the door of the cottage and had never seen the occupants. Joseph and Gabriel visited the cottage that was run down and neglected. The windows and curtains were so filthy that it was impossible to see in. They received no answer after knocking on the door several times, so they went round the back of the house. The garden was wild and overgrown. Then Gabriel remembered that Jack's wife Elizabeth had not seen her mother and sisters for a long time, and that they lived somewhere in this village. They pushed the back door open and were overcome with the smell of musty decay. Layers of dusty cobwebs hung like hammocks from the ceiling and the torn curtains disintegrated at a touch. Silvery clouds of dust, illuminated by the rays of the sun, billowed into the air as they entered the house. They heard a muffled sound from another room and discovered a painfully thin, virtually bald creature, with huge terrified eyes, cringing behind the dilapidated furniture. It was Emily. Her mother and sisters had died years before and were reduced to powdery bones and still in their beds upstairs. Emily had gone slowly insane living with the corpses and dreading the return of her malevolent brutal husband. Joseph and Gabriel tried to talk to her, to assure her they meant no harm and would take her to her sister Elizabeth. Emily failed to understand and skittered around in panic. By the time they had caught her and subdued her violent struggling with a blanket and put her in the cart to take her to her sister, she had died of fright like a little trapped bird.

Joseph organized the mass funeral of Emily, her sisters and her mother, burying them next to the long-suffering Farmer Paine. Then he was tormented by the thought that poor Farmer Paine had begun turning restlessly in his grave. Elizabeth was consumed by a crisis of conscience and bitterly regretted neglecting her mother and sisters, even though it had been them that had turned her away.

It was a miserable summer. The skies were overcast and the rain fell quietly and persistently further dampening the depleted spirits of the grieving family. Even Mary was struggling. Lily consoled herself with the knowledge that she had had thirty years of happiness. Mustapha's grief was the most wretched. He was haunted by the memories of Aziz Shadi Rashad Salamar Badr al din's parents, who had died when he was a small child. Mustapha had promised them that he would protect their beloved son. He believed that he had failed. The family's misery was further exacerbated as they awaited the return of Sam and Sal who had no idea that their father was dead. Their return would doubtless provoke a renewed period of grieving. Mary's remedy for the sadness enveloping the family included persuading Gabriel and Ellen Lily to move back to the big house with their brood of small children. They now had four and a fifth was imminent. She also insisted the family all celebrate Aziz Shadi Rashad Salamar Badr al din's birthday in August as elaborately and extravagantly as he would have done, inviting the whole village. Mary, Joseph and Gabriel organized the event and even the sun managed to shine. The villagers arrived with bunches of flowers and in the evening a long procession spontaneously occurred as they made their way to the grave of Elijah carrying the flowers. The musicians followed. Gabriel and Joseph carried lanterns that they hung from trees. Individuals took turns to sing songs, with everyone joining in the choruses. Lily was visibly moved, a few people cried quietly. The musicians, motivated to avoid a somber atmosphere, began to play some lively dance music and people began to dance up and down the path. Even Mustapha began to smile again, knowing that Aziz Shadi Rashad Salamar Badr al din's spirit was dancing among them. Ellen Lily gave birth effortlessly to her fifth child that evening, naturally, they named him Aziz Gabriel. Mustapha held him aloft in the moonlight and shouted unintelligible sentences. Mary believed he was showing him to his namesake.

The evening proved to be the turning point for the family and for the weather. The harvest kept everyone busy and Elijah's first 'grand-foal' was born, so he was named Elijah. His mother was Bess's first filly Betty, his father the dark brown stallion named Joe. Mustapha was back in his garden nurturing the plants he had neglected over the previous months. He was pleased that they had thrived so well without him, unaware that the tireless. Mary had been tending them with unstinting regularity during his absence.

Lily and Rose waited on the dock when the ship arrived, dreading delivering the news to the twins. Both Sam and Sal instinctively knew something was wrong. Rose told them quickly, explaining that he had not suffered and died with Elijah. The twins took the sad news like mature men. They put on a brave face and comforted their mother and sister. Then Sam introduced them to a beautiful young woman, with long straight black hair and amber coloured eyes who had been standing quietly at a respectful distance. Her name was Mina, she was his wife and she spoke no English apart from 'Hello'. Lily hugged her son and Rose, sensing the nervousness in the young Mina, hugged her warmly and asked Sam to tell her that she was very welcome to the family. Sam translated and Mina looked visibly relieved, but nothing prepared her for the welcome she received when they arrived at the big house. All the strange, pale faces talking to her in a language she could not understand, the little children tugging at her clothes and the excited dogs sniffing her. Mustapha rescued her, he spoke her language and he took her to his peaceful garden with a tray of hot sweet tea and explained who everyone was. He asked about her family. He completed the introduction to the family that would have been delivered by Aziz Shadi Rashad Salamar Badr al din, believing it to be his duty. Mina instantly warmed to the skinny, chirpy man who reminded her of the old men in her village.

That night Mustapha accompanied Sam and Sal to the place their father had died. The twins were touched by the amount of flowers people had planted there. Away from the women, the twins were able to show their grief. Mustapha comforted them and promised that he would be there for them as a father for as long as he lived. Rose and Maria joined them, bringing Mina and refreshments, and they sat talking quietly until the mosquitoes and moths reminded them to return to the house.

Sal and Sam did not intend to sail again until spring and they began transporting their cargo to London. Mary and Mustapha began teaching Mina to speak English. Mina fell in love with baby Aziz and Ellen Lily, like her mother before her, was happy to share her child with Mina. Despite the sad loss of Aziz Shadi Rashad Salamar Badr al din, the family had a happy Christmas that year. Lily missed her husband acutely, but she had her sons at home, a new daughter and the house was alive with the laughter of children again. It snowed at Christmas, to the utter consternation of Mina, who insisted on going outside to play in the snow with the children. By the time that the twins were due to sail in the spring, Mina was expecting a child and Sal and Maria had fallen in love.

Chapter 21

Mustapha was euphoric. His precious daughter was going to marry the son of Aziz Shadi Rashad Salamar Badr al din, the man he had loved dearly. From the day that Maria was born he had worried about who would care for and protect her after his death. He trusted Sal absolutely and just wanted nothing more than to live long enough to see them married. The wedding would be in the late autumn when the ship returned, hopefully in time for the birth of Mina's child. Mina's initial sickness was relieved by one of Mustapha's remedies made of ginger root. Apart from that she was well and her command of English was improving slowly.

Joseph was also very happy, due to the hours he spent with Lily who helped fill in the account books. He watched her as she sat beside him at the table, her elegant head bent over the books, long curls invariably escaping from her scarf. Sometimes he began to tremble so much that he would excuse himself by volunteering to collect refreshments from the kitchen. He began to accompany her on her walks in the countryside as he had done when they were children. Lily sometimes talked about her husband. Joseph listened to her soft voice rather than the content. He was contented and comfortable to be in her company, he knew he could never replace her husband, he knew she would never love him with the passion she had felt for Aziz Shadi Rashad Salamar Badr al din and he did not mind. He was satisfied to be her companion, to be of use to her, to share her task of managing the farms. Isabel watched them together and felt at peace in her old age.

The summer was a very hot one and Mustapha and Mary were kept busy in the garden, watering the plants and suspending old sheets on sticks to shade the plants from the scorching midday sun. Mina, undaunted by the heat, organized games for the children and taught them songs that only Mustapha could understand. The children loved her and followed her everywhere. Anna Isabel was almost five and was a quiet, affectionate little girl with striking green eyes and a lovely smile. Charles Edward was four and he was a happy laughing child with bright blue eyes like his mother and a mop of dark curly hair and a love of animals, particularly the camels. Henry Thomas was a boisterous, accident prone, green-eyed whirlwind of a child. He was three and needed constant supervision. Little Mary Ellen was fair-haired, fearless and besotted with her elder sister and toddled along behind her from morning until bedtime. The baby Aziz Gabriel was dark haired and had hazel eyes like Mary Ellen and towards the end of summer was taking his first steps. Ellen Lily was grateful to spend the first summer for six years without a swelling belly.

The horse races drew huge crowds. The blond stallion Adam, son of Elijah and Molly fulfilled his early promise of being a winner. He won so many races, proudly ridden by Robert, that Gabriel was regularly offered large amounts of money for him. He refused to sell him and charged a high price for his stud services. The horse breeding business flourished and Gabriel employed over a dozen workers and was forced to build extra stables. He reported regularly to Lily and Joseph and always asked permission before embarking on his next idea. Lily trusted him implicitly and following her husband's example, signed the farm, stables and horses over to him and Ellen Lily.

Sam and Sal's marriages, coupled with the tendency in the family for the number of births to outweigh the deaths, necessitated a massive reorganization in the house. Gabriel, Ellen Lily and the children returned to the their own house, disturbing the peaceful, solitary existence of Robert. Mary and Edward moved to one end of the house with Mustapha and Ida. Lily and Rose moved into the central section with Isabel and Joseph. Mina and Maria were given free reign in the vacated section to create their own little homes in which to begin their married lives. They took to the task with enthusiasm. They raided the attics for discarded furniture. Lily showed them the rolls of fabrics stored in wooden trunks. With the help of Ivy they made curtains, cushion covers and bedspreads. They dug out the wall hangings from the old house. Mina chose to use a mixture of deep reds and oranges for her bedroom and Maria favoured violets and blues. Lily gave the carved wooden crib, made for the birth of Sam, to Mina. To Maria she gave the violet-blue bedspread with the thousands of mirrors embroidered into it that her husband had given her prior to her own wedding. In the upheaval Lily found the warm green dressing gown that had belonged to her father. She gave it to Mustapha. Lily and Joseph made plans for a large extension to the house to be undertaken in the following spring.

The twins arrived home in early autumn, driven as much by the impatient, relentless winds of love and desire as by the wind in the sails of their ship. The family intended to have a quiet wedding, but in a village grown accustomed to the excesses of Aziz Shadi Rashad Salamar Badr al din this proved impossible. Mustapha proudly escorted the exquisite daughter he never dreamed he would have down the aisle of the church, watched by a crying wife who had assumed her life to be over until the day that Mustapha had appeared at her door, dragged there by an impatient Mary, determined that they waste no more time. He handed her to the tall handsome Sal, the unexpected son that no one knew existed until he followed his brother into the world. The ceremony went ahead, but the grinning Mustapha was not listening, he was marvelling at the sheer amount of wonderfully unexpected events that had had to become realities in order for this day to happen. The villagers unable to cram into the church were assembled outside, and welcomed the couple with cheers and good wishes. Then they followed them home to share in the celebrations that followed all major events in this family.

A month after the wedding, Mina went into labour. Her pains were very mild throughout the day and Mary encouraged her to walk around to aid the descent of the child. Mustapha collected his potions and threw a rope over the kitchen beam. Mina was not alarmed by this development, due to it being a common practice in her home village. She was unused to a man being present during childbirth, but Mustapha was the only one she could really communicate with, apart from her husband. Mary assured her that Mustapha had been present at all of the family's births, with the exception of Ellen Lily's, whose babies fell out like beasts in the fields. Her pains increased during the night and Mustapha gave her the first of his concoctions and along with Mary, helped her into the deep warm water in the candlelit bathhouse. Mina had expected to feel pain. She had listened to many women giving birth in her family. It was blissfully pain free in the warm water and she thought her labour had stopped. Mary kept the water hot by topping it up with steaming bowls from the stove. Mustapha watched Mina closely for the first signs of involuntary pushing. He intended to take her to the kitchen for the last stage, after fortifying her with another concoction. Mina began to sing the songs from her village and Mustapha joined in. Mary supported her head as she floated in the water singing at the top of her voice. She had become so relaxed Mary feared that she would sink. During a particularly rousing chorus, the top of a little head bobbed to the surface of the water. Mustapha fished out the child and wrapped him in warm towels and took him to meet his father. Mary attended to Mina, who was still singing and had completely missed the birth of her first child. Mary was dressing Mina in a clean nightdress when she heard the familiar shouting at the stars by Mustapha, Sam and Sal. Then she carried the smiling Mina in and sat her in the chair beside a roaring fire and placed her son in her arms. The men had decided he would be called Khalid, meaning 'eternal and glorious'. His other names would be Aziz John. When Mina regained her senses she was insistent that they add Mustapha to his list of given names. Mustapha smiled until his old face began to hurt.

Consistent with her own traditions, Mina kept Khalid at her side for forty days and nights. At Christmas she was willing to allow other people to cuddle him. He was a quiet, content baby and he rarely cried. He resembled the twins when they were babies. He had the same mop of dark hair, his skin was darker than theirs and his eyes were a deep amber colour. He possessed a penetrating stare that reminded Isabel of his grandmother Lily's stare when she was tiny. Mustapha fussed around him. He had achieved his wish of staying alive to witness the marriage of his beloved Maria, but now he had a new dream. He wanted to stay alive long enough to be a grandfather. Mary attributed Mustapha's extreme longevity to his perpetual revision of ambitions and his unyielding, dogged resolve to reach the next one.

It was the second Christmas without Aziz Shadi Rashad Salamar Badr al din and Lily missed him intensely at times, but the house was so full of joy that she was genuinely happy. Counting the children, there were over twenty family members to feed. It was necessary to employ help from the village to cook and clean so that Mary did not exhaust herself. Both Mary and Mustapha interfered in the cooking, adding spices and supervising the meticulous construction of Mustapha's famous puddings. The men pushed tables together and collected every chair in the house to make room for everyone at dinner. They had roasted lamb, beef and a pile of chickens cooked in Mustapha's sauce. There were trays of crisp, golden roasted potatoes, parsnips, onions and carrots. Dishes of cabbage, jugs of steaming gravy, stuffing and pots of horseradish were the final items to be brought to table by the women from the village. Lily then insisted that the women sit down with them to eat. The flustered, red-faced women sat down nervously, wiping their hands on their aprons. Mustapha, who had adopted the role of host, served them first and the family congratulated them on their culinary skills. Close to tears the women tucked in to the best meal they had ever had. Mary and Ellen Lily served the puddings, combatting the women's attempts to help. After the numerous pots of tea were drunk they finally allowed the women to clear the table and wash the dishes. They were each sent home with a box of food for their families as well as their wages.

Gabriel and Ellen Lily took their children home to bed, armed with a box of food. Sal took over the job of keeping the fires roaring that had been Gabriel's task. The family, who were too full to eat anything else, dozed on the sofas and cushions and watched the first snowflakes falling.

By the time they had all retired to bed the snow was falling heavily and the wind had begun to blow. Mina woke Sam during the night petrified by the screaming gale blowing outside. By morning, the windows on the North side of the house were opaque with snow and the front door was buried under a huge snowdrift. It was still snowing. It snowed remorselessly for days, icicles hung from the eves of the house and Mina's former love of snow was significantly diminished. The water pump froze necessitating thawing the snow in buckets. Fuel, the only defense in this weather, was not a problem. Joseph admired the foresight of Aziz Shadi Rashad Salamar Badr al din, building houses in the shelter of a wood and fervently hoped this winter would not be a repeat of the previous harsh one that had killed so many villagers. He went to see Gabriel, battling his way through the drifts, and told him about the tragedy of so many villagers frozen to death. They took the wheels off an old cart and constructed a makeshift sledge, harnessed it to a pair of the strongest heavy horses, filled it with dead trees and dragged it to the centre of the village. They repeated the arduous journey everyday, with the help of Sam and Sal who dragged the dead trees though the wood ready for loading. Men in the village, moved by the heroic efforts of Gabriel and Joseph, chopped and sawed the wood and made sure that the old people had enough to prevent them from freezing to death. A few did die that year, the very frail and the inevitable drunks who fell into temptingly comfortable snowdrifts on their way home. Nobody died from the lack of a decent fire.

Gabriel attacked the frozen water pumps with buckets of hot embers, and lagged them with hay and sacking, succeeding in bringing the bathhouses back into use. This gallant achievement backfired when the water from the previous evenings welcome hot baths froze solid in the backyard, forming a lethal sheet of ice from the back door to the stables. Mary sprinkled it with a whole sack of salt to avoid anyone breaking bones or even necks. Overnight it froze again and the men had to resort to breaking the ice up with shovels and moving it to the side of the house. Gabriel was relieved that he had had stoves built in to the new stables. He worked unflaggingly, keeping his horses well fed and watered and covered in warm blankets, trudging through the woods to make sure the ponies and camels were warm and fed. Ellen Lily frequently had to wake him from a deep sleep in front of the fire in the evenings to go out and stoke up the fires in the stables before retiring to bed. She was kept busy with the children. Anna was a helpful little girl and Charles at four was already starting to help his father in the stables. Henry was another matter. He ran about from morning until night, creating havoc. At three he had already broken an arm, had his head stitched by Mustapha several times and managed to get his finger trodden on by a horse. He jumped out of windows, climbed onto the roof of the house and fell off trying to get down again. Mustapha suggested putting him on a leash and his father was tempted to build him a cage.

The first rays of the spring sunshine and the snowdrops were welcome sights, heralding spring at last. Most people in the big house were pleased, with the exception of Mina and Mustapha. Mina knew that her husband would be sailing in a month's time and poor old Mustapha had been thoroughly devastated by his daughter's announcement that she wanted to go to sea with her husband as Lily had done thirty years ago. Mina thought she was mad and vowed she would never set foot on a ship again. Once had been enough. With Mustapha's encouragement Mina told Maria about the seasickness, the maggots in the biscuits, the storms and the constant embarrassment of being the only woman on board and no access to a lavatory. Without his knowledge Mina reminded Maria that her father could die while she was away and how would she be able to live with her conscience if that happened. In the end the warnings were unnecessary as by April, a few weeks before departure, Maria realized that she was expecting a child and Sal refused to take her with him. Mustapha immediately prostrated himself on the floor and thanked Allah, whom he had pestered constantly with his desperate entreaties for over a month. Then he ran around the house, hugging everyone and crying with laughter and jumping about until Mary, fearing for his life, unceremoniously manhandled him into a chair in the kitchen and poured him a cup of tea. She threatened to tie him to the chair if he got up again. She reminded him that he was no spring chicken and far too old for that sort of silly gallivanting about and showing off and as a prospective Grandfather he should show a great deal more decorum! He stayed there, smiling triumphantly. Maria eyed him with amused suspicion, firmly believing he had cast some sort of smell that had thwarted her attempt to sail away from him.

It was Lily's turn to fret when Rose asked her brothers if she could sail with them. She reminded everyone that she was the only member of the family who had never been. Her father, brothers and even her mother had all sailed the seas and it was in her blood! Her brothers agreed with her and Lily accepted defeat. As she watched the ship sail away, containing all of her children, she understood how utterly desolate her poor father must have felt when she sailed away with Aziz Shadi Rashad Salamar Badr al din.

'Don't worry Lily, they'll come home, just like you did.' Joseph said quietly.

She turned and looked into his eyes, her own brimming with tears.

'Promise me they will.'

'I promise.' Answered Joseph as he put his arm around her shoulders.

They sat in silence as Joseph drove the cart home and Lily was glad he was with her.

.

Chapter 22

Mustapha took on the role of broody hen and rarely let Maria out of his sight. She spent the summer helping him in the garden, making him rest by insisting that he keep her company every time he made her take a rest.

Most of the village attended Aziz Shadi Rashad Salamar Badr al din's birthday celebrations. Anticipating a large turnout, Gabriel had cleared the area in the woods and built seats and tables and a solid floor for the musicians. The event became a permanent feature in village life and continued for so long that people forgot why it had begun.

Virtually all of the children in the village attended school and even children from nearby villages walked several miles in order to learn to read. Joseph managed the staffing, selecting the brightest children and employing them as teachers when they were old enough. There were six classes, two for the little children, two for the ones that had mastered their reading and counting and two for the ones studying specific, more advanced subjects. The school continued to provide a hot meal for all of the children, prepared by ex-pupils who had learned to cook. Joseph employed a dozen young people to run the school, lifting another dozen families out of poverty.

The ship had been expected to return in the

autumn but failed to arrive, causing slight concern in most of the household and sheer dread for Lily, Maria and Mina. Mary reminded them that there could be all sorts of reasons why they were late and there was no need to worry. Mustapha agreed with Mary and maintained they would return in the spring. Lily, feeling isolated and out of step with the mounting excitement surrounding the imminent birth of Maria's baby, resumed her long walks in the countryside. Life, it seemed to her had turned full circle. Her husband was dead and all of her children were gone and at times her marriage took on the quality of a distant dream. Joseph accompanied her as he did when they were young.

In early October Maria's labour began. Mary took charge, preparing the warm bath that had become the favoured method since Mina's baby's birth. Ida wanted to be present at the delivery, as did Isabel, who believed that this would probably be the last birth she would be alive to witness. Remembering how incapacitated he had been at his daughter's birth, everyone tried to keep Mustapha in blissful ignorance and sent him to deliver a message to Ellen Lily. This plan had been pre-arranged, so that Ellen Lily would detain him for as long as possible. He happily played with the children for most of the afternoon, but when invited to remain for the evening meal, he smelt a rat, and skittered off through the woods. He stopped briefly at Aziz Shadi Rashad Salamar Badr al din's shrine to inform him that his grandchild was on the way. Contrary to everyone's expectations, Mustapha appeared in the bathhouse and calmly assessed the situation. He told Mary to raise the temperature of the bath water, sent Isabel to make pots of hot sweet tea and sent Ida to get a sheet. He mixed a concoction for Maria and twisted the sheet into a rope. He encouraged Maria to kneel in the bath and pull on the sheet whilst he held the other end. He watched his daughter closely and when she began to arch her back he stationed Mary behind her to watch for the emerging head. Isabel and Ida watched the fragile old man of uncertain age, whose glittering eyes never left his daughter, and his quiet voice never failed to encourage her. Mary caught the baby and passed him between Maria's legs for her to hold. Ida burst into tears, Maria and Mary laughed and Mustapha fell to the floor. For an awful moment the women thought he had died but he was fervently thanking Allah. He wrapped his grandson in a warm towel and went outside to present him to the sky. The family gathered around the fire while Mary tended to Maria. Mustapha refused to part with his grandson, he pottered around the room talking excitedly to the child. Eventually he reluctantly allowed Ida to hold him briefly, but hovered so close that Ida gave him back with a smile.

Maria sat beside the fire and announced that she and Sal had already decided on names for the child. Had he been a girl it would have been Lily Ida, but as he was a boy it would be Mustapha

Aziz, for his grandfathers. Mustapha danced around the room babbling incoherently until Mary sat him down with a cup of tea and passed the startled baby to his mother.

The ship arrived home on a wet day in early December. The family had resigned themselves to wait until spring, so were shocked when the twins and Rose arrived in the kitchen. Lily was overcome with relief and Sal was overjoyed with the birth of his son. Joseph was the first to notice that Sam and Rose seemed ill at ease. Sam explained they had been delayed due to damage to a mast in a storm that had necessitated a month of repairs in a Portuguese dock. Later in the evening he and Sal asked to speak to Lily alone. They informed her that whilst they were docked in Portugal, Rose had secretly become involved with a local carpenter. When it was time to leave she insisted she was in love with him and refused to sail without him. Sam had refused to take the carpenter and pointed out to her that she knew nothing about this man, the whole idea was ridiculous, and they were leaving in the morning whether she agreed or not. In the morning Rose was not on board. It had taken the twins almost a month to locate their sister. She was living with the carpenter's family in a cottage near the mountains. Sam was angry and could not decide between dragging his sister back to the ship, tied up if necessary or washing his hands of her and leaving her there. Sal, the more sensitive twin reminded his brother that he had married a stranger he met during a voyage and he had taken her home. Sam had tried to insist that it was different as Rose was a woman. Eventually, they reached a compromise, Rose agreed to return home and her brothers agreed to take the carpenter to meet the family. They made him work his passage to England and refused to allow their sister to be alone with him during the voyage.

Lily went to speak to Rose. She was tearful, apologetic and pleaded with her mother to meet the carpenter whose name was Paulo Vidal Salazar. Lily remembered how she had loved Aziz Shadi Rashad Salamar Badr al din the moment she saw him. It would not have mattered whom he was or if he had been rich or poor. She understood how her daughter felt and agreed to meet with her carpenter. He would be invited to dinner the following day.

Joseph was given the task of collecting Paulo from the ship. The young man's English was limited and he was visibly nervous. The family had assembled in a random crowd outside of the front door, all very curious to see the stranger. Poor Paulo was terrified. Rose was blushing and clinging to her mother's hand. Joseph introduced the trembling Paulo to each member of the family in turn. Lily watched the tall, slim young man nodding politely. His skin was pale and his black hair hung in tight, shiny ringlets onto his shoulders. He had large, bright blue eyes, black eyebrows and a full mouth. Lily smiled at him as Joseph introduced her as Rose's mother. Paulo smiled back and in that instant,

Lily was left in no doubt why her daughter loved him. During the meal she watched Paulo and Rose, she saw the way they looked at each other. It was obvious that he was besotted with Rose, and Lily was happy with that. Mustapha, believing it to be the responsibility of the family elder, vetted Paulo after the meal and introduced him to little Mustapha. Paulo smiled at the baby. He had a smile that lit up his entire face from within and little Mustapha smiled back and kicked his little legs. That was enough for Mustapha, who firmly believed that his tiny grandson possessed the innate ability to effectively assess the character of a person.

The family organized a wedding just before Christmas. The vicar was relieved that he was marrying Christians this time and kept quiet the fact that one was obviously a Catholic. Paulo was astonished at the size of the extravagant celebrations that included the entire village dancing around a vast bonfire in the field at the front of the house, whilst deafening fireworks sparkled in the night sky.

Sam and Sal and their wives and babies had moved into the new extension built on the west side of the house during the previous summer and Rose and Paulo took up residence in Sal and Maria's old rooms. At Christmas, the family discovered that Paulo had a beautiful singing voice and played a guitar. He entertained them in the evening while they digested the meal, although nobody understood a single word of any of the songs.

In the spring, Gabriel showed Paulo around the large woodland at the back of the house. Paulo was speechless when he learned that he could cut down any of the trees and immediately set about selecting the most suitable. He converted an empty stable into a carpentry workshop and with Gabriel's help began felling the mature trees, which he stacked in the workshop for drying. He produced drawings of furniture and waited impatiently for the timber to dry.

Isabel, who was well into her seventies, found it increasingly difficult to move about. She was unwilling to remain in her bed and wait to die, so Mary and Paulo moved her bed downstairs and attached wheels to a suitable chair so they could push her around the ground floor. She spent considerable time in the kitchen, peeling vegetables and harassing the cooks. On sunny days Mary wheeled her into the garden with Mustapha to give the cooks some welcome respite. Mustapha believed that her bones were crumbling, for which he had no cure, but he kept her pain free with his remedies and sleeping draughts. The remedies loosened Isabel's tongue to such an extent that, during dinner, she announced to Lily that Joseph had been in love with her since he was a child and that they should get married before she died. Lily stared at her, stunned. The initial silence was interrupted by other members of the family, laughing. Joseph stared at his mother red-faced and horribly embarrassed, too shocked to get up and leave the room. Isabel, blissfully unaware of the level of discomfort, asked Mary to pass the salt.

Later in the evening, during which Lily and Joseph had strategically managed to avoid each other, Mary and Lily sat at the kitchen table drinking tea. Lily was surprised to learn that the entire family knew of Joseph's feelings. Lily was very fond of Joseph and depended on him a great deal. The thought of re-marrying had never entered her head. She still felt married to Aziz Shadi Rashad Salamar Badr al din. Mary pointed out that she already spent so much time with Joseph that marriage would make little difference. After Mary left the room, Lily sat and thought. In a way, she did love Joseph. Not with the blind passion she had felt for her husband, but with a quiet, comfortable companionship that old couples settle into after many years together. He had been a loyal friend all of her life and she could not imagine life without him, she had always been secretly grateful that he had never married. Mary, who had little patience with the luxury of embarrassment, hauled the reluctant Joseph into the kitchen and insisted that they discuss the situation. She then flounced out of the kitchen, slammed the door and warned the rest of the family to avoid the area. Left alone together, Lily and Joseph remained silent for a while. Joseph looked sheepish and fiddled with a dent on the table and Lily started to giggle helplessly.

'Lily, I can only apologise for my mother's untimely outburst.'

'So, you do not love me then Joseph?' she laughed.

Joseph's mouth dropped open, which resulted in a renewed bout of laughter from Lily.

'Oh Joseph, we have known each other all of our lives and are too old to be embarrassed now, I think we should consider what to do.'

Joseph valiantly tried to regain his composure.

'Lily, I have always loved you. I know I can never take the place of Aziz and would not want to.'

'Do you think we should marry? It would mean so much to your mother.'

Joseph had tears in his eyes.

'Lily, if you should ever agree to become my wife I would be the happiest man in the world.' He whispered.

'Then I agree,' said Lily with a smile. 'And I think you should tell your poor mother!'

They sat and drank a pot of tea whilst Lily tried to discuss their forthcoming marriage, but Joseph just sat and smiled, unable to make any useful response.

Chapter 23

During the decades that Mustapha had lived in the village he had administered his remedies to all the families during times of illness and death. In the early years, the locals were suspicious of him and his remedies. It was the women that had overcome their fears first, allowing him to relieve the pains of childbirth and death. The men, in particular the devout Christians had been the most reluctant to request his services. The vicar refused his wife's pleas and forbade her any contact with Mustapha, and his wife, unable to benefit from his remedies during childbirth, never forgave her husband.

Mustapha was fascinated by sickness. He was interested in all the different types of illness and the patterns of incidence amongst the villagers. He was well aware that extreme poverty rendered people much more vulnerable to illness and death. He deduced that adequate food and decent shelter was essential for good health. The death rate of village children had reduced considerably since the school had opened and provided them with meals. Illness also followed a seasonal pattern. Mustapha knew that winter increased the incidence of chest problems, whereas hot weather produced more stomach and bowel disturbances. Some illnesses passed from one person to another, particularly within families. Other illnesses did not. Malaria was a disease of damp summers, when the mosquitoes invaded from the marshes. He had made balms that deterred the mosquitoes from biting, and oils, that when burned, gave off a smoke that rid the area of flying insects. He believed that the excessive heat generated within the body during the fevers suffered by malaria sufferers was what killed them. He made potions to reduce the heat and induce sleep, whilst cooling the body with damp cloths and bellows.

Smallpox, the sickness most feared, was no respecter of social standing. It attacked anyone, the rich, the poor and at any age. It was more common in the towns and made an appearance in the village less frequently. Mustapha noticed that some families were invariably spared, despite contact with sufferers. The cowmen, the milkmaids and the families with cows that had suffered an attack of cowpox appeared to be immune to the disease. Contact with an infected cow, according to Mustapha, somehow protected the person from contracting the deadly smallpox. He encouraged the villagers to catch cowpox. It was an irritating outbreak of blisters, but far from life threatening. Many people thought he was mad, but over the years they were gradually convinced. Eventually, villagers were often seen gathering around an infected cow, waiting for their turn to stroke it's udder and squeeze it's blisters.

Mustapha also observed that illnesses generally limited to children, like measles, chicken pox and mumps, only happened once in a person. During a subsequent bout, all the children that had suffered the illness in previous outbreaks were untouched. This led him to believe that the body somehow learned to defeat the illness, in the same way that cowpox taught the body to ignore smallpox. He recorded the medical histories of the families. He believed that his remedies and potions supported and assisted the body, helping it to fight against the illness. It also seemed to him that a person's character had a bearing on their health. Cheerful, indomitable people like Mary and Ellen Lily had not suffered a day's sickness in their lives and yet some individuals, prone to sadness and worry, appeared to be much more likely to suffer illness.

Mary's had gained extensive knowledge of Mustapha's remedies and she was a great help to him in both production and prescribing. Anna, Ellen Lily and Gabriel's eldest daughter, always close to her grandmother, began to spend her spare time with Mustapha and Mary in the garden, learning the care and harvesting of the plants. She showed great promise and constantly asked to help them when nursing the sick. Anna had helped her mother nurse her younger brothers and sister, sitting beside their beds during the night to allow her mother to rest. She had nursed Henry, her accident- prone brother, when he broke his bones with alarming regularity. She was never happier than when nursing the sick, as her mother had been when teaching children to read and write.

It was Anna who first suggested the idea of having a designated building in the village where the inhabitants could go if they were sick or injured and needed help. Stocks of remedies, potions, splints, clean bedding and dressings could be stored ready for any eventuality. Mustapha agreed and called a family meeting and the decision was made to obtain a piece of land near the centre of the village, allowing easy access for the inhabitants. Mustapha had a new wish, to stay alive long enough to see the building in operation.

Chapter 24

Lily and Joseph, now in their early fifties, insisted on a small quiet wedding in early autumn, with just immediate family, followed by a meal at home with the family. The villagers had other ideas. They assembled silently outside in the churchyard whilst Mustapha led Lily up the aisle to Joseph, and greeted the couple with cheers and flowers as they left the church. Despite being uninvited, the entire village arrived in the field outside of the house, where they had attended parties for the last thirty years. This time they took their own food and musicians and invited the startled family to join them. The children from the school lined up and sang them a song. The women of the village had each made a beautifully embroidered patchwork square, depicting a flower. They had then sewn all the pieces together to form a quilt. They had sewn bluebells, anemones, primroses, wild roses, snowdrops, forget-me-nots, daisies, buttercups, poppies, clover, iris and water lilies. The family joined the villagers in the field and danced under the full moon. Isabel sat in her chair with wheels and cried with happiness at the smile on Joseph's face as he danced with his wife.

It was early November when the storm arrived. Mustapha had predicted it was on the way. Storms were fairly regular events, and rarely caused much damage. This one was different. It was heralded by three days of darkening skies and strong winds. Vast black clouds built up in layers above the estuary and were swept along by the strong winds. People watched the clouds disappear to the east and breathed sighs of relief. Even bigger clouds formed and hovered menacingly above the marshes. The first thunder sounded in the distance, many seconds behind a flash of lightening. Everyone hoped the storm was moving away. There followed an eerie silence as the sky took on a greenish colour and the air became heavy and oppressive. The birds became silent, the animals shifted nervously in the fields and Gabriel's horses clamoured to enter their stables.

The first lightening, accompanied by an ear-splitting roll of thunder, hit the weathervane of the church steeple and blew a hole in the wall of the ale house, knocking some disorientated drinkers to the sawdust covered floor. The lack of rain heightened the oppressive silence. The next casualty was the tall sycamore in the centre of the village. The lightening split it into three, crushing a cottage, blocking the lane and leaving a black, smoking shard standing fifty feet tall. The first people to emerge and see what had happened were greeted by the sudden hailstones, some the size of eggs, crashing to the ground. The people retreated as the hailstones broke windows and smashed onto the homes, breaking tiles. The storm continued unabated throughout the evening. Thunder rumbled constantly with varying intensity and the lightening illuminated the clouds like firecrackers. Several building caught fire. Men ventured out with sacks folded over their heads against the driving, stinging rain to assess the damage. Gabriel was torn between comforting his squealing children and reassuring his terrified horses. Mina refused to come out from under the bed and the babies both slept soundly. Mary made tea for the family huddled around the fire, waiting for the storm to abate and worrying about the damage. Mustapha watched the storm and worried about his garden.

Around midnight the rain subsided and the wind increased from the west. Mustapha announced that the shutters should be closed. The younger men went out to shut them, without the help of Mustapha, who was so frail that in his green dressing gown that he resembled a sparrow in a horse blanket and would have been blown away. The wind came in gusts that built slowly in strength, increasing in force until the men were incapable of doing anything but cling on to each other. The men managed to close the ground floor shutters during the rhythmic lull between the gusts. The upper windows were more challenging, requiring a ladder. The men sheltered at the side of the house, waiting for the wind to subside, then ran to a window with the ladder and Paulo climbed the ladder whilst Sam and Sal tried desperately to hold it fast before the next gust arrived. They managed to close the shutters on the east of the house, which was taking the brunt of the wind, but gave up after

Paulo was blown from the ladder and disappeared into the darkness rolling like tumbleweed. He returned muddy and disheveled but unharmed. The family barred the doors and listened to the wind roaring and the random crashes outside. Mustapha and Mary had forced a remedy down the throat of Mina and she was sleeping peacefully in her bed. Isabel was unable to remember wind as strong as this in all of her life. Mustapha did, but not since he had lived in the village. It reminded him of tropical storms. The women meandered into the kitchen and started to cook, providing a welcome distraction from the increasing screaming of the wind and the clatter of objects hitting the house. The wind abated just before dawn, to the relief of everyone and they waited for daylight.

Mustapha unbarred the door to go and investigate his precious garden and was so alarmed by the sky that he forgot all about the garden. Huge, forbidding storm clouds towered motionless, miles high into the sky. He shut the door, deterred the twins from opening the shutters, and suggested everyone go into the kitchen for a good hearty breakfast to prepare them for a busy day. Mary was puzzled by Mustapha's behaviour. She noticed an unfamiliar troubled look in his eyes. She made some tea and Maria and Rose began cooking eggs and mushrooms and slicing bread. The family sat at the table and due to the shutters, failed to notice the sky darken again as the menacing clouds crept soundlessly across the marshes. The resounding clap of thunder, coinciding with lightening so bright it shone through the cracks in the shutters, made the family jump and sent Mina screaming out of bed. The storm raged ferociously, shaking the house to the foundations. Mina cried under the kitchen table. The babies woke up and corrupted by the tension in the family, wailed pitifully. Joseph and Paulo went upstairs and looked out of the back window in time to witness a fork of lightening explode the massive oak tree containing the old tree house. The house shuddered as the tree fractured and lurched to an undignified sprawl beside the stables. Mina yelped and jumped, banging her head on the underside of the table. Mustapha gave her a hot, sweet tea, liberally laced with his potion.

It was midday before the storm finally subsided, almost twenty-four hours after it had begun. The family wandered outside to a wilderness of destruction and littered debris, fences were torn down, trees uprooted and fires burned in the distance. Within an hour, villagers arrived requesting help to free the friends and neighbours trapped in collapsed buildings and to set broken bones and stitch cuts. Gabriel arrived to see how everyone had fared. His own family was unhurt and his horses were fraught but uninjured. He returned home to collect a cart pulled by his strongest heavy horse and arrived with Ellen Lily and Anna, leaving Charles to look after the other children. Isabel, Ida, Mina, Sam and the babies were the only ones left at home, the rest joined forces with Gabriel and headed off to the village. The damage was extensive, several of the cottages had been crushed under the weight of fallen trees, and the men and women were already clearing the timber and rubble to rescue the trapped. The streets were littered with casualties, limping and bleeding. Joseph opened the school and told everyone to take the injured there. The more seriously injured arrived on carts and tied to doors or carried on chairs. Mustapha assessed the broken bones, sending Paulo to cut the wood for splints. Sal lit the fires. Mary administered the pain relief to the seriously injured. Anna cleaned and dressed the minor cuts and grazes. Ellen Lily and Lily stitched the larger wounds and passed them to Anna for dressings. Women arrived with sheets that they tore into strips for bandages. Ivy boiled water and several women from the village arrived with vegetables and meat and began making soup for the survivors. Many of the families had no homes to return to.

By nightfall, many of the walking wounded with homes still standing, following a fortifying bowl of hot soup and bread, had returned to their homes. Some were told to return in the following days to have their dressings changed. Gabriel and his horse and cart moved the belongings of the homeless to the school where they could stay until other alternatives were found. The seriously injured remained in the school and were nursed around the clock. Most of these patients had broken bones or lacerations resulting from flying debris. Mustapha and Mary administered the remedies and kept them virtually pain free. Ellen Lily and Anna fed, washed and comforted them. The village women took it in turns to man the kitchen. Miraculously, there were only two fatalities during the disaster, an elderly couple whose cottage had collapsed. Joseph took care of them. Over the next few days, the patients with broken bones and no sign swelling and heat around the area, were transported to their homes on Gabriel's cart. Anna cleaned the lacerations each day with warm boiled water. Mustapha checked the healing and applied one of his balms if necessary, and Anna redressed them with clean bandages. Ivy boiled the bandages, dried them and stacked them for future use. Mary and Mustapha slept in shifts. Anna refused to take a break from nursing and was eventually found fast asleep at the kitchen table, beside her soup, the spoon still in her hand. She had worked non-stop for four days.

Mustapha was so impressed by Anna's efforts that he took her with him, several days later, to visit the homes of the patients and check of their progress. He showed her how to remove stitches with sharp scissors and tweezers. Then, with the help of Mary they tackled the ravaged garden.

The village animals had fared better than their owners. The sheep on the marshes had huddled together in the shelter of hedgerows. There was little flying debris on the marshes and what there was stuck in their thick fleeces rather than their bodies. Most of the cattle had been in sheds. The roof had blown off a chicken shed and the chickens were blown about and found wandering aimlessly about the village for days afterwards.

Chapter 25

Clearing up after the storm took weeks. Paulo and Gabriel were kept busy collecting and storing the trees damaged by the lightening. Paulo had already begun planning the furniture he would build. The village men sawed and chopped the fallen trees and delivered the logs to the elderly. The crew repaired sails and ropes ripped by the wind. Winter set in early that year, in late November the village was under a blanket of snow that failed to melt until March.

Isabel's health was failing and she needed help dressing and washing. Mary and Lily, fearing it may be her final Christmas, made sure that all of her sons and grandchildren would be present for Christmas dinner. There were so many members of the family that the young children sat at a separate table where Anna tried desperately to maintain some semblance of order. Isabel sat surrounded by all of her sons and realized that of all the people in the room, she loved Mary the most. Paulo had made sledges for the children and after dinner they skidded around the field until their fingers were red and aching.

It took the family several days to recover from the chaotic, pandemonium that was Christmas. The twins spent time at the docks, preparing for a spring voyage and the women passed the long dark evenings in the warm bathhouse.

Isabel died in the spring, sitting in her chair in the garden with Mary and Mustapha, in the middle of a conversation. They realized she had died when she stopped joining in. Mustapha checked for a pulse and nodded to Mary, who tried to control her emotions, failed, fell to her knees and sobbed, her head in Isabel's lap. Mustapha sat beside her and stroked her hair. The two women had lived in the same house for over thirty years and had formed a friendship closer than most mother and daughter relationships. Mary had been, for Isabel, the longed for daughter she had never had. Mustapha pottered into the kitchen to get some tea. He told no one of Isabel's death, firmly believing that Mary would not wish the family to see her grief. They sat on the ground beside Isabel and drank their tea until Mary had stopped crying. She was grateful that it had been a good, painless death, and was glad that she had been with her at the end. Mary blew her nose on the apron and with a sigh rose to her feet. Mustapha flailed like an injured bird in an attempt to get up and needed Mary's assistance, which made her laugh and restored her invincible spirit.

Joseph organized the funeral. Edward, the eldest son walked in front of the coffin and Isabel's other six sons carried her from the cart to the church. Mary had decorated the coffin with primroses. Isabel was buried beside her husband, watched by a large number of villagers who remembered her as a kind, hard working woman who had been very fortunate to die before any of her children. Both Mary and Mustapha missed her presence keenly, and even the village women who worked in the kitchen missed her heckling interference.

The Parish Relief committee, responsible for the distribution of financial relief for the poor, a small group of the more affluent villagers included Joseph. He had been asked to assist the committee after the death of Aziz Shadi Rashad Salamar Badr al din. The committee had been impressed by the family's response to the villagers injured after the great storm, and agreed with the suggestion that a small designated building to treat the sick and injured would be advantageous. There was an empty cottage near the church, in need of repair. The committee donated the cottage and a small sum of money for materials for the necessary refurbishment. Paulo was put in charge of the rebuilding. The crew from the ship helped him to replace the roof, but when the ship sailed Paulo was struggling on alone. Word soon permeated through the village about the 'sick house' as they called it. Local men, who had worked all day, offering their services for a few hours before dark, joined Paulo during the evenings. Women arrived during the day, babies slung across their backs. They swept and scrubbed the walls and floors. Mustapha and Mary helped Paulo draw plans for the rooms, with shelves, cupboards and beds. People donated chairs, sheets for dressings and cooking pots for the kitchen. By June the 'sick house' was complete. It had a functioning kitchen, with stoves for hot water and a chest with a lock to store the potions and remedies. There was a waiting room with chairs and table. The remaining two rooms were furnished with beds for the patients in need of extensive treatment and nursing. The shelves in the kitchen held rolls of bandages made by the local women. Mustapha wanted a bathhouse in the yard at the back of the cottage. Joseph agreed, but this was a massive undertaking and was postponed to the following year. The 'sick house' was open from Monday to Friday from ten in the morning until mid afternoon. Anna was there everyday and Mustapha and Mary attended on alternate days. Ivy arrived most days, willing to help with out in any way she could. Anyone who needed help at night sent a messenger to Mustapha and Mary as they had always done.

The first person to arrive at the 'sick house' was a frantic young mother with a screaming small child with scalded feet. Mustapha sat the child with her feet in a bowl of cold water. He gave her a remedy for pain and changed the cold water every hour. Finally, he lanced the blisters with a boiled needle and dressed the burns with bandages soaked in paraffin wax to avoid it sticking to the skin. He gave the mother a potion to help the child sleep and instructions to return for dressing changes. Anna began writing down all of the treatments given by Mustapha and Mary, in case an emergency occurred when she was alone. During the first few months, they had two broken legs, a broken arm, two cases of malaria fevers, several deep cuts and a nail through a foot. Births and deaths were still dealt with in the homes of the villagers.

Ivy arrived to open the 'sick house' on a Monday morning and was astonished to discover a tiny naked baby wrapped in and old ragged tweed jacket on the doorstep. She took the baby in, not sure if it was dead or alive. When Mustapha arrived he declared the baby girl just alive, but unlikely to survive. He cut and tied the long umbilical cord. He estimated her to be a day or two old and in desperate need of breast milk. Ivy, believing the child's survival was her responsibility, rolled her in a clean sheet and set off around the village to the houses of nursing mothers, pleading with them to feed the child. She found two mothers willing to feed her. Every four hours, day and night, Ivy took the baby for a feed. After several days the baby was feeding well and her colour had improved. After two weeks, Mustapha decided that she had a good chance of survival. Her parentage remained a mystery. Nobody came to claim her and nobody knew where she had come from.

Ivy's only child Jack, the quiet shepherd, had not married and she had no hope of grandchildren. She pleaded with her husband Charles, begging him to allow her to keep the child. He had not seen her so animated and happy for a long time and had not the heart to refuse her. She named the child Isabella Mary after the women she loved most. She was christened in the church, Jack was godfather, Anna was delighted to be godmother and little Isabella, the foundling, became part of the Martin family. She remained utterly bald for the first six months of her life, eventually growing thick, very fine, very straight pale blond hair. Her eyes were a light hazel. She grew into a slender, very shy child who hid in Ivy's skirts at the first glimpse of a stranger or a spider. Ivy loved her and reveled in the role of Isabella's chosen refuge.

Chapter 26

Khalid grew into an adventurous, fearless child. He was very protective of his cousin Mustapha, who was quieter and more sensitive. Paulo built them an expansive, resplendent tree house, using his unique carpentry skills. Instead of a rope ladder, he built a spiral stairway with banister rails for safety. He made intricately carved tables, chairs and cupboards and carved their names on the door. He made a slightly larger chair for Mustapha senior, who chose to spend considerable time in the tree house with his grandson, passing on the secrets of his garden that grew below the tree house. Little Isabella was a nervous child and a little scared of Khalid, but she liked both Mustapha's and would run up the stairs to join them, followed by the cries of 'Careful, hold tight!' from the over-protective Ivy.

Khalid was happier running through the woods to play with his cousin Aziz, so the tree house became the chosen refuge for little Mustapha and Isabella. Ivy arrived most days with Isabella, who ran off to find Mustapha. Ivy sat sewing with Lily, and Mary, who possessed no skill in that area made the tea. Ivy rose and went to the window to check on Isabella. She was holding hands with little Mustapha, whilst he showed her around his grandfather's garden. Mustapha senior sat watching them from the tree house above and waved to Ivy. Ivy waved back, smiled and struggled with the urge to cry.

Mustapha remembered when he was little Mustapha's age, living with his father and grandfather in a remote area in Northern Afghanistan. The land was parched and dry. He was unable to recall his mother, who had died when he was a baby. In fact, he was unable to evoke memories of any women in the early years of his life. His grandfather succumbed to a protracted, agonizing death, finally relieved with the sap of the poppies. Mustapha was left with an inability to bear human suffering. His father buried the little old man in the dusty soil, sold their meager belongings and embarked on a journey westward, searching for a better life for his only son. Mustapha could remember the hunger and being carried on the shoulders of his father when he was too weak to walk. The small amount of money ran out and they were reduced to begging. The walked for so long that by the time they approached the home of a wealthy merchant Rashad Badr al din, to beg for food, they were only days from death. Rashad had them put in a building with the camels, provided them with food, water, a change of clothes and when Mustapha's father was well enough to stand, offered him the job of tending to the camels. To Mustapha hunger was a constant, gnawing sensation and the smells escaping from the kitchen of the merchant's home tormented him and caused him to salivate profusely. He lurked beside the kitchen, eyes closed, breathing in the aromas, whilst his father was working.

'You are wearing my clothes!' the child's voice was loud and startled Mustapha.

'I said, you are wearing MY clothes!' he repeated.

Mustapha just stared at him, fiddling nervously with the hem of his long shirt. He had no idea whose clothes they were.

'Take them off!' demanded the child.

'I said, take MY clothes OFF!' the child moved closer. He was a head taller than Mustapha.

'NOW!'

Mustapha removed the clothing and stood naked, he was so emaciated that he resembled an insect, rather than a boy.

Hearing the shouting, two women came out of the kitchen to investigate. They saw the tiny bag of bones, the discarded clothing and Salamar, the son of Rashad. One grabbed Salamar by the ear and marched him to his father and the other helped Mustapha back into the clothes. Tears rolled quietly down his dusty cheeks. The woman picked him up and carried him into the kitchen. It was the closest he had ever been to a woman and he thought she smelled as nice as food.

Later in the day, Mustapha was summoned to the house and Salamar, severely admonished by his father, was made to apologise to Mustapha and present him with another set of clothes.

'Thankyou.' Whispered Mustapha, his head bowed.

From then on, Mustapha took care to avoid Salamar, and spent most of his time in the kitchen, fetching water and washing dishes. The women were kind to him, they washed, combed and braided his long hair and answered his interminable question about the food.

Salamar spend much of his day with his tutor. He was a boisterous, competitive boy and lacked the concentration for studying. Rashad despaired at his son's lack of academic progress and several months after Mustapha's arrival, he asked Mustapha's father if he would allow his son to study with Salamar, believing that a competitive element may speed his own son's efforts. Mustapha was initially sad to be removed from his beloved kitchen and very wary of Salamar. The tutor was a kind man and the lessons fascinated Mustapha. They learned to write and to read, they studied mathematics, history and geography. Both of the boys liked geography. Mustapha was shocked to see how large the world was and how many different countries there were. Salamar refused to believe that the great blue patches on the maps were water. He had seen a river but could not imagine that there was so much water on the world, and that in many places one could not see any land. Gradually the boys became friends, Salamar always won all of the races they had, and the wrestling matches, and Mustapha gracefully accepted defeat and did not care in the least.

Life had been good for the next few years, Mustapha had put on weight and grown taller, he and Salamar had eventually formed a close relationship and their education was progressing well. Rashad had grown fond of Mustapha. Mustapha still loved the kitchen and spent all of his spare time there, learning skills and enjoying the laughter and the companionship of the women.

Mary arrived with hot tea, startling Mustapha out of his reminiscences.

'Where were you?' She laughed.

'I was in Iran with Aziz's father Salamar.' He answered. 'When we were just boys together, just before my own father died'

'How old were you?'

'I cannot be certain, between eight and twelve I think.'

They sat in silence for a while and Mustapha thoughtfully sipped his tea.

'I was orphaned that day and Aziz's grandfather welcomed me into his family and treated me almost as a son, he was a compassionate man.'

Mary collected the cups and teapot, kissed Mustapha on the top of his head and descended the spiral stairs, leaving him to his memories.

Following the death of Mustapha's father and years of pleading from Salamar, Rashad arranged a treat for the boys, a journey to see the sea. They travelled to the South east of the country near the border with India and saw the vast Indian Ocean. Salamar was speechless, the long, flat horizon of shining blue water touching the sky. He worried his father to take them on a ship or a boat so they could get out into the sea far enough to be unable to see the land, but Rashad refused. They saw large ships moored close to the beach and dozens of smaller craft ferrying goods to and from the land. Salamar fell in love with the sea. He stood in the water and was astonished by its coolness and its colossal weight and strength as the waves pushed and tugged at his legs. He saw people swimming in the water and thought he would be able to do the same and had to be dragged out coughing and choking. By the time they left the coast and returned home several days later, Salamar had already mastered the art of swimming in an ungainly fashion that made the locals laugh.

Salamar's obsession with the sea increased relentlessly and he confided in Mustapha that he intended to run away to look at the sea again and he wanted Mustapha to run away with him. Eventually, the harassed Rashad agreed that the boys, now almost fully grown, could have two weeks, two camels and some money to return and look at it again. When they set off on their trip, Mustapha believed they would return. Salamar had other plans. He paid a ship's Captain to take them aboard, and teach them about the sea. Mustapha was horrified. He had no wish to go to sea, no wish to leave the benevolent Rashad, who had cared for him like a son. He spent hours pleading with Salamar, who would not be dissuaded. In the end, Mustapha agreed, as he was unable to face the unthinkable alternative of returning home to Rashad and admitting that he had failed to prevent his only son from sailing away.

Salamar soon achieved his dream of reaching the middle of the sea and unable to see land in any direction. He worked on deck, learning with the sailors, and below deck learning navigation with the Captain. Mustapha worked in the galley, and to the joy of the entire crew, vastly improved the quality of the food. The crew consisted of a mix of nationalities and Mustapha soon discovered that he possessed a gift for learning languages.

The ship made two voyages, the first down the east side of Africa and the second to India and China. Very similar journeys that Salamar's son and grandsons were destined to make some fifty years later. Salamar loved the tiny white islands and the emerald waters of the Indian Ocean. Mustapha was more impressed by the vast amount of tall rocky islands cloaked in dense forests that littered the South China Sea. They were at sea for almost three years and had grown into men. They were barely recognizable when they once again entered the house of Rashad, scaring him almost to death. Everyone had believed them to be dead of some misfortune. Rashad struggled between extreme anger and blessed relief. The following day, Rashad threw a party for the returning young men, who entertained everyone with fantastic accounts of their travels and Mustapha demonstrated his ability to speak in tongues few had heard before.

Rashad and Salamar negotiated the future. He conceded his son's point that trade by sea was faster and more profitable and that to own one's own vessel was essential. Rashad agreed to purchase such a vessel, but only if Salamar agreed to a marriage that must take place before he returned to sea. Salamar agreed to a marriage with DaryA, whose name meant 'sea'. She was a beautiful young woman, almost as tall as him, clever and fiery. She was the granddaughter of Rashad's cousin.

Six months after the wedding, the ship was purchased and furnished with a trusted, experienced crew and Salamar and Mustapha sailed to China for silk, tea and porcelain and India for spices and gemstones. Salamar studied charts and Mustapha learned the secrets of medicinal potions from an aging Chinese man who worked in the galley and administered to the sick and injured. When they returned after almost two years, DaryA had given birth to a son named Aziz Shadi Rashad Salamar Badr al din. It was then that Salamar fell in love with his wife and his child. Rashad was a happy man. There was a male heir in the family and he rested easier when the restless Salamar returned to sea. Their next voyage was to east Africa for gold and spices. Salamar talked to other sea Captains who had made the journey around the Cape of Good Hope in southern Africa. They then sailed north to Britain and Europe where there was an insatiable market for silk, tea and porcelain. Salamar decided that his next voyage would be to China and directly on to Britain. DaryA was with child again by the time the ship set sail for China and then south around the Cape of Good Hope. The Atlantic Ocean differed from the seas they were used to. It was frequently grey and angry. The further north they sailed the colder the weather became, Mustapha shivered and found it difficult to comprehend how Salamar could cope with separation from his wife and child. Mustapha accepted that he would never marry. He had nothing to offer a wife, no money, no security and no home. In a strange way, he was glad.

There was indeed a huge market in Britain, particularly for porcelain and silk and destined to become a regular destination. It had been a long arduous voyage, and even Salamar was content to stay at home for several months with his family. DaryA had given birth to a daughter named Dorri, meaning 'a sparking star glittering like a gem', and she did sparkle. Rashad was besotted with his tiny granddaughter. Little Aziz was five and viewed her with mute suspicion. Salamar and DaryA were about to take the children to meet her parents, several days journey by camel, when Aziz became unwell. Mustapha believed he had eaten something that had upset his stomach and advised rest and plenty of fluids, and definitely no camel rides. Salamar and DaryA entrusted Aziz's care to Mustapha and set off with Dorri.

They were the victims of bandits and ambushed during their return journey, less than half an hour from home. DaryA refused to hand over her jewels and they snatched Dorri from her grasp and severed her head and ran a sword through DaryA as she lunged for them. They held Salamar whilst they stripped her of her jewels, robbed him and beat him mercilessly, took the camels and finally left the little family for dead beside the track. A group of young goatherds found the bodies and ran to find Mustapha. Mustapha left Aziz in the kitchen with the women and took a handcart and followed the boys. He stared at the massacre in disbelief. The beheaded baby was the worst sight he had ever seen. DaryA lay dead several feet from her daughter and Salamar lay face down in the dust. He lifted DaryA onto the cart and when he picked up the pieces of Dorri he could not contain the scream that almost rent him in two. He placed Dorri with her mother and fell to his knees beside Salamar. As he attempted to turn him over, he heard a groan and realized that he was still alive. His face was swollen and purple and splattered with drying blood. One of the boys passed him water, which he trickled into Salamar's mouth, causing him to choke and splutter, eventually he was able to swallow some.

'Mustapha.' He whispered hoarsely. 'They are all dead, all dead. Promise me.' His voice tailed off.

'Anything.'

'Look after Aziz, raise him for me.'

'I promise.'

With super human effort, Mustapha

managed to lift Salamar onto the cart beside his wife and baby, tied a rope around his shoulders and set off towards home, dragging the cart. The cart became easier to pull after a few minutes. Mustapha struggled on, unaware that the four young boys were pushing with all their might from behind, trying desperately not to look at the ruination of the baby. Salamar died on that journey. He had stayed alive long enough to entrust his son to his best friend, the man he trusted more than anyone else. Rashad never recovered from the deaths. He thanked Allah that Aziz was not with them, but cursed him for failing to protect them. Mustapha and Aziz stayed with Rashad until his death five years later, during which time he rarely smiled. He put his fortune into gold and buried it for Aziz. The ship continued to trade with a hired Captain. After Rashad's death, Mustapha packed up Aziz and his gold, headed to the coast to wait for the ship and vowed never to return.

Mustapha looked up in response to Ivy's call for dinner and wiped away the tears. He struggled to extract himself from the swamp of sad memories. Little Mustapha and Isabella ran up the steps to hold his hands on the way down.

'Come on Grandaddy, we're having chickens tonight!' announced little Mustapha with a triumphant smile.

Isabella giggled and kissed Mustapha's hand. He smiled as the children led him down the spiral stairs and through the garden. Their small warm hands enabled his spirits to soar and he had returned to his usual chirpy self by the time he sat down to eat. He mentally thanked Allah for his wonderful life. That evening he went to visit Elijah's grave and had a chat with Aziz Shadi Rashad Salamar Badr al din.

Mustapha's memories, successfully buried for many years, had been unearthed by Rose's questioning. She had asked for his help in the construction of a family tree that she could give to the children when they grew up. Aziz Shadi Rashad Salamar Badr al din had never discussed his childhood, not even with Lily. He had maintained that he was unable to remember his life prior to going to sea.

Mustapha was able to tell her the names of Aziz Shadi Rashad Salamar Badr al din's parents, his grandfather and his great grandfather, also named Aziz. He knew the names of some of Rashad's brothers and Salamar's cousins that Lily would have met when she visited with her husband. Rose turned her attention to Lily, who was able to remember a useful amount of information.

Poor Mustapha was having difficulty re-burying the past. Obscure, often painful scenes would emerge without warning. He resorted to one of his own remedies that made it worse and enabled him to recall entire conversations. Mary, sensing his discomfort, asked if he was unwell. Mustapha, unable to keep anything from Mary, told her the truth. She, who believed that bottling up feelings was as dangerous and as useless as hesitancy, self-doubt and tact, advised him to talk about them. Mustapha told her about his own childhood, his journey with his father, the kind Rashad, his kitchen, Salamar and the sea. He told her of their voyages, the old gentleman from China who taught him medicine, and the massacre of Salamar and his family. At times they were both moved to tears. Mary held his hand and she asked him questions and succeeded in eliciting some of the happier circumstances. He recalled the adventures that he and Salamar had in the many countries they visited. He remembered the relief he was able to bring to the women during childbirth, armed with his knowledge of potions. He remembered the change in Aziz Shadi Rashad Salamar Badr al din when he saw the sea for the first time. Like his father before him he could not wait to sail away in a ship. During their first voyage, his quiet sadness was washed away and replaced with a zest for life that remained with him until the day he died.

Mustapha taught him languages and the crew taught him to splice rope, mend sails, climb to the crow's nest and the Captain taught him the charts.

That night Mustapha slept well for the first time in days and he spent the following days in the garden with Mary, remembering the past.

He told her of his second visit to Britain, when Aziz Shadi Rashad Salamar Badr al din was about twelve. Mustapha had not liked Britain, with her grey, malevolent seas. Her shores covered in jagged, sharp stones. With her lashing rain, her drab skies no higher than the topmast, and her persistent cold dampness that encouraged the proliferation of fungi in cupboards and a powdery orange rust to grow on cooking pots. He had never ventured ashore. Aziz Shadi Rashad Salamar Badr al din pleaded with the Captain and Mustapha to be allowed to go with the crew to London to deliver the cargo. He returned with stories of rolling green countryside, fertile land and majestic buildings. Mustapha remained unconvinced. He admitted to Mary that the first time he had dared to set foot on the land was many years later, when he was persuaded to teach her and Isabel the secrets of cooking with spices and herbs, and he had not set foot on a ship since that day. At the time he had been unaware that the short journey from the ship to John's house would be such a final one, no inkling that he would meet a wife, have a daughter and become an Englishman, which he firmly believed he now was. He even thought in English.

Mustapha recalled that, at eighteen, Aziz Shadi Rashad Salamar Badr al din used some of his gold to purchase a new vessel, promoted himself to Captain and hired an experienced crew. He bought a young black stallion, named him Elijah and took him aboard. Despite having four legs, Elijah proved unsteady at sea and took months to develop his sea legs and even then his disapproval was evident. The vessel was larger and faster, and they made regular journeys to China and back to Britain until Aziz Shadi

Rashad Salamar Badr al din fell in love with Lily. Mustapha remembered thinking that of all the beautiful countries that they visited, he had to choose Britain to fall in love, the one place that Mustapha had no fondness for.

.

Chapter 27

Rose's enquiries about the past brought back memories for Lily as well as Mustapha. Her memories of Grandfather William were happy ones, but the memories of her cold, critical mother, her timid Grandmother and violent drunken Grandfather, who had smashed her mother's head were not happy ones. As a small child she had feared her Grandfather. She dreaded the visits with her mother when her Grandfather would grab her roughly, tickle her, slobber on her head and insist that she sat on his lap. She had sat quietly, eyes downcast until he called her a miserable little bitch and pushed her away. She had seen her Grandmother's bruised face and occasional black eyes and wondered why she fell over so many times.

Lily knew the names of her uncles and aunt on her father's side of the family, despite them having died or run off prior to her birth. This information she had learned from the long talks she had had with her father as they sat minding the sheep. Rose's family tree grew rapidly. Anna became interested and asked if she could include her father Gabriel's family. No one knew much about Gabriel's past, except that he was from Ireland and had been raised with horses. Ellen Lily had asked about his family years before and Gabriel had invariably changed the subject. Anna proved more persistent, she explained that Rose was drawing out a family tree for the children, to hand down to their children, before the old people died, so that their ancestors were remembered. Gabriel tried to say that his family was not part of it, but Anna pointed out that he was her father and although she had never met his parents, they were her grandparents. His brothers and sisters, if he had any, were her aunts and uncles and he would get no peace until he complied with her wishes.

Gabriel very rarely thought about his family and his past life. He liked to believe that his life had begun when Aziz Shadi Rashad Salamar Badr al din had offered him work. Although at times he did remember some of the fine horses he had known.

He remembered the names of his parents, Maeve, his hardworking, downtrodden mother who spent her days desperately trying to find enough food for her fourteen children and failing almost every day. Daniel, his father was a large, robust man who had a rare way with the horses. His skills as a breeder and trainer were widespread and admired. Unfortunately his skills as a betting man with a fondness for alcohol, also widely known but less admired, had brought the entire family to ruin. His mother would take in washing and mending to earn a few pennies to buy food, but no matter where she concealed her wages, her husband, with the searching skills of a gambling spaniel in need of a drink invariably managed to locate the hiding place. Gabriel was one of the youngest children in the family. He could remember some names of his siblings, but not the order of their births. As a small child he could remember the farm filled with horses, in the days when his parents could still smile at each other. Before the bitter resentment turned to venom. Before the physical fighting started. Gabriel had left home and headed for London, where everyone said that the streets were paved with gold. He hated the filthy city, the inebriated, homeless, hopeless men that fought each other for a days work, so that they could buy another drink. Attracted by the carter's horses, he eventually obtained work, driving carts to the docks in the countryside. That was where Aziz Shadi Rashad Salamar Badr al din had found him.

Gabriel's memories had a similar effect upon him as Mustapha's had had. He was disturbed by dreams and felt dreadfully ashamed of his background. Mustapha successfully diagnosed his mood and invited him to spend the evening in the bathhouse. They lay in the steamy, hot room, Gabriel wallowing in the hot water easing his aching muscles. Mustapha sat submerged apart from his head, resembling a walnut in a puddle, his long white beard fanning out on the water's surface. Gabriel was the first to mention Rose and the family tree, admitting that he was finding the intrusion unsettling. Mustapha acknowledged his discomfort and told Gabriel a little of his own life, the poverty, starvation and rescue by Aziz Shadi Rashad Salamar Badr al din's grandfather. Gabriel has assumed that only he had the difficult start in life. When Mustapha related the killing of Salamar and his wife and child, Gabriel was able to put his own experiences into perspective. His father may have reduced the family to destitution by his gambling, but at least they had stopped short of killing each other. They were permanently hungry, but not actually starving to death. Gabriel walked home through the woods with a spring in his step, remembering some of the happier times during his childhood, blissfully unaware that Mustapha's plan had been swimmingly executed.

Gabriel recalled the rest of his brothers and sisters names by the time he reached his home. He checked the horses and went inside to relate the names to Anna, who had come up with the idea of writing a book about the family. Henry, who was now fourteen declared he wanted to go to sea, and would Gabriel ask his uncles if he could go on the next voyage. The family stared at him and then at each other. Then they all agreed that it was the best idea Henry had ever had.

The women were less disturbed by Rose's enquiries. Mary, Ida and Ivy sat at the kitchen table for hours, remembering their parents, grandparents and occasionally great grandparents. Ida had a deranged great aunt Jane who had insisted she was the Queen and paraded around the village with a cooking pot on her head, expecting her subjects to bow and curtsy to her. The women exchanged stories throughout the afternoon. Occasionally they were quiet, and at times in tears, but most of the time they giggled or laughed so much they cried. Mustapha listened to them from the next room and was struck by the dissimilar, virtually diametrically opposed reaction to memories by men and women. He decided that women appeared to enjoy, or at least manage powerful emotions, whereas men shied away from them. This led him to wonder if this was an actual physical difference between the sexes. Mustapha decided it was not, as he had met some individuals that did not fit that strict criteria.

Chapter 28

Maria was with child again and the ship was due to sail. Sal, having missed the birth of his firstborn, was reluctant to leave. So, for the first time in the twins' life they were to be separated. Sam sailed away, taking Henry with him and Gabriel and Ellen Lily's home had never been so quiet.

Ida began to suffer from disabling headaches, accompanied by a loss of balance. Mustapha concocted a remedy for the pain, which gave her some relief but failed to improve her balance. The headaches persisted and Mustapha realized that her sight was beginning to fail. She was not suffering from a loss of balance. She fell because she could no longer see obstacles. Her eyes were clouding over with a pale blue opaque layer. Mustapha had seen this before and he knew he could do nothing to help her. Ida became depressed and tearful and pleaded with Mustapha to concoct something to help her die. He refused. The family tried to lift her spirits. Maria reminded her that soon she would have a new grandchild but Ida's response was a renewed bout of tears, as she would never see the child. Mary tried a different approach and reminded Ida that blindness was not the end of the world. Many people lived their whole lives blind. Mary begged her to think of her daughter who needed her. She told her in no uncertain terms that is was utterly selfish to ask her husband to end her life. Mary's 'dressing down' appeared to be successful. Ida rallied for a time and allowed Mary to help her downstairs to the kitchen and even joined the women in the bathhouse.

Mustapha was so busy with his wife's care that Anna was called upon to help him. Then Mina's sickness started and she realized that she was pregnant and Mustapha was busy making ginger root tea. Mary's time was spent in the garden caring for the plants and cooking for the family. Maria helped in the kitchen. Rose and Lily entertained the children. Then Gabriel broke his leg when one of the horses fell badly, landing on his left leg. Charles ran to get Paulo and Sal to help him transport his father to Mustapha. They carried Gabriel through the woods on a door. His leg was bent out of shape and he was sweating with agony. Mary prepared the kitchen table for Mustapha, who was busy brewing a strong pain potion. Gabriel was a strong man, but he was unable to control the scream when they lifted him onto the table. Mustapha administered his remedy and waited for it to take effect while Mary forced some hot sweet tea into Gabriel. He studied Gabriel's leg. The skin was unbroken but it was twisted to one side and the foot was pale and Mustapha was unable to detect a pulse. He knew he had to restore the circulation of blood quickly to avoid gangrene and amputation. Sal, the strongest, was given the task of gripping under Gabriel's arms to prevent his from sliding when his leg was pulled. Paulo held his upper leg, white in the face due to his unfamiliarity with this type of event. Mary pulled and twisted Gabriel's ankle, ignoring the screams, bringing the foot back into line while Mustapha felt for a pulse. It was a tense few minutes. Mary and Mustapha glanced at each other, made minor adjustments, waited for a pulse. Then Mustapha nodded so slightly that only Mary noticed, he had found a pulse. Mary bound the ankle to the table to prevent it moving and was about to send Paulo to fetch splints, when his eyes rolled back in their sockets and he fainted away below the table with a dull thud. Sal went to find splints and Mary and Mustapha shared a chuckle as she collected the pile of bandages from the cupboard. Paulo remained under the table. Mustapha bandaged the splints to Gabriel's leg. He checked regularly for a pulse and ensured that Gabriel was able to feel sensation and to wriggle his toes.

Finally, they moved Gabriel to the big sofa beside the fire and Mary gave him some more tea and Mustapha gave him a sleeping draught. Then Mary gave the wobbling, shocked Paulo a cup of hot sweet tea.

When Mustapha went upstairs to check on his wife, she was already dead. Ida had capitalized on the calamity and grabbed the opportunity to grope around in the bedroom until she found a vial of her pain remedy and she had drunk the entire contents. Mustapha sat on the edge of the bed and held her hand. He felt no anger towards her for taking her own life. He understood that, for her, the price of staying alive was too high for her to pay. She wanted everyone to remember her as a wife and mother, not as a blind person. Mary joined him a few minutes later, instinctively sensing that all was not well. They sat in silence, side by side on the bed with Ida. Eventually Mustapha slowly rose to his feet and plodded away to find his daughter. Mary waited with Ida until Mustapha and Maria came in. She left them alone then, went to the kitchen and made herself some tea. She stayed up all night, quietly delivering tea to Mustapha and Maria, who had been joined by Sal, checking the pulse in Gabriel's foot and making ginger root tea for Mina.

During the following few days, Anna stayed to nurse her father as Mustapha would not risk moving him. He banned Gabriel from putting any weight on his foot for six weeks. Paulo redeemed himself by making a stout pair of crutches for Gabriel. Joseph arranged Ida's funeral. It was a sunny day in early autumn and attended by just about everyone. Ida would have been aghast, but she was the wife of Mustapha the Magician and he had administered his remedies to almost every family in the village. He had stayed all night with their sick and dying loved ones, relieving their agonies and fears. He had delivered hundreds of their babies and he had always refused any payment. They were all there to support him in his own time of need and he was touched. There were so many flowers that they formed a vivid carpet that engulfed the surrounding graves. One by one the inhabitants of the village filed past Mustapha and warmly shook his hand and offered their condolences. He held his composure until a small girl smiled up at him and gave him a grubby, well loved, toy sheep whose straw stuffing was beginning to escape. Tears rolled silently down his crumpled face and Mary took his arm and quietly led him away from the crowd.

Gabriel's eldest son Charles took over the care of the horses. He arrived at the house each morning and Gabriel gave him a list of tasks for the day. Ellen Lily visited daily and laughed at Gabriel's attempts to master his crutches. Mustapha pottered around making ginger root tea for Mina, whose sickness was improving. Later in the week, Rose confided in Lily that she thought that she might be expecting a child as well. She had not told Paulo yet as she was not certain. Lily told Mary, who was not at all surprised, as she had noticed 'a look about her'. Mary told Mustapha who clapped his hands in delight at the prospect of three new babies in the family next year. By the time Rose told Paulo, and he proudly announced the news to the family, they all knew, but managed to act as if they did not. Paulo made a splendid crib, suspended from a stand on wheels. Ivy made the bedding and Ellen Lily knitted a blanket.

By Christmas, Gabriel's leg had mended, although it continued to ache at the end of the day. Maria, Mina and Rose were comparing the sizes of their bellies and wondering in what order they would give birth. There were twenty-one for dinner that year, plus the four women from the village who had helped Mary with the food. Sal was thinking about his brother and Ellen Lily wondered how Henry was behaving at sea. Isabella sat between Ivy and Charles and grinned across the table at little Mustapha who sat next to his grandfather. Mustapha sat at the head of the table and was grateful for the many happy years he had spent with his wife and how proud he was of the daughter she gave him, who was soon to give him his second grandchild. He hoped it would be a little girl. Then he looked at Mary, her face flushed from the heat of the kitchen, her thick, curly, chestnut hair streaked with grey, her bright blue eyes had lost none of their sparkle. She was laughing with the children. Mustapha wondered whatever he would do without her and fervently hoped he would never have to find out.

Chapter 29

During the first couple of weeks at sea, Henry suffered a disabling bout of seasickness, which was not his fault and he wished he had not gone to sea. When he recovered, he suffered from a severe bout of not listening to instructions, which was his fault and then Sam was the one who wished Henry had not come to sea! Gabriel had warned Sam to keep Henry 'on a short reign' as he was prone not to listen and possessed a rare talent for misfortune. Henry was told not to climb the rigging in high seas. Henry ignored the warning and climbed to the crow's nest. He then managed to get his foot stuck fast in a loop of rope, which necessitated two of the crew to climb up and rescue him, putting them at risk. Sam was furious and he dragged Henry below and lectured him on safety at sea. It could not have been entirely successful as two days later Henry was almost washed overboard whilst trying to balance on the side of the ship. Sam made a rule. Henry was only allowed on deck if he agreed to being attached by a storm rope. Sam told him of the first time he and Sal had gone to sea with their father. They were younger than Henry when they left and they had been able to obey orders and not put themselves and others at risk. Henry was unimpressed. He failed to see what all the fuss was about and wished he had not come, he had thought that life at sea would be exciting, but it was boring and relentlessly tedious.

When they docked in North Africa, Henry was off the ship before the crew had tied the ropes. Sam watched his as he ran around on the shore resembling a caged animal that had finally been given liberty.

Sam decided to take Henry with him to collect the leather hides. The rest of the crew were already tired of his antics. The tannery was located some three days ride into the desert. Henry's camel took a distinct dislike to him instantly and spat in his face. Sam realised that Henry was indeed a strange young fellow and he did seem to attract calamity.

Sam visited the family he had stayed with as a child and they were distressed to learn of the death of Aziz Shadi Rashad Salamar Badr al din. He informed them of his own and his brother's marriages. A loud crash heralded the demise of a large terracotta urn that Henry had collided with. The following day, fearing for the family's chinaware he took Henry to the tannery, purchased the hides and took Henry to visit the souks. For once Henry was fascinated by what he saw. The snake charmers, the performing monkeys and the Bedouin tribesmen who had come in from the desert to sell their wares caught his attention.

The following morning, Henry was nowhere to be seen and neither was his cantankerous camel. Sam spent the day searching and wishing

Sal was with him. How could he return and admit he had lost Gabriel's son. Then he discovered that a quantity of gold was missing from the saddlebags. Henry was not lost somewhere, he had run away. Next day Sam visited the souks and made enquiries and was told that a young man with a white face and hair the colour of the sand had left with the Bedouin tribesmen early the previous morning.

Henry had almost two days start, in an immense desert landscape that left no tracks. He could be anywhere. Sam journeyed back to the ship with his purchases, fervently wishing he had left Henry shackled aboard the vessel. He paid a fair price for the cantankerous camel and watched as the crew loaded the hides into the hold. Sam left instructions with the locals that if Henry were to arrive there, to tell him the ship would be returning in a couple of months.

The ship sailed to Turkey, and then to Crete, a busy trading port. Some fifty ships were anchored and their wares were frequently bartered and exchanged without ever reaching the shore. Sam loaded the ship with packages containing silks, tea and crates of the popular blue and white porcelain from China, made for the European market. Sam found a large bronze statue of a horse. He purchased it as a peace offering for Gabriel and it was a nuisance for the entire voyage until the crew buried it amongst the packages of silk to stop it moving.

The ship visited the port where Henry had disappeared. There had been no sight of him.

Sam was not surprised and the crew was quietly jubilant. They encountered a severe storm in the Atlantic. The men spent a grueling, backbreaking night. They were so engrossed with keeping the vessel afloat that nobody noticed Gabriel's horse rhythmically destroying a crate of porcelain with its hooves and puncturing a tea chest with the tip of its its tail. Several of the sails ripped to shreds and the men were exhausted by the time the storm abated. It had been a frustrating voyage and everyone was relieved to sail into the estuary that led to home. Sam suffered a mounting dread. He prayed that Henry's family would not be at the dock. He had a desperate need to speak to his brother and to Mustapha before he saw Gabriel or Ellen Lily.

Chapter 30

The winter was very cold, with deep frosts and very little snow. It was too cold to snow. Paulo and Sal were struggling to keep the house warm and Gabriel organized the dead tree deliveries to the village. Having all of the women of childbearing age in the house pregnant at the same time proved a recipe for chaos. They bundled around and their mood swings causing prolonged bouts of tears, days of panic and episodes of hysterical laughter. Mary did her utmost to reassure them and Lily tried to keep out of their way. Edward spent all of his time at the other farm. Mustapha was trying to ascertain who would give birth first and stockpiling a range of remedies. Anna pleaded with her grandmother Mary to be present during one of the births. Mary agreed and Mustapha could see no reason why she could not help with all of them. She would be needed if all of the women coincided their deliveries.

Spring arrived and the sun encouraged the carpet of bluebells and purple orchids in the woods. Anna began stalking the trio of bulging women as they struggled up the slope in the woods, picking bluebells. Mary suggested to Anna that she move to the big house, rather than running through the woods at the crack of dawn every day, praying that she had not missed a birth. It was Maria who won the race, her pains starting suddenly at the kitchen table during dinner, causing Sal to spill his cup of tea. Mustapha sent Paulo to light the fires in the bathhouse and put the pans of water on to heat. Maria sat beside the fire and her pains were initially mild but regular. By ten o'clock they were stronger and Mustapha gave her a hot tea laced with pain relief. Paulo and Mary filled the bath. Sal hovered around, everyone else appeared to know what to do and he felt helpless. Having missed the birth of little Mustapha he did not know what to expect. Mary announced that the bath was ready and told Sal to help Maria to the bathhouse. Maria waddled to the bathhouse holding Sal's arm and talking about chickens. Her waters broke just before she reached the bathhouse but she failed to notice. Sal helped Mary to lower Maria gently into the hot water and knelt beside the bath holding her hand, she continued to discuss the chickens in depth, a look of avid concentration on her face. Anna arrived as Maria widened her discussion to include snails. Mustapha gave Maria a further potion and she relaxed and leant back in the water, Mary's arms supporting her from behind. Everyone forgot about Sal who sat holding her hand. Mustapha watched his daughter closely and Mary watched Mustapha's face for the slightest signal. Anna stood open-mouthed holding a pile of clean towels. The room would have been silent but for the monologue about chickens and snails. Maria raised her knees from the water and braced her feet against her father's body, almost knocking the slight, insubstantial Mustapha over. He grasped her feet as she bent her head forward and growled deeply as a black shape appeared between her legs. Mary told Anna to grab the baby as the rest of it slowly emerged. Anna dropped the towels and gently lifted the child from the bathwater, tears rolling down her face. She passed it up to Mustapha and picked up a towel for him to wrap the baby. Mary cut and tied the cord.

'Well Mustapha, you have your granddaughter.'

Mustapha smiled at the baby, who stared back with the same intense glittering black eyes as her grandfather.

'I'd like to call her Sophia Mary.' Maria had finally stopped talking about chickens and snails. Sophia had been Ida's second name.

Sal was still holding Maria's hand, and he had to be helped to his feet by Mary.

Mustapha passed Sophia to him and they went outside to offer her up to the sky as usual, watched by the astonished Paulo.

'They always do that.' Rose said nonchalantly, by way of explanation.

Mary dressed Maria in a clean nightdress and helped her to the chair beside the fire and sat at the kitchen table with Anna and explained that not all births are that easy, that second children are usually quicker, but that without Mustapha's potions it would be a much more harrowing business.

Little Mustapha woke that morning and was

surprised and excited to have a little sister and he worried Anna until she agreed to take him to tell Isabella.

'She's called Sophia and her second name is Mary just like yours is!' he shouted to Isabella as Ivy opened the door.

Mina and Rose waited for their pains to start. They became grumpier as the days passed into weeks. They were not amused when Edward suggested that they were not with child, they just had a bad case of wind.

Just over a month after the birth of Sophia, Anna woke Mary to tell her that Mina's pains had begun. Anna had been sleeping in Mina's room due to her being alone. Mary woke Mustapha with the news and a cup of tea, then she lit the fires in the bathhouse and Anna helped Mina to the chair beside the fire. Mina's pains were already quite strong and Mustapha arrived with his potion. He had a feeling that the baby was coming quickly. The four of them were sitting beside the fire, waiting for the water to heat up when Rose appeared at the door complaining of a chronic backache, so severe that it had woken her up. Mary and Mustapha exchanged a knowing look, remembering that her mother Lily's labour had begun with a backache. Mustapha gave her a potion and laid her on the sofa and she soon drifted off into a peaceful pain free sleep. Mustapha sent Anna to wake Lily up, as he did not want Rose to be left alone when they took Mina to the bathhouse.

Paulo woke up to an empty bed and went

downstairs to find his wife asleep and Mina about to give birth. Mustapha scuttled in to tell Mary that the water was hot and she left to fill the bath. Anna arrived with Lily. Mustapha told Lily that he thought Rose was going into labour and Mina would be likely to deliver very soon. Following Paulo's previous ill timed fainting fit, everyone agreed that it was best not to expect too much from him. Mina's contractions were getting closer together and her discomfort was apparent. Mustapha gave her another concoction and waited for a few minutes until she became more relaxed. Anna went to the bathhouse and Mary and Mustapha slowly helped Mina to her feet. She took one or two steps, then she abruptly bent over, her knees buckled and her waters, closely followed by her son, gushed to the floor. Mary rescued the baby and Mina, with a confused frown, sat back down on the chair. Paulo passed out. Mustapha was consumed by a giggling fit. Mary and Mina joined in and Rose woke up. Anna came back from the bathhouse to see where everyone was, unprepared for a roomful of people laughing, Paulo lying unconscious on the floor and a new baby in his mother's arms.

Rose's back continued to ache and when Mustapha examined Rose's belly it was as tight as a drum and he was sure the baby was on its way. Paulo regained consciousness, but remained traumatised and excitable, especially when he discovered that his wife was in labour. Everyone agreed that Mustapha should give him something to calm him down. Rose sat in front of the fire and drank another of Mustapha's potions that resulted in a pain free hazy semi consciousness, in which all the colours in the room became extraordinarily bright and people's voices sounded very far off. Paulo snored quietly on the sofa. Mary sent Mustapha to bed to regain his strength in time for the birth. He left a further dose of the same potion in case Rose needed it. Mary dozed in the armchair and Lily and Anna sat with Rose. Rose sat and watched the first rays of the dawn sunshine creep slowly across the curtains. She wanted a cup of tea but had lost the power of speech. Anna brought her one anyway and she sat watching the steam curling above the cup for quite a while until she remembered to drink it. Eventually Rose dozed off for a while and was then abruptly woken by a deep cramp below her belly that took her breath away. She gasped and grabbed the arms of the chair. Mary was immediately at her side and gave her the potion Mustapha had left for her. The cramps slowly eased but did not disappear completely. Mary went to wake Mustapha up and Anna went to stoke up the fires n the bathhouse and reheat the water. They moved Rose to the bathhouse and lowered her into the hot water. The relief on her face was evident as the soothing water covered her tense belly. Mary and Anna stayed with her while Mustapha was brewing his next potion, one that would give her the stamina to push this baby into the world. Progress was slow and it was not until evening that Rose showed signs of needing to push. Mustapha gave her the potion, and soon after the earnest pushing began. Rose knelt in the bath and pushed like one possessed and in just over an hour Mary caught the baby girl. She waited for Rose to move and take the baby between her legs, but Mustapha had realised that like her mother before her, Rose was bearing twins. Mary quickly cut the cord and passed the baby to Anna. Rose, who was tiring, remained squatting in the bath, breathing heavily, her long dark hair stuck to her back. Mustapha sent Mary for more of the potion and sent Anna off with the first baby to give her to her grandmother. Mary returned and topped up the hot water as Mustapha gave Rose the potion and words of encouragement. Anna returned and Mary watched for the second baby to appear. After fifteen minutes Mustapha put his hand in the water and was alarmed to feel not a head emerging, but a foot. He whispered to Mary and she and Anna hauled the alarmed, disorientated Rose up out of the water and balanced her buttocks on the wide edge of the bath. They supported the weight of her upper body and Mustapha clambered into the bath and knelt down. Both of the feet were out and he eased the tiny body down. He inserted his fingers and one by one pulled out the arms. Mary reassured Rose who was becoming agitated and fearful while Mustapha allowed the tiny body to hang as he gently twisted it. Everyone held their breath, Anna began to shake and even Mary displayed a worried frown. He shut his eyes and felt around the neck then he suddenly tilted the little body and the baby plopped into the water. He fished out the disgruntled little boy who spluttered and howled in protest. All four of them cried with relief. Mary and Anna slid Rose back into the bath and passed her the baby. Mary hauled the bedraggled Mustapha out of the water and hugged and kissed him to within an inch of his life. Anna took the baby to Lily. It took Mary and Mustapha a while to tend to Rose and change their own wet clothes. They finally emerged with Rose to a round of applause from the family and a welcome pot of hot sweet tea.

After the tea, Paulo had a quiet word with Mustapha, who smiled and spoke to Sal. Then the three men went outside, Paulo with his son and Sal with his daughter. Then Paulo passed his son to Mustapha and watched as he and Sal shouted the usual unintelligible torrent into the sky whilst holding the tiny babies aloft. Paulo thanked them although he was not really sure what they had done.

Mina did not want to name her son until his father returned and chose the name, but Mustapha believed it unlucky to have an unnamed baby, so Mina called him Joey. He was Joey for almost two months and he began to look like a Joey and the name remained throughout his life. Paulo wanted to name his son Mustapha as he believed that Mustapha had given him life, but the family complained of the confusion that would result in having three Mustapha's under one roof, so he was named George Mustapha and his daughter was named Olivia Lily.

The babies all with dark hair and eyes, and looked remarkably similar. During the initial few weeks only their mothers could be relied upon to tell them apart. George and Olivia shared their majestic swinging crib, as their uncles had done when they were babies.

.

Chapter 31.

Sam slipped quietly into the kitchen under the shadow of darkness in search of Mustapha and Sal. He found Mary in the kitchen, brewing tea for the nursing mothers. She rushed upstairs to wake Mina so she could present him with his new son that he knew nothing about. Barely able to conceal her excitement, Mary bustled around the kitchen singing quietly, waiting impatiently for Mina and Joey.

'I am so sorry Aunt Mary, but I have lost Henry, he ran away in North Africa and I could not find him.'

Mary, transfixed, with a plate of cakes in her hand, stared at Sam.

'How can I face Ellen Lily and Gabriel?' he asked, utterly distraught.

Mina scurried into the kitchen with a huge smile and Joey in her arms, oblivious to the atmosphere. Sam thought it was Sal and Maria's child and nodded politely and turned his worried face to Mary.

'Sam, this is your new son Joey!' said Mary, resuming her composure.

Sam turned again to Mina, his despair evolving rapidly into stupefied confusion.

'I found I was with child just after you left.' Explained Mina. 'And Rose has had twins!'

Demolished, Sam gaped at Mina, and then at Mary and when Mustapha pottered into the kitchen he broke down and cried.

Mina and Mustapha looked at Mary.

'He's lost Henry in Africa.' She explained.

Mustapha shut the kitchen door in an attempt to avoid waking the household and elicited the whole story of Henry's disappearance. It was obvious to him that Henry had made his choice and that Sam was not to blame. Even Mary understood that he could have done no more and was certain that Ellen Lily and Gabriel would understand as well. They would obviously be upset and worried, but they would not blame Sam. Sam was not convinced. He looked at his new son, if anyone lost him in a desert, he would want to kill whoever was responsible!

Mary and Mustapha said they would go and see Ellen Lily and Gabriel in the morning and explain to them what had happened, but Sam would not agree. He felt responsible and wanted to tell them himself, but he did ask Mustapha to accompany him. Sam was unable to sleep and felt unable to face the family until he had been to see Gabriel. At first light, when he knew that Gabriel would be up with his horses, he and Mustapha set off through the woods. They stopped briefly at the clearing where Aziz Shadi Rashad Salamar Badr al din and Elijah died, and them continued through the woods to find Gabriel.

Gabriel waved and greeted them warmly as he caught sight of them from the stables. Mustapha beckoned for him to come and speak to them. Sam blurted out what had happened, that he had lost Henry, that he had searched for him, that he was told he had gone off with a nomadic tribe, that he did not know where to look for him in a limitless desert, that he was so, so dreadfully sorry. Gabriel listened in silence and them he flung his arms around the distressed Sam.

'Sam, I am so sorry.' He said. ' That is just the sort of thing that Henry would do, there is nothing you could have done to prevent it!'

'Perhaps if I had been more patient with him?'

'Don't blame yourself, that boy never settled to anything, he's like an unbroken horse with a brain full of rashness and stupidity and not an ounce of common sense.'

'But.'

'Don't you be worrying yourself now Sam, he'll be fine, he always is! It's the rest of us he distresses!'

Gabriel took Sam and Mustapha into the house where Ellen Lily was making breakfast. Gabriel told her the news before Sam could open his mouth. She shook her head sadly.

'Sam, I am sorry he put you to so much trouble and he promised me faithfully that he would behave and not let us down.'

'I am truly sorry Ellen Lily.' Whispered Sam.

'He'll be back!' said Ellen Lily. ' I know he will, the little devil!'

Throughout the many months since Henry

disappeared, Sam had played this scenario in his head countless times, and he never, ever expected Gabriel and Ellen Lily to be apologizing to him. The months of dread, dismay and occasionally sheer terror melted and Sam was starkly depleted and drained of all emotion. He sat at the table, his head in his hands. Gabriel and Ellen Lily congratulated him on the birth of his son, who he had almost forgotten about during the last hour. He asked Gabriel if he would mind if he added Gabriel to his son's name.

'I would be surely honoured Sam, now drink that tea!'

Back at the house, everyone was up and waiting to see Sam, and to proudly introduce him to the clutch of babies and share the news. Since seeing Gabriel and Ellen Lily, he was able to relax and enjoy the moment. Much later in the day he remembered the bronze horse that he had brought home for Gabriel. He and Sal borrowed Gabriel's strongest cart and two of his strongest horses and headed off to the ship. Gabriel assumed they had a lot of provisions to move and offered to help. They declined the offer.

It took a lot of time, men, rope, sweat and a considerable amount of cursing to extract the extraordinarily heavy, awkward horse from the hold of the ship. They almost lost it over the side of the gangplank. They erected a sturdy ramp leading up to the bed of the cart. They stabilised the cart with chocks under the wheels and used the horses to drag the statue up the ramp. They succeeded on the fourth attempt. The cart wheezed and creaked and threatened to collapse entirely on the journey to Gabriel's farm.

Sam would have liked to stand the horse outside of Gabriel's house as a surprise, but they needed his help to unload it. So Sam found him and said he had a present for him on the cart. Gabriel was astonished to see his cart full of a horse made of metal. He loved it even before he saw it stood up. It took quite a time, several puzzled horses, a lot of shouting and the removal of the side of the cart to unload and stand upright the bronze horse. It stood proudly at the gate to the stables. It was as large as a normal horse and its tail and mane blew in a constant, silent breeze. It held its dignified head high and calmly surveyed its surroundings. Gabriel looked up at his horse and stroked its cool, smooth, gleaming neck. He loved it.

'Henry.' He said. 'I'll call him Henry!'

At the kitchen table, Sam related the story of the horse's journey from Crete. The problems getting it on board, the damage it wreaked below deck, the difficulties removing it from the ship. Gabriel laughed.

'Sure, tis aptly named then!'

Henry stood at the gate to the stables and startled the other horses for several weeks until they became accustomed to his presence.

Gabriel patted his flanks as he passed by.

'Morning to you Henry!' he would say and secretly believed he had done well in that exchange, but kept that thought to himself.

Chapter 32

It was a pleasantly warm summer that year and the babies spent a lot of time in the garden with Mustapha and Mary. The babies took up a lot of time and Joseph hired two cooks to lighten the load for Mary, who had taken over delivering the babies in the village with Anna. Ivy had taken over the responsibility for the 'sick house', where she had enlisted the help of two young women from the village. Most days she dropped Isabella at the big house to play with little Mustapha.

The party for Aziz Shadi Rashad Salamar Badr al din's birthday was destined to be a particularly lavish affair, due to the addition of his four new grandchildren and to both of his sons being home from sea. The village was buzzing with excitement. The women were sewing new dresses and mending old ones and making tiny baby clothes to give to the family on the day. Everyone was hoping for a sunny day.

This activity coincided with the arrival of a new vicar and his family at the rectory. He was a stout middle-aged, well-educated man of calm disposition and a fascination for science. He had been provided with a brief history of the village prior to his arrival. He was aware of the ambivalent relationship that the church had forged with the Martin/Badr al din family. The doubtful relationship had varied over time, dependent on the personal inclination of the individual vicars. Generally they had been conquered, or at least silenced, by Aziz Shadi Rashad Salamar Badr al din's consistent generosity. His donations had undoubtedly saved the church roof and kept pace with general repairs. All of the vicars had experienced their own crisis of conscience. They had agreed to conduct the marriages of Christians and Muslims and even a couple of Catholics. They had christened their children and buried their dead. The family was popular in the village and powerful, and no vicar was confident enough to risk complete alienation.

The real thorn in their sides had always been Mustapha the Magician. One vicar in particular, who forbade his wife from seeking pain relief during childbirth, firmly believed that Mustapha should have been burnt at the stake. He was a vicar who preached that suffering was good for the soul and deemed that he was relentlessly usurped and undermined by Mustapha's potions that largely obliterated pain and suffering. He believed that Mustapha purposely averted incidents that would have been seen as acts of God. The villagers, who had traditionally called in the somber, funereal vicar at times of suffering and death, thereafter had sought the services of Mustapha. They preferred the quiet, peaceful, painless deaths, sometimes preceded by a hilarious interlude during which their beloved dying relative unexpectedly spoke to their dead loved ones or saw God waiting for them with a smile on his face, rather than the fervent prayers of the vicar who often needed to shout above the agonizing screams of the dying to a God that did not appear to be listening.

So when the new vicar tapped on the door of the big house, having walked all the way from the church following the Sunday service, Mary was quite taken aback. No vicar had ever visited the family home in over forty years. He introduced himself as the Reverend James Knightly and shook Mary's hand warmly. She invited him in for tea. He sat on a sofa, waiting for his tea and surveyed his surroundings. It was a beautiful room, full of inviting sofas and chairs with cushions of vibrant colours. The gleaming wooden floors were strewn with sumptuous rugs and the walls hung with tapestries. Mary arrived with his tea in a tall, red glass teapot, accompanied by a matching drinking glass and a bowl of sugar. A number of members of the disconcerted family tumbled into the room to look at the vicar. Mustapha, dressed in his usual striped long shirt and baggy trousers, his head swathed in a long white scarf, wandered into the room as Mary was pouring the tea, oblivious to the presence of the vicar. Mary was about to introduce them when the vicar stood up and took a step towards the unsuspecting Mustapha.

'You must be the famous Mustapha.' Said the vicar and proffered him his hand. ' It is indeed an honour to meet you Sir!'

Mustapha was momentarily flabbergasted, keenly aware of the animosity he had engendered in the past.

'The honour is all mine.' Answered Mustapha, bowing his head, as he shook hands with a vicar for the first time in his long life.

Mustapha introduced the family to the vicar and the conversation covered conventional matters such as the weather and crops.

'Actually Mustapha, it is you that I came to see.' He admitted eventually.

Mustapha invited the vicar outside, an easier option that emptying the room of the large, inquisitive family, and they ended up sitting in the tree house, overlooking the garden. Paulo carried a chair up the spiral stairs, as unlike Mustapha, the vicar was too stout to fit the tree house chairs.

The vicar was very interested with regard to the history of the family. He was even interested in Mustapha's potions and felt a great sense of relief, and a deep respect, when Mustapha explained that his remedies were a gift from God and therefore free to whoever needed them. They sat up the tree house for so long that Mary delivered them another pot of tea and warm biscuits and shooed away the small crowd of curious children gathering at the foot of the stairs. Mustapha invited the vicar and his family to the birthday party for Aziz Shadi Rashad Salamar Badr al din, despite his being dead and buried for these last ten years.

The Reverend James Knightly headed for the rectory with a happy heart, a feeling of humility and a vague disappointment that his predecessors had been unable or unwilling to see that no matter what religion these people may be, they were God fearing and sincere. He felt extremely fortunate to have the family in his parish and looked forward to the party on Saturday.

The preparations for the party started during the week. Gabriel and Charles cut back the branches and grass in the clearing in the woods and repaired the benches and musicians platform. Sam and Sal cut the grass in the front field and Paulo made makeshift benches from planks of timber. They built the fires for the spit roasts and the women began the cooking on the Friday morning. The kitchen was crammed with sacks of flour, potatoes, onions and carrots. There were trays of butter and cheeses and boxes of tomatoes and lettuces. The several sheep and sides of beef were to be spit roasted outside. Several of the villagers were hired to help with the cooking and serving of the food. The villagers and the musicians began arriving early on the Saturday afternoon. It was a bright sunny day with a gentle breeze. By three o'clock the music was playing and the smells from the spit roasts were enhancing the appetite of everyone who walked past them.

The Reverend James Knightly arrived with his family. His wife, Faith was a stately woman with a warm smile and a ready laugh. With them were their three sons. The two eldest, John and Matthew were approaching adulthood and James was considerably younger. Members of the congregation were happy and relieved to see the vicar at the big house. The more devout members having been uncomfortable in the past, sensing the resentful acrimony on the part of one or two of their vicars.

The Reverend James Knightly, whilst introducing his family to Mustapha, suggested that Mustapha feel free to call him Jim. Mustapha was about to ask if he and his wife would like to see the house and the famous bathhouses, when they were interrupted by a distraught, apologetic woman, dragging her reluctant husband towards Mustapha. Her husband's cheek was swollen and red and his face contorted in pain. He was suffering from severe toothache.

'E's more upset about not being able to eat the food than 'is blessed toothache!' she explained.

Mustapha smiled and as he led the couple towards the house, he asked if the vicar would like to accompany him. Jim readily accepted, keen to see the Magician at work.

Mustapha took them to the bathhouse and sat them on a bench. The woman held her husband's hand while Mustapha pottered to the kitchen for a potion and tools. On his return, he kept the pliers hidden until he had administered several spoonsful of his potion. Within a relatively short space of time the man began giggling and announced that his toothache was better. Mustapha calmly explained that the tooth had gone bad and needed to be pulled out. The man refused, fearing the excruciating pain of having a tooth pulled, so Mustapha gave him another drink that very quickly reduced the man to a drowsy state and unable to put up any useful resistance. With the help of the man's wife and the vicar, Mustapha laid him on the bench, instructed the vicar to hold the man's head tight on the bench and in one swift movement pulled out the offending tooth with a pair of vicious looking pliers. Then Mustapha sat the men up and encouraged the puzzled individual to rinse his mouth with salt water and he plugged the wound with a small piece of white cloth. He instructed the wife to tell her husband to chew with the other side of his mouth when he was able to understand, which would be in about half an hour. He gave her a tiny bottle of pain relief to be given to her husband if he needed it later.

The grateful woman, still apologizing for the trouble, led her unsteady, chortling husband out of the bathhouse. The vicar sat and smiled at Mustapha, he shook his head slowly.

'You truly are a magician Mustapha, I know where to come if I am ever stricken with the toothache!'

The party was a great success. The village women brought little packages of clothes for the babies and they were welcomed inside to see the new arrivals. The food was plentiful and the music soon resulted in the people dancing around the field. The man relieved of his bad tooth managed to eat roasted meat and vegetables. Then he got up and danced, a spectacle that his wife had never before witnessed in the forty years of their marriage.

As the light faded, the musicians and partygoers headed for the woods, along pathways lit with lanterns so that Aziz Shadi Rashad Salamar Badr al din could enjoy the section of the proceedings that were especially for him. Mustapha and Anna found the vicar and his family and escorted them along the lantern lit pathways, explaining that this was where Aziz Shadi Rashad Salamar Badr al din had met his death, falling from his dying horse Elijah. The vicar and his family sat on a bench in the large candlelit clearing, and marveled at the amount of flowers blooming, and watched as the musicians played and the villagers sang at the tops of their voices. Paulo made an appearance and played his guitar to the crowd while the other musicians had a short rest and refreshments. Sam and Sal helped Mustapha up on to the musicians' platform and he thanked the villagers for coming to the party and wished them all a good year. The round of applause was drowned by the spectacular firework display, set off by Gabriel and Charles. Mustapha watched the smiling, awed faces of the villagers lit up by the fireworks. It was then he noticed that Matthew, the vicar's middle son, was staring in awe at Anna as she watched the fireworks, her blue eyes shining and her exuberant mass of chestnut curls moving in the breeze. Mustapha was reminded of Mary, when he first met her so many years ago in the kitchen of John Martin. As he turned to walk to the house he bumped into Mary who was looking for him, they linked arms and wandered along the woodland path, looking at the lanterns.

Chapter 33

Edward went off to work at Henry and Charles's farm as normal on the Monday morning. He and Henry were due to plant the spring cabbage in the top field. They took it in turns to make a shallow trench with a hoe, along the line of string that kept the rows straight, whilst the other followed along sprinkling the tiny seeds into the trench and treading the earth over them with a foot. At around ten o'clock Sarah arrived with hot tea in a jug. They sat and drank their tea, and watched her disappear up the path towards the house. Edward stumbled as he stood up, looked at his brother with a puzzled expression in his eyes, as though he was about to ask him a question. Then he fell backwards and was dead before he hit the soil. Henry stood and stared at his brother, then he looked towards the house, but his wife had disappeared inside. He removed his jacket and covered his brother's face and slowly walked along the path in search of Charles.

Henry, Charles and Sarah stood in the top field and stared down at the figure of Edward, lying as he fell. Then Charles rode to the big house in search of Mustapha. He returned within the hour with Mustapha, who had reluctantly agreed to ride behind him on the horse, due to the urgency of the situation. Mustapha said that Edward's heart had just stopped beating. Charles went to get a cart and Mustapha waited with the body, unwilling to get back on the horse. Henry and Charles placed their brother in the cart and Sarah went back to the house.

Mustapha sat in the back of the cart with Edward on the way to the house. He found Mary in the garden watering the plants. She knew by Mustapha's face that someone had died.

'It's Edward.' He said quietly.

Mary blinked a couple of times and then sat down heavily in the chair, placing the watering can on the ground.

'Where is he?' she asked with a sigh.

'He's on the cart, he collapsed in the field, Henry said he just fell down dead. His heart stopped'

'He didn't suffer then?'

'No.'

'I'm glad he didn't suffer.' She said. ' Edward didn't deserve to suffer. I'd like to see him now.'

Mustapha took Mary into the stable where they had placed the cart. Mary stroked Edward's face, kissed his forehead and covered him up again.

'I'm going to tell the children.' She said as she left the stable.

She plodded slowly through the woods. Mustapha followed her, but at a distance great enough that she would not notice. Mary saw Gabriel first and asked him to find Robert and Ellen Lily. Gabriel could see something was wrong as Mary looked desperately tired but he did as she asked without question. When he returned with her children she said.

'It's your father, I'm afraid he died this morning.'

Ellen Lily burst into tears and fell into Gabriel. Robert stood and stared at his mother. Mary turned and plodded away. Robert made to follow her but Gabriel held his arm and shook his head.

Mustapha was waiting for Mary. He was sitting on Elijah's grave. She plodded up to him and sunk to the ground, laid her head in his lap and sobbed. They remained there for some time, Mustapha stroking her hair.

'Well.' Said Mary. 'This won't do, Mustapha, I've got a husband to bury!'

She wiped her face on the bottom of Mustapha's shirt, took a deep breath and got up and pulled Mustapha to his feet. They strolled back through the woods and just before they reached the house, Mary looked into Mustapha's eyes.

'Thankyou.' She said.

Joseph had taken control of the situation when they got back to the house. Lily had made some tea. Mary and Mustapha sat at the kitchen table and the family left them alone. It was less than a year since she had sat with him after Ida had died.

The funeral was a quiet modest affair, just as Edward would have wanted it to be. He never enjoyed a fuss. His mother Isabel had been like his wife, gregarious, lively and loved the company of others. Edward had loved them both, but he much preferred his own company and the solitude of the fields that he worked all of his life. He had lived at the big house as Mary had insisted that they live there. He would have favoured a little cottage outside of the village, but Mary would have pined for company. He was a man of few words and much of the time went unnoticed at the house, as he went about his business of working the land. The funeral was well attended, as everyone in the village knew Mary, the indomitable force that arrived at their homes in times of crisis. As with Ida's funeral, most of them came for Mary, in truth, many could not quite remember who Edward actually was. He was buried beside his parents. Ellen Lily, Anna and Mary Ellen were tearful. Mary remained composed, the only person who ever saw the vulnerable side of Mary was Mustapha.

The Reverend James Knightly arrived at the house to discuss the forthcoming mass christening of the babies. Joseph and Lily were the main organisers of the event. After they finalised the details, the Reverend joined Mustapha, who was perching in the tree house. Jim admired the tree house and when he discovered that it had been built by the twins father Paulo, he asked Mustapha whether he thought that Paulo would take on the commission of building new choir stalls in the church. They mentioned it to Mary when she delivered the tea and cakes and she summoned Paulo and sent him to see the Reverend.

Paulo could not wait to begin. The following day he was at the church with his measuring tape and sketchbook. The Reverend showed him the old decrepit choir stalls and they discussed what was required. It was a large undertaking that would keep Paulo busy for months. The Reverend gave Paulo a free hand with the design and the decoration. A few days later, Paulo arrived at the rectory with his sketches for approval, but the Reverend liked all of them and told Paulo to do as he saw fit.

The wood in the stable that Paulo had been collecting since he arrived was well seasoned. He had a lot of oak and ash, some poplar, willow, holly, beech and yew. He asked around the village for two young lads interested in becoming apprentices and was inundated with a queue. Mustapha suggested assessing their aptitude with wood and tools rather than guessing. There were nine lads, ranging from twelve to seventeen. Paulo demonstrated a mortise and tenon joint, the mainstay of the carpenter. It proved an interesting day, one failed to understand the measuring tape, another cut their finger with a chisel, requiring the urgent attention of Mustapha. Yet another had no aptitude for a saw. Two decided it was not the occupation for them and another was very slow in the brain department. The remaining three showed some promise, with one, named Roland, even managing a reasonable joint for a first attempt. Paulo could not decide so he took all three lads on as his apprentices. One of them, a large lad named Harold, was as strong as an ox and able to lift large timbers with little effort. He proved invaluable on the other end of the long saw. The final one, known as Pip, was the quietest and most careful, and wanted to learn to carve with a chisel.

Joseph and Mustapha watched the activity from the tree house. It was obvious that the stable was not big enough for what was turning into a major undertaking. The wide variety of dangerous tools would be hazardous to the numerous young children, and the intrepid Khalid was already poking his nose in the enterprise.

There was a large property to rent near the church, previously used for storing fleeces. Joseph negotiated a year's lease and all the men in the family, with the exception of Mustapha, who Mary said would just get in the way, transported the timber, tools and workbenches from the stable to Paulo's new workshop. Ro, Harry and Pip, collectively known as' Paulo's chippies', cleaned out the stoves and the chimneys and by the end of the week there was a sign on the building.

Paulo Salazar & Son. Carpenters and Joiners.

Paulo stood back and admired his sign and wished that his parents could see it.

The workshop was near to the lads' homes and to the church and the work progressed well.

Just before Christmas the first set of choir stalls were complete and installed on the left side of the church. Constructed mainly of oak, with Gothic arches at the top of each seat and an intricate cross, carved into each of the backrests. The oak had been polished with beeswax and shone like gold. The Reverend James Knightly was astonished. He had asked for choir stalls and received works of art. He insisted on paying for the completed half. It was a handsome sum, more than Paulo would have asked for. He gave his chippies a generous Christmas bonus and their families were able to afford meat for their Christmas dinners for the first time in years. On Christmas Eve, Paulo shut the workshop at midday, he gave the lads a Christmas pudding each, that Mary had made, and told them they would start work again on the day after Boxing Day.

It was a good Christmas, the babies were healthy and Paulo sat proudly at the table for the first time since his arrival, as he was now able to contribute financially. The weather was cold and clear and as yet there was no sign of snow. After Christmas, Mina and Maria decided to take on much of the cooking, to ease the burden on Mary. Rose was not required as, like her mother, she needed help to boil and egg. Paulo took his chippies into town and purchased new tools for the workshop. He bought brand new brown overalls, long aprons, matching caps and jackets for each of them, to save wear on their clothes. The following day Harry arrived with his own clothes over the top of his new overalls, as he did not want to spoil them. Paulo made him change and assured him that when the overalls wore out he would be provided with another pair. Due to the development in the skills of Paulo's chippies, the final set of choir stalls were finished and installed in early March. The lads were morose as they left the church, believing that this would mean that their apprenticeship was at an end. Paulo assured them that there was a lot of work to do. Orders for furniture had begun to arrive shortly after the installation of the first choir stalls. The chippies sang all the way back to the workshop.

Chapter 34

Mustapha and Mary had lived in the rooms at one end of the house for many years. He and Ida had a bedroom and a sitting room and Mary and Edward had the same. Now they were both alone, Mary decided that they should reorganize the largest room that had a window overlooking the woods as a shared sitting room. Mustapha agreed. Later, the family heard loud creaks and the odd bumping noises from above and found Mary, in her sixties, and the frail Mustapha of unknown age, trying to move sofas and armchairs from room to room and laughing at their shared inadequacies. Maria told them both off and sent Sal and Sam to move the furniture to the destinations required. They wanted the large cream leather sofa with the violet cushions in front of the window so they could watch the woods and see the stars at night. They wanted the purple footstools in front of the sofa so they could put their feet up. They wanted the table and two chairs from another room brought in, in case they fancied eating upstairs. The armchairs were placed one each side of the fireplace, with a table in between for the tea. Mustapha's bookcase was tried in several places, eventually taking root against the wall nearest to his armchair. Sam and Sal, who had responded reasonably patiently to the constant instructions. 'Move it a bit further that way!' and 'No, too far, back just a bit!' Then they detected the poorly concealed, stifled giggling of Mary and Mustapha, clutching their stomachs, tears rolling down their faces. Sal and Sam looked at each other, and back at Mary and Mustapha, they watched the old couple as they slid down into the chairs hooting with laughter. They left the room without asking if anything else required moving.

That evening, Mary and Mustapha sat in their respective armchairs in the candlelight, the kettle singing on the hob beside the roaring fire, the snow beginning to fall outside, and they talked about anything that entered their heads. They had never felt so comfortable and at peace.

After that Mary and Mustapha spent most of their evenings together in that room. They continued to tend the garden and replenish the stocks of remedies and potions and Mary continued to attend many of the village births and pass on her skills to Anna, who was now 'walking out' with Matthew, the son of the Reverend James Knightly.

Mary had thought that she would never relinquish her control of the kitchen. She had toiled in various kitchens for fifty years. First in her parents' kitchen, then John's and finally the busy kitchen of Aziz Shadi Rashad Salamar Badr al din, where she learned so much from Mustapha. However, she was now content to let the young women take over the responsibility and each day she looked forward to her evenings with her best friend, who read stories to her and listened to her prattling about life without falling asleep. As for Mustapha, he had never been happier. He had a daughter, grandchildren and his Mary for company. In the soft light she was as beautiful as the day he first saw her. He told her so and she blushed, although he didn't notice it in the firelight.

The winter was a fairly mild one. There were several light snow falls, just enough to cover the landscape, but nothing severe.

The four babies all began crawling at the same time and Rose was at her wit's end trying to keep them all together whilst Maria and Mina were busy in the kitchen. Paulo built a portable enclosure of wooden railings, curtailing the most adventurous ones from becoming lost in the big house. He brought home a bag of small wooden blocks for them to play with, but Joey, the largest, tended to throw the blocks at the others. Ivy and Lily made some softer playthings and Isabella was recruited to supervise the imprisoned babies.

Paulo's order book filled up. He had orders for tables, dressers and a four-poster bed. He assembled sketches of his designs, and during the quiet evenings when the noisy brood was safely in their cribs, Rose and Maria copied his drawings and made several pamphlets of his work to show to new customers.

Mustapha and Mary sat upstairs and began writing in detail the ingredients and preparation methods used in the potions.

Matthew Knightly visited Gabriel and Ellen Lily and formally asked Anna's father for her hand in marriage. Gabriel agreed.

In the spring, when the babies started to walk, Paulo built a fenced area, with a gate for access, near to Mustapha's garden for the toddlers to run around in. Joey soon unlatched the gate, freeing the toddlers and allowing them access to the garden where they trampled about and severely disturbed Mustapha's plants until discovered by Isabella. Paulo replaced the latch with a two bolts, one at the top and the other at the bottom of the gate. Joey merely squeezed his small hands through the gaps and undid the bolts and the marauding bunch found their way into the woods so Paulo, admitting defeat, nailed the gate permanently shut.

The ship was due to sail. A lengthy voyage was planned, to East Africa and India and Sam and Sal promised Paulo that they would bring back some unusual timbers, they had seen wood in many colours in the past, deep reds, dark browns and black. Paulo began to think about the spectacular inlaid patterns he could achieve with those colours.

They set sail in early summer and most of the family went to the dock to see them off. They wanted to be in the Indian Ocean, still their favourite part of the world, before autumn descended onto the volatile Atlantic Ocean. As they sailed north on the east coast of Africa, they saw the whales and dolphins they had seen as children and the tiny islands surrounded by emerald water. They anchored a few times, to take on fresh water and food. They purchased sacks of spices and found a heavy, black timber that was so heavy that it failed to float in water like other woods. They spent several weeks, moored near a beautiful uninhabited island and the entire crew had a well-deserved break. They swam in the warm, crystal clear water, caught fish, warmed their bones in the sun and recovered from the damp chill of a British winter. The ship meandered around the islands, often becalmed for short periods of time. By the time they reached India it was winter in England. They loaded sacks of ginger, peppercorns, cumin, coriander, cardamom, turmeric, chili and long plaits of garlic bulbs.

Whilst they waited for a consignment of tea and the delivery of a red wood called mahogany, Sam and Sal went to the markets. Sam purchased two saris for Mina, one in a deep orange with strong yellow detailing, the other in purple and cerise. Sal bought Maria a long gold necklace and matching bracelet. For Rose and Paulo they found a wall hanging and for the children, numerous drums of different sizes. For their mother and Joseph they found a new bedspread that they liked so much that they bought another two, one for Ellen Lily and Gabriel, the other for Anna's wedding present. Finally, for Mustapha and Mary they purchased a breathtaking chess set, in which the pawns were tiny monkeys, all different. The kings and queens were mounted on elephants, the bishops were holy men, the knights were camels and the rooks were towers with tigers on the tops. The set was carved in two different woods, one darker than the other and came with a matching chess table.

The timber arrived, two massive trunks of a deep, red mahogany that were too big to go below and were lashed to the top deck and adopted as a seat by the crew on the journey home. The tea chests were packed into the hold and the remaining space filled with bolts of silk. Then they left India and sailed slowly through the islands to time their rounding of the Cape of Good Hope in early spring. They arrived home at the end of spring, in time for Anna and Matthew's wedding.

Mustapha skipped around the kitchen like a child when he saw the chess set, and Mary kissed the twins. During the summer months they sat up in the tree house in the shade of the huge oak and played games that often lasted for days.

When the twins delivered the ebony and mahogany to Paulo's workshop, that had required three of Gabriel's strongest horses to drag the tree trunks, one at a time across the marshes, he was in such awe that he lapsed into his native tongue for the first time in year.

Chapter 35

During the year before Matthew Knightly's marriage, he had been studying at the London Hospital Medical College in Whitechapel. He learned anatomy, and under the supervision of surgeons and physicians at the hospital, he treated some patients and watched operations. Matthew was horrified by the operations, from which most patients appeared to die within hours. The surgeons used none of the potions that Mustapha made available to the villagers. In particular, Matthew dreaded the sound of the Operations Bell that sounded to summon staff to hold down the unfortunate patient who had summoned the energy to put up a fight. The surgeons were aloof individuals and dismissive of students. Matthew had attempted to inform one surgeon of Mustapha's substances that obliterated pain and received a humiliating barrage of insults and thereafter kept his views to himself.

Matthew discussed the issues with his father, who had witnessed Mustapha extract a tooth, causing no discomfort. The villagers all had stories about the potions and remedies. Childbirth and death no longer held the terrors that had been all too familiar to the people before Mustapha arrived. Matthew studied hard and vowed that, one day he would witness surgical operations in which the patients were either asleep or at least not writhing in indescribable agony. The vicar took his son to see Mustapha to discuss the potions. Mustapha was visibly distressed when Matthew told him about the surgical operations, the screaming patients and the Operating Bell. Matthew asked what Mustapha used in his potions. Mustapha explained that he used many different plants that he grew in his garden. Many of the plants could be lethal in high doses. He did not know the names of many of the plants but he knew then by sight. Matthew was mostly interested in Mustapha's ability to obliterate pain.

'Ah!' answered Mustapha. 'That will be the power of the poppies!'

Mustapha talked of the terrible death of his grandfather, his own inability to watch the suffering and finally the poppy juice that relieved the agony. Then he talked of the old gentleman from China, from whom he learned the skills of the potions and how that knowledge changed the lives of the people in the village in Southern Iran and allowed him access to the women's secret world of childbirth. He had honed his skills aboard ship, dealing with the injuries and bouts of sickness amongst the sailors. In those days he had purchased the raw poppy juice during the voyages, but now he grew the poppies himself and harvested them in the traditional way he had seen as a child in Afghanistan. Mustapha added that the poppy can also kill and if used too frequently can cause a desperate need in the user. The poppy, a wonderful gift from God, must be used wisely, and never abused.

Mustapha took Matthew into his garden where the tall poppies grew. The flowers were of various colours from pure white to a deep purple and all the pinks in between. He showed him the fine cuts in the poppy heads oozing with juice that quickly set into a greyish-cream gum, that he collected and dried. He knew all the different strengths and weaknesses of the individual types of poppy, some he favoured for pain relief, others for inducing sleep. He had many other types of plants in his garden, those that helped the healing process, others that settled stomachs and some that relieved fevers.

Matthew was fascinated and thanked Mustapha profusely. Mustapha warmed to the young man and recognized in him the same abhorrence to human suffering that he himself felt. An unyielding abhorrence that would motivate him to do the best he could for his future patients and not rest until he had discovered a way to silence the Operations Bell forever.

On the way to the rectory, Matthew announced to his father that Mustapha's knowledge put to shame the surgeons and doctors at the London Hospital. If Mustapha would agree to educate him and share his knowledge, then he would promise to strive his utmost until the time came when no person would go under the surgeon's knife without a potion to numb the pain.

The Reverend James Knightly looked at his

son and was exceedingly proud and thanked God for sending him to this parish that contained the unusual creature that was Mustapha the Magician.

Lily, Mary, Ellen Lily and Anna were busy planning the wedding and Matthew visited regularly. But he and Anna would invariably disappear and Mary would locate them in the tree house with Mustapha. Then the four of them would become engrossed in lengthy discussions that invariably led to potions and the like. Lily and Ellen Lily gave up trying to lure then back to the wedding plans and organized it themselves.

The wedding was held at the beginning of July. It was a warm sunny day and Anna was resplendent in ivory silk and her abundant chestnut curls were loose and reached to her slim waist. Mustapha had made her a crown of pink and white poppies and gave her a matching small bunch to carry, with strict instructions that he wanted them back after the ceremony. Gabriel smiled broadly as he walked her up the aisle of the church. The Reverend James Knightly smiled equally broadly as he conducted the wedding ceremony. His tall, fair-haired son smiled too. Mustapha had pinned a lone purple poppy on his jacket and told him he could keep that one.

The Reverend and his family were startled to see the crowd of villagers that had assembled outside the church during the ceremony, and even more startled when the entire population began to make its way to the big house, on horses, in carts and on foot. The party was as lavish as the birthday party for Aziz Shadi Rashad Salamar Badr al din and he would have been proud. He had believed that the happiness of the guests at a wedding was endowed upon the couple and would carry them through the first few years of their marriage. A queue of villagers waited patiently for the couple to appear and presented them with little gifts, most of which they had made themselves. There was singing, dancing and a lot of eating, rounded off with the inevitable fireworks, after which the tired, well-fed villagers ambled slowly home.

Anna stayed at the rectory with her husband until he returned to London for his studies. While he was away she returned to live with her parents, and continued to help Mary deliver the babies. In fact, she now delivered many of them herself and Mary rarely needed to intervene. Anna visited the rectory regularly and her parents-in-law made her very welcome. They had always hoped to have a daughter and came to love her as their own. Faith in particular benefitted from her presence in what had always been a male dominated household.

When Matthew returned home in the autumn, he brought with him an object that tantalized and absorbed Mustapha. A microscope. He showed Mustapha the wonders of magnification, revealing wondrous secrets unavailable to the naked eye. Mustapha, mad with excitement scuttled to and from his garden with tiny slivers of plant matter to place between the slides and then dragged Mary to look and them. Matthew also brought drawings from his anatomy classes, some that he had made himself and some he had copied that were very old, and originally made by a man called Leonardo Da Vinci. Mustapha was transfixed. He had knowledge of the bones of the body and the major organs, but these drawings showed details beyond his wildest dreams. Within a day, Mustapha and Mary's sitting room had largely disappeared under piles of drawings and objects that Mustapha just had to view under the microscope. With Matthew and Anna's help they cleared out the unused sitting room, ferreted around the rest of the house, brought in tables, chairs and a tall cupboard with numerous drawers. They removed the curtains to maximize the light, pinned the drawings on the walls, and dug out Mustapha's old notes he had made during his study of the villagers and their illnesses, when he had discovered the relationship between cowpox and smallpox, a fact that sent Matthew into paroxysms of admiration. Pride of place in the room was given to the microscope, on a polished table under the window.

Matthew and Anna became regular visitors to the quarters of Mustapha and Mary, often working late into the evenings. Matthew made copious notes when Mustapha carefully explained the harvesting and preparation of his potions, balms and poultices. On a night in the autumn, when the rain fell in great sheets, Mary insisted that the couple stay the night. She gave them her bedroom and she slept with Mustapha in his large feather bed, declaring that they were far too old to cause a scandal. She never moved back to her own room.

Matthew left the microscope with Mustapha when he returned to Whitechapel. Little Mustapha joined his grandfather at the microscope table, avidly investigating anything that Mustapha placed on the slides. Mustapha stared wistfully out of the window, waiting for night, when he could bask in the extraordinary soft warmth that Mary brought to his bed, and he secretly believed that, given the opportunity on a good night, he may well be able to manage a scandal.

Chapter 36

In order to avoid the inevitable quandary that Matthew and Anna would face, trying to decide which family to spend Christmas with, the family invited the Reverend James Knightly and his family to spend the day at the big house. The small army of village women, who had drawn straws for the prestigious jobs of cooking at the big house, arrived on Christmas Eve to begin the preparations. The Knightly family arrived mid-morning with a new, larger microscope and a box of glass slides for Mustapha, causing him to disappear upstairs and requiring Mary to forcibly retrieve him in time for dinner.

Dinner consisted of goose, lamb, roast potatoes and parsnips, winter cabbage and carrots, stuffing and mint sauce, followed by Christmas pudding, mince pies and cream. As usual the women who cooked the meal were expected to sit and eat with the family. James and Faith Knightly, greatly impressed by the gesture, vowed that in future, their staff would eat Christmas dinner with them. When Maria and Mina carried in the plates of cheese, butter, biscuits and fruit, Mustapha experienced a sudden, momentous flash of clarity. What he wanted more than anything in his life was to be able to say of Mary. 'This is my wife, Mary.' He turned to Mary, who was seated several places away, the other side of little Mustapha and Isabella.

'Mary, would you do me the honour of becoming my wife?' he whispered, although everyone around the long table heard him.

Mary choked on the biscuit she was eating, and a small fragment hit the butter dish and ricocheted into Maria's tea, causing a snort of laughter from Isabella. All eyes were on Mary during the silence in which everyone held their breath. Her mouth was still full of cheese and biscuit and she found herself unable to swallow, so she nodded her head eagerly. The family erupted into laughter, applause and shouts of congratulations, startling the Knightly family. There was also an unspoken element of relief, as the entire family knew that they already shared a bed.

Mustapha and Mary decided on a spring wedding in case of snow causing disruption, as Mustapha had predicted that this year the snow would be heavy. From the moment Mary had accepted his proposal he had referred to her as 'my future wife,' at any given opportunity. He was right about the snow, as it began to fall at the end of December and continued erratically until March. Gabriel began the tree delivery to the village and Paulo trudged through the deep snow to his workshop. The chippies were invariably there first and had lit the stoves before he arrived. Mustapha was delighted to discover that no snowflake was the same as the next one. The two Mustapha's took the small microscope outside for this experiment, as the snowflakes quickly reverted to water when taken indoors. Mary discovered them sitting in the snow, fiddling with the slides, their hands swollen and red, their noses dripping. She dragged the pair of them indoors and lectured them as they thawed out in front of the fire, grinning quietly at each other. The snow was at its worst at the end of January, when a blizzard lasted almost three days. Paulo decided to remain indoors and hoped his chippies had the sense to do the same. When he was able to get there several days later, he was surprised and humbled to see that not only had his loyal chippies struggled to the workshop, they had virtually finished the large dining table they were working on. He mentioned to the lads that they could do with another pair of hands and did any of them know a young lad who would be interested. Harry said that his little brother was keen to work there and Paulo suggested he bring him to the workshop the following day. Harry's 'little' brother Ernest was even bigger than Harry, and immensely strong. He was known as Big Ern. There were several others with the same name in the village. There was Lily's uncle Ernest, Long Ern, Round Ern and Daft Ern. The two of them delivered the large dining table a week later. The solid oak table would have required four or possibly six normal men. They made short work of sawing the mahogany tree trunks into eight feet lengths, and then into workable planks. Ro, the one most skillful in fine sawing and measuring was given the task of cutting the black timber, known as ebony, and the mahogany with the most beautiful grain into thin strips an eighth of an inch thick to use as veneer. Paulo and Pip made a small ash table, inlaid with a lily made from mahogany with stems and leaves of ebony. Paulo presented it to Rose's mother Lily on her birthday. The little table caused an influx of orders for furniture adorned with family crests, flowers and even animals.

Lily and Ivy spent the snowy days making Mary's wedding dress. The used a soft, warm blue silk, with a hint of lavender that would enhance her eyes. They also made Mustapha new baggy trousers and long shirt in darker blue and white striped cotton. Ivy added a black embroidered pattern around the neck, the cuffs and the bottom of the shirt. They both hoped that the bluebells would be out in time for the wedding.

Mary couldn't decide who should give her away. She considered the twins, but only wanted one person and felt unable to choose. She was uncomfortable about asking her brother-in-laws. She thought of little Mustapha but he burst into tears believing that he really had to give her away and would never see her again. So, in the end, she asked Gabriel, her son-in-law.

Family celebrations were traditionally lavish and included the entire village. Due to the popularity of the couple, this wedding was likely to outstrip anything they had seen before. Mustapha was jubilant, as he wanted the whole world to see his wedding. The villagers had known about the wedding since Christmas afternoon, when the women who had been at the big house returned home. They had knocked on doors with the news on their way home. In the days preceding the wedding, villagers with little to offer but their time and energy arrived to help the family prepare for the wedding, and in a short time the field and the house was ready. The villagers had no intention of staying outside of the church for this wedding and they crammed themselves into every inch of the church. The Reverend Knightly had never seen a church so full. Mustapha arrived in his new clothes, without its usual long scarf. His long white hair and beard had been washed and brushed by his daughter Maria. Then Mary entered on the arm of the smiling Gabriel, now an expert at giving away the women in his family. Mary's still abundant curly chestnut hair, with a sprinkling of silver hung loose and was decorated with tiny silk flowers that matched her dress. She carried a bunch of bluebells. The silk shimmered as she walked down the aisle and Mustapha had to be steadied by the Reverend as she approached. Mustapha grinned inanely throughout the ceremony. When the Reverend Knightly declared them man and wife, Mustapha clapped his hands, he kissed his wife, the Reverend and even Gabriel.

Outside of the church the villagers had stationed a horse and cart decorated with flowers and ribbons. It had a driver and cushions in the back for the couple to sit on. Harry and his little brother lifted them up onto the cart. At the house, Mary and Mustapha stayed in the cart as the villagers delivered their little gifts, then they retired inside for a rest and some tea. They joined the party later when it was in full swing, they walked arm in arm and Mustapha frequently said, 'This is my wife, is she not lovely?' and Mary frequently elbowed him in the ribs.

Paulo and his chippies had made them a chest of drawers, with dozens of tiny compartments and the top was inlaid with poppies. When they finally went upstairs that night, they discovered on their bed the famous deep blue/ purple quilt with the thousand glittering stars that had been Aziz Shadi Rashad Salamar Badr al din and Lily's, then Maria and Sal's and now it was their turn. The room smelled strongly of jasmine.

Chapter 37

Matthew came home during the summer and was ecstatic to discover that Anna was with child. She suffered no sickness, just a surge of boundless energy. The couple visited Mustapha and Mary and Matthew told them stories from the hospital and of his continued frustration regarding the treatment of patients. His ambition was to qualify as a doctor and eventually set up a practice in the village, using the knowledge he gained from his studies, coupled with the even greater knowledge he had gained from Mustapha.

Little Mustapha, at ten, spent his days with Mustapha in the garden. Mustapha was impressed with his grandson's instinctive ability to know when the poppies were ready to begin harvesting. He watched him moving carefully around the plants, sniffing and gently squeezing the seed heads. He nurtured the bugle, lavender and the figwort, used in the balms, the feverfew for high temperatures, the chamomile, used for both sleep problems and upset stomachs. The dandelion and the nettles, both robust plants needed no nurturing and grew everywhere and were used to treat stomachaches and bloating. Little Mustapha was currently learning the uses of the dried spices from India. As well as being used in the kitchen, the ginger, chili, turmeric, fenugreek and cayenne, were all incorporated into his grandfathers potions. Little Mustapha also knew when to collect the elderberries and the hawthorn fruit.

Mustapha loved to sit in the tree house and watch him in the garden. Isabella remained a frequent visitor, and Mustapha would listen, with a sense of satisfaction, to the quiet, studious boy explaining to her what the plants were used for.

Khalid, on the other hand, ran around pestering his father to go to sea. He knew that he was the same age as his father and uncle had been when they first went to sea. His pressure became relentless and eventually the twins agreed to take him in early autumn when they intended a fairly short voyage to North Africa and Crete. Mina, unlike Lily before her, was happy for him to go, knowing how difficult he would be if they left him behind.

The crowd of toddlers were now three and slightly more manageable. Joey remained the leader and George and Olivia followed him everywhere. Sophia deserted the pack and was drawn to the gentle company of her grandfather and elder brother, like a moth to a flame. She would sit in the tree house with Mustapha and follow him around holding onto the hem of his long shirt. Maria was delighted to see them together, to see that both of her children appeared to have inherited her father's calm temperament. Sophia was growing into a beautiful child, with her long, virtually black curls and Mustapha's eyes.

The ship sailed in early September, with the

irrepressible Khalid aboard and the house was considerably quieter. Matthew was back in Whitechapel and Anna spent her time between her parent's home, the big house and the rectory. Faith was impatient to have a grandchild and she prayed on a daily basis for a granddaughter. As the days grew shorter and cooler, the two Mustapha's resumed their explorations of familiar objects with the microscopes. Mary made their tea and biscuits and Sophia helped her. Out of the blue, Sophia asked when her grandfather's birthday was, and Mary realized that even she did not know, neither did Mustapha himself. Sophia was astounded, as all three year olds would be, birthdays being very important milestones in their little lives. Sophia's solution to the problem was to let Mustapha choose what day he would like to have as his birthday. The three of them stood in the microscope room and waited for Mustapha to invent a birthday for himself. He could see by the children's faces that they would have been disappointed should he decide on very distant date.

'I think it's next week!' he announced with a smile.

'What day next week?' asked Sophia, requiring more detailed information.

'Why don't you choose the day?'

'No Granddaddy, you have to choose!' she insisted.

'What day of the week is your favourite?' suggested little Mustapha, desperately trying to break the deadlock.

'Um, I think it is Friday.' Said Mustapha at last.

'Oh, goody!' chirped Sophia and trotted off to tell the whole family that it would be Mustapha's birthday on Friday.

As Mustapha had missed every birthday throughout his life, the family rallied round organizing one that he would remember. During the week, a pile of little presents built up beside the hearth downstairs, causing mounting excitement in the children. Maria and Mina prepared Mustapha's favourite food and Mary baked him a cake. Very early on the Friday morning Sophia woke her grandfather by tugging on his beard.

'Happy birthday granddaddy!' she squeaked, her dark eyes shining with excitement.

She hopped around the room until Mustapha and Mary had hauled themselves from bed and put on their dressing gowns. She skipped up and down the stairs in front of them and grabbed Mustapha's hand when he reached the bottom and pulled him into the room where the entire family had assembled. There was a tray of hot tea on the table beside the armchair and a pile of presents on the floor. Maria poured his tea and everyone sat down to watch him open his presents. Lily and Ivy had both made him new white scarves. Lily had embroidered each end with tiny purple poppies and Ivy had frayed the ends of hers and tied them into tassels. Paulo and Rose gave him a wooden box made in the workshop and Pip had carefully carved his name on the lid. Maria gave him a set of handkerchiefs embroidered with a fancy 'M' in the corners. Joseph gave him a large bound book with blank pages for him to write the ingredients of his potions, and the children had gathered him a large bag of fresh walnuts, of which he was very fond. Mary gave him a long nightshirt in thick, soft cotton and a pair of wooly bed socks. She loved him very much, but the glacial temperature of his feet at night had regularly given her quite a turn.

Later in the morning, Gabriel, Ellen Lily and their children arrived with a pair of slippers that they had collectively constructed from a sheepskin. Jim Knightly delivered a new box of slides and Anna gave him a box of pencils, a new pen and a bottle of ink. Mustapha was overcome, and forced to agree that birthdays were well worth having. Later, the family sat down to dinner, spicy chicken and roasted vegetables, fresh bread, Mary's delicious cake and the randomly shaped biscuits that the children had made.

It was the best, and only, birthday that Mustapha had ever had. The date was the third of October.

Chapter 38

The year's lease on Paulo's workshop was up for renewal. His business was doing so well, his order book full and his four young chippies were reliable and hardworking. So he made an offer on the building, which was accepted. He raised the lads' wages and they all embarked on a future with the security of their own premises.

Anna and Matthew stayed with Mary and Mustapha from the week before Christmas, as Anna wanted to be with both of them for the birth. If Anna was anything like the generations of women in her family that gave birth with ease, and considerable speed, the big house was the best place to be. Mustapha requested that the bathhouse be kept in readiness. Anna woke Mary early on Christmas morning and they pottered downstairs and Mary lit the fires in the bathhouse. Mustapha, sensing the absence of Mary, got up to see where she was. He found Anna making tea in the kitchen and Mary putting water on to boil in the bathhouse. The three of them sat at the kitchen table drinking tea. Anna was looking forward to experiencing one of Mustapha's potions. He had one in readiness for when her pains increased. Matthew arrived to find them chatting and laughing, very early in the morning, unaware that he was about to become a father. Mustapha asked if he wished to be present at the birth. Matthew was shocked. Even though he was training to be a doctor, he still assumed that birthing remained the prerogative of women.

'Not in this house it isn't!' chuckled Mustapha.

He explained that he himself had been present at all of the births, that Sal had been present at the birth of Sophia and that poor Paulo had inadvertently witnessed the birth of Joey, when Mina delivered onto the floor beside the fireplace and he fainted clean away. To the family's constant amusement, and his own embarrassment, Paulo was renowned for fainting during medical procedures.

Matthew helped Mary to fill the bath as the rest of the family was beginning to wake. Mustapha took Anna and the potion to the bathhouse and they helped her into the bath. Her pains were stronger and Mustapha gave her the potion he had prepared for her. Matthew watched as she visibly relaxed, giggled and then asked of Mustapha.

'Since you have married my grandmother, shall I call you granddaddy?' and she laughed raucously.

'Anna, you may call me whatever you please.' Chuckled Mustapha.

Anna laughed even more, a list of absurd words that she could call Mustapha tumbled through her brain. She laughed so much it was impossible for her to tell anyone what was so amusing. The she stopped laughing abruptly. Matthew noticed an almost imperceptible glance pass between Mustapha and Mary. Then Mary reached under Anna's arms and gently lifted her as Mustapha took her wrists and without exchanging a word, they deftly moved her into a crouching position. Anna grabbed the side of the bath and began to push. Mustapha held her face in his hands, looked into her eyes and spoke to her quietly. Mary hung over the side of the bath, her hand in the water, ready to catch the child. After several minutes of involuntary pushing, Mustapha telling her quietly to relax and let her body do the job it was designed for, Mary caught the baby, glanced at Mustapha who lifted Anna's leg and Mary passed the baby under her leg and into her arms. Anna sat back into the water with her baby, who spluttered, opened its eyes and looked around the room at everyone. Matthew was speechless. Anna briefly lifted the baby form the water.

'She is a little girl!' she announced happily.

Mary cut the cord and took the baby, rolled her in a warm towel and sent her father out to show the family that she knew was clamouring outside the door. Then she sent Mustapha out as well and set about cleaning Anna up and making her presentable. It was Christmas Day after all. Mustapha asked Matthew for permission to present the child to Allah. Matthew had no idea what he was talking about. He was so in awe of Mustapha at that moment, he would have agreed to anything. He followed the fragile old man outside and watched him hold his daughter aloft, and in an alien language, shouted into the sky. A shaft of morning sun broke through the clouds.

'That's a good sign.' said Mustapha with satisfaction. 'This little girl has been especially blessed.'

By the time the Knightly family arrived, Anna was in the armchair in front of the fire with Holly. The name was a unanimous decision, very fitting for a baby that arrived on Christmas day. Faith cried when Anna passed her the tiny granddaughter she had prayed so hard for. Holly had wispy fair hair and bright blue eyes. The Reverend Knightly hugged his son.

'Father, it was the most amazing thing I have ever seen!' Matthew was still in shock. He looked over at Mustapha and Mary, who sat laughing together on the sofa, still in their dressing gowns and he had his birthday bed socks and slippers on. He had seen them deliver his daughter, painlessly and with an unspoken communication that defied explanation. He knelt down beside them and hugged them both.

Mustapha and Mary wandered off to get dressed, Mustapha dropping the unsubtle hint that they could do with a hearty breakfast when they came down again. Maria laughed and headed for the kitchen.

Paulo volunteered to deliver the news to Ellen Lily, who was unaware that she had become a grandmother, and Gabriel. He returned in half an hour with the whole family impatient to see the new baby. Mustapha and Mary were eating breakfast in the kitchen when they arrived.

'Ooh!' they heard Ellen Lily shriek. 'I am a grandmother!'

.

'Oh Lord!' muttered Mary to Mustapha. ' I've just realized that it makes me a great-grandmother! That makes me feel very old!'

'Mary, you will never, ever be old in my eyes, just more beautiful.'

She smiled, and blushed.

Maria collected the plates and shooed the old couple from the kitchen as the women from the village were trying to begin the cooking. They adjourned to their sitting room and made fresh tea and kept out of the way until it as time for dinner. They could hear the small army of children running around downstairs and the occasional raised voice of a harassed mother. They were grateful to be out of the way in peace and quiet. The gentle tap at the door was made by little Mustapha and Sophia, unable to cope with the chaos. Little Mustapha squeezed in the armchair beside his grandfather and Sophia with Mary. The four of them sat in blissful silence until one by one they all dozed off. Maria came up to make sure her children were not disturbing her father and found them all fast asleep, she shut the door quietly and left them until it was time for dinner.

Mustapha woke first. He sat looking at his beloved wife and his sleeping grandchildren and believed he was the happiest man in the world. He sat smiling quietly until his daughter arrived with a tray of tea and the news that dinner would be in about ten minutes.

Dinner was roast beef and chickens in a spicy sauce, Mustapha's favourite. Jim agreed, stating that he had never tasted anything so delicious. Instead of Christmas pudding, Maria and Mina had tried their best to follow two of Mustapha's famous pudding recipes and had succeeded fairly well. Due to the arrival of Holly, dinner was later then usual and the exhausted troop of three year olds were in bed by six o'clock, to the abject relief of their parents. Anna, Matthew and Holly retired early. Mary heard the quiet cry of Holly in the night when she woke for a feed and she heard the quiet footsteps of Matthew as he made Anna a cup of tea. Then she went back to sleep.

Matthew returned to his studies after Christmas and Anna remained with Mustapha and Mary for the first few weeks of Holly's life. She needed their support and advice, their safety net, in case of anything untoward occurring. She had delivered many babies, but was unprepared for the overwhelming attachment and fierce love she felt for her own first daughter. Faith, who visited regularly, understood Anna's need to be with her grandmother and remembered how vulnerable and helpless she had felt with her first child.

Chapter 39

Khalid loved the sea as his father, grandfather and great-grandfather Salamar had before him. He spent his days on deck watching and learning from the crew and the evenings with his father learning the mysteries of the charts. His father promised him that if he worked hard on this voyage, he would take him on the next voyage to his favourite place in the whole world, the emerald green Indian Ocean.

Sam pointed out the coast of Portugal to his son, he told him that it was the country that Uncle Paulo came from, and that it was the land of great explorers, who had discovered strange lands that nobody knew were there. Khalid immediately wanted to be an explorer when he grew up.

Sam and Sal decided to go the Crete first, having been surprised by the amount of commodities available there, and fill up the remaining space with hides from North Africa on the return journey. The weather in the Atlantic had been very windy and the seas choppy and rough, but Khalid appeared to have been born with sea legs and barely noticed. It was a relief for the crew when they sailed into the calmer waters of the Mediterranean Sea. The ship sailed east for several weeks and they were becalmed on occasions. They stopped a few times for fresh water and provisions. Khalid was staggered to see the hundreds of vessels anchored off the island of Crete. Tiny, countless boats rowed to and fro between the ships and in and out from the shore, ferrying people and crates of all shapes and sizes. The air was full of strange smells and languages, and for the first time in his life, Khalid fervently wished that he had tried harder when Mustapha had diligently attempted to teach him other tongues. Following a challenging and rather undignified clamber down a rope ladder, slung over the side of the ship. Sam, Sal and Khalid went ashore in a tiny boat, rowed by two burly men with enormous moustaches. The dock was crowded with people, bartering and making deals, exchanging money and gold. Sam negotiated a good price for six crates of porcelain from China after carefully examining the consignment. They purchased crates of tea and packages of silk. Khalid saw his first octopus and large turtle, brought ashore by fishermen. He heard his first whale, saw it spit a fine spray into the air and saw its huge tail as it dived. Sam informed him he would see hundreds next year, and in clearer waters. After several days when the hold was carefully packed with goods, the vessel sailed west to North Africa. Khalid sat on deck and watched the coast, sometimes flat and featureless and other times mountainous, the peaks tipped with snow. The climate was warm and Khalid could not understand why the snow on the mountains failed to melt.

In North Africa, the three of them set off south on camels. Khalid had learned to ride on

Lumpy, the decrepit survivor from the pair of camels that his grandfather had returned with when his twins were small. These camels were much more lively and inconsistent than poor old Lumpy and Khalid fell off a number of times. After three days of toiling through the increasingly warm desert, where Khalid had never seen so much sky, they arrived at their usual destination, where Henry had disappeared from several years ago. The family was excited to meet the grandson of Aziz Shadi Rashad Salamar Badr al din and they made a great deal of fuss over him. Sam and Sal bought a selection of hides from the tannery, where Khalid held his nose throughout the bartering. They bought the finest thin leathers made of goat for the London glove makers, thicker leather for coats and jackets and the very thick, stiff hides for boots, belts and saddles. Then they visited the souks and Sal bought a thick, heavy, woolen djellaba for Mustapha who felt the cold. They bought Moroccan spices for his famous lamb stew and several sacks of oranges, a delicacy they had promised, and failed miserably, to take home many times before. Khalid thought they were the loveliest taste he had ever experienced and he was warned not to eat too many oranges, ignored the advice and was stricken by a severe case of loose bowels, delaying their departure for several days before he could be trusted not to soil his camel. It was early spring when they left North Africa and headed for the moody, mercurial north Atlantic. The wind was behind them, a brisk wind from the south that speeded their journey and blew the warmer weather further north. They arrived home at the beginning of April.

Sam and Khalid took a sack of oranges to the children at the school, distributed the fruit between then with clear instructions to take them home to share with their families. Khalid, with an air of authority, and in rather more graphic terms than was absolutely necessary, warned the wide-eyed children to never eat more than one orange a day. Some, as Khalid had done, ignored the advice and were so taken with the flavour that they exceeded the advised limit, culminating in a disparate variety of embarrassing consequences.

Mustapha was scandalised to discover that nobody was saving the orange peel. He sent Khalid to retrieve as much as he could. He put a bowl in the kitchen and instructed everyone place the peelings there. He used the zest from the peelings in cakes and puddings and stewed the rest in hot sugar water and made candied peel that he dried and saved for winter.

Chapter 40

Joey, Sophia and the twins started school in the spring. They could be seen meandering across the fields, led by little Mustapha. They were joined most mornings by Mary Ellen, who had begun teaching the little ones, as her mother had done in the past. The procession generally consisted of Sophia clutching her brother's hand, the twins one each side of Mary Ellen and Joey running around, circling the others like a sheep dog. By the time they reached the school, Joey had travelled at least three times the distance of the others. Sophia was a good student and had learned to read and write in the tree house with Mustapha. George and Olivia learned quickly and George excelled at mathematics. Joey found it difficult to sit still, fidgeted, and wished he was playing in the woods, climbing trees and finding bird's nests.

Aziz, Gabriel's youngest son had finished school and with his brother Charles and his Uncle Robert now worked with his father's horses.

Little Mustapha was in his last year at the school and Isabella still had a year of studying to complete. It was during that summer that Ivy became ill. She had not been blessed with a robust constitution, but Mary noticed that she was becoming thinner and her face more ashen. Isabella confided in Mary that her mother ate very little and was frequently sick. Despite the best efforts of Mustapha, Mary and Matthew, she continued to fade, plagued by a gnawing pain in her abdomen. Her main concern was not for herself but for her precious Isabella. Mary promised her that she and Mustapha would take care of Isabella. Mustapha made a potion that kept her free of pain during the final few weeks and Mary moved in to nurse her and care for Isabella and Charles.

Isabella's grief was terrible, but Ivy begged her to remember the years they had together and to be brave. She made her promise to have a good, happy life. She died peacefully in Isabella's arms, with Mary and Charles at her side.

After the funeral, Isabella moved into the room beside Mary and Mustapha and Charles moved to the farm to spend his last years with his aging brothers. It was little Mustapha who finally helped Isabella escape from her nightmare of despair. He encouraged her to talk about Ivy and every week he helped her to pick flowers and went with her to Ivy's grave. He comforted her when she cried. Mustapha watched them in the garden together, silently tending the plants. Little Mustapha, with his dark eyes and dark curly hair, was a head taller than Isabella, whose long, straight hair was bleached almost white by the sun. Physically they were opposites, but Mustapha could sense a close bond between the pair, there since early childhood, that became stronger as the years passed. Mustapha set himself a new goal, to live long enough to see them become man and wife.

Anna, Isabella's godmother, took her role seriously. She nurtured the girl's interest in the garden and the potions and suggested that when she finished her schooling, she could assist in the sick house. Isabella was delighted, as it would mean spending her days with little Mustapha.

Little Mustapha's studies continued with his grandfather, they measured and weighed the ingredients of the potions and little Mustapha wrote the recipes down in Mustapha's birthday ledger. They dried and crushed the poppy sap, the herbs from the garden and the spices from abroad. Isabella labeled the airtight jars and placed them in rows on the shelves in the microscope room. They listed the common ailments and the types of potions used to treat them. Some potions could be made in advance and would keep for a considerable time. Others had to be made fresh each time.

The overall plan was that when Matthew finished his studies at the hospital, he would set up a practice in the village, with little Mustapha as his potions maker. It was agreed that Matthew would charge a fee from patients that possessed the means to pay, but the potions would remain free of any charge. Paulo and his chippies were already beginning to build the extra room at the back of the 'sick house', and to furnish it with a desk, examination table, shelves and cupboards.

Thomas, the only son of Henry and Sarah, the first baby to have been born in the big house, and Jack decided that Henry, Ernest and Charles, all well into their sixties, deserved a rest after fifty years of toil on the farm. They told them to choose a horse each and the old brothers rode off most days to discover the outskirts of the village that they had never had the time to explore since their childhood. They gathered winkles, cockles and mussels from the shore, walnuts and hazel nuts from the woods, blackberries from the hedgerows, and duck eggs, mushrooms and watercress from the marshes. They would arrive at the big house, and at Gabriel's farm, at random intervals with the fruits of their foraging expeditions. One spring they collected a large jar full of tadpoles, and took it to the school so that the children could watch them evolving into frogs.

Ellen Lily, whose children had grown up, or in the case of Henry, disappeared, formed a friendship with Faith, initially due to a shared interest in Holly. Faith had never had a close female friend. Ellen Lily, with the boundless energy of her mother, motivated Faith to tackle the overgrown gardens and reclaim the unused, forgotten, dusty rooms at the rectory. Ellen Lily rode to the rectory two of three times a week. When she discovered that Faith was unable to ride a horse, she arrived one morning with a gentle bay mare, a descendent of Elijah and one of his conquests. Faith was not keen and stared warily at the horse. Ellen Lily encouraged her to make friends with the horse, known as Mabel. Faith fed her an apple and stroked her soft nose.

She led her around the garden, talking to her quietly, but was not at all certain about climbing onto her back. Ellen Lily tied a rope to Mabel's halter, led her to a bench in the garden and insisted that Faith stand on the bench, put one foot in the stirrup and mount the horse. Faith, red-faced and giggling nervously obeyed, and when her feet were both firmly planted in the stirrups, Ellen Lily slowly led Mabel along the garden path. Mabel, well aware that the person on her back was a complete novice plodded along the path, head low and ears swiveling. Faith remained aloft, gradually relaxing and looking around. She declared that horse riding was a pleasant surprise, but when Mabel, on Ellen Lily's signal, broke into a trot, Faith unintentionally dismounted and landed with a resounding thud on the ground. Ellen Lily laughed and Mabel hung her head guiltily. Faith, with some reluctance, climbed back into the saddle and Ellen Lily told her to practice standing in the stirrups, explaining that putting her weight in the stirrups would reduce the chance of falling off. After an hour of practice, Faith, bruised and disheveled, actually remained aloft during a short period of trotting, Mabel was fed up and Ellen Lily was in dire need of a cup of tea. During the following few weeks, Faith's skills gradually improved and she became very fond of Mabel. The essential trust between rider and horse developed and after a couple of months Faith was confident enough to ride into town with Ellen Lily. The Reverend James was pleasantly surprised. He had tried unsuccessfully in the past to persuade her to learn to ride. Gabriel gave Mabel to Faith, and she moved to the rectory, where she was cossetted and fussed over for the rest of her days.

Isabella became a regular visitor to the rectory, to see her godmother Anna and little Holly who was crawling with enthusiasm by the summer. She was a happy little girl with the abundant chestnut hair that ran in the family. James, the youngest son of the Reverend, thought that Isabella was the most beautiful creature he had ever seen, she was like a fragile angel with her long pale hair and appeared light enough to float away on the breeze. James was afraid to talk to her and watched her in the garden with little Holly from his bedroom window. He lost his appetite and his nights were besieged by unhealthy, sinful dreams. He would awaken sweating, sticky and ill at ease. His parents thought he was sickening for something and took him to see Mustapha, who only needed one brief look at him to know what was ailing him. At that stage, Mustapha was unaware of the identity of the individual responsible for his inexorable suffering.

Chapter 41

Joshua was rudely awakened, for the first, and last time in his life, by the master at one o'clock in the morning. The master held a lantern, a gentleman's overnight bag, a spade, a horse and a gold coin. He ordered Joshua to ride hard for an hour, find a remote, secluded spot and bury the bag. He was then to return and never speak of the incident again. Joshua tied the bag and the spade to the saddle, and mounted the horse that suddenly bolted due to the resounding slap it received on the rump from the master. With the gold coin in his pocket and a great deal of confusion in his head, he rode for an hour, following the river. After an hour, he found himself in marshland. There were miles of marshes, separated by ditches and thickets. He dismounted and searched for a suitable spot in which to bury the bag. By the light of the moon he dug a hole near a ditch. The reeds and tall grasses providing cover.

Curiosity got the better of him as he picked up the bag. It was a good bag, too good to bury. Then he remembered his gold coin. He had never had a gold coin. With that gold coin he could buy his own bag without risking the wrath of his master. He had worked for the master since he was a small child. His father before him had been the gardener and Joshua had taken over after his father died. The master was a fair man, unless he was drunk. He was a widower with an only daughter and for many years had been selling off parts of the once extensive estate to make ends meet. Joshua continued to dig the hole when he heard an unearthly sound, a tiny high-pitched whine. Startled, he looked around, his heart thumping loudly. The sound was coming from the direction of the bag. Joshua stared at it, holding his breath. He opened the bag and found a newly born baby. He dropped the bag in horror and sat down with a thump. The baby was silent again and he thought it looked dead. He shook the bag and the baby's arms jerked upwards and it whined again. It was very cold and its eyes were tightly shut. It looked more like a baby bird than a child.

Joshua could not bring himself to bury the baby alive, even for a gold coin. He could not bring himself to kill it with the spade either. He had no idea where or how the master had come by a baby, or why he wanted rid of it so badly. Joshua sat with his head in his hands wondering what to do. Then, with a sigh, he got to his feet, lifted the baby out of the bag and laid it on the grass, and noticed that it was a female child. Then he buried the bag in the reeds and lifted the child. It was silent now and cold as death. Joshua took off his jacket and rolled the baby in the old threadbare garment, he threw the spade into the ditch and headed up a gentle hill that led to a village. The horse followed him, ears twitching. Joshua could see a square church tower off to the right and a number of small houses on the left.

The he saw a larger building with a small flight of steps, sheltered by a porch. He placed the baby on the top step close to the wall and tucked his old jacket around her. He prayed that someone good and kind would find her before she died. Then Joshua mounted his horse and rode hard for an hour until he reached home. He put the tired horse into the stable and returned to his bed, a place that tormented him with terrifying nightmares from that night onwards.

Fifteen years later, Joshua married the young woman who worked in the kitchen. Her name was Jane and her mother had been a Lady's maid to Eliza, the master's daughter for over twenty years. Jane moved into his cottage in the grounds and set about making it habitable. She removed the dogs, the chickens, straw, twigs and the layers of dirt, cobwebs, dead mice and dust that had accumulated over the years. She scrubbed the walls and floors. She washed bedding and clothing and made curtains for the windows. She boiled water and soaked the filthy pots and pans and wondered how Joshua had not poisoned himself.

Jane was at a loss when it came to Joshua's dreadful nightmares. Every few days she was woken by him screaming and thrashing about, his eyes staring blindly, sweat pouring down his contorted face. She would shake him awake, reassure him and hold him until his breathing slowed. He maintained he could not remember the dreams, but she did not believe him. Sometimes he shouted words and whole sentences and Jane wrote them down. Then she began to question him before he woke. After several months of painstaking research, she gleaned that the nightmares were about a baby that he refused to bury. When she had enough information, she waited for the next nightmare, woke him and confronted him with the things he had said. Joshua broke down and told her the terrible whole story. Neither of them had any idea what to do next.

The old master had died a year before, leaving his spinster daughter to manage the dwindling estate. Eliza was a kind, quiet woman, and treated the staff better than her father had done. She did not drink. Jane's mother Maria was still her Lady's maid. Jane finally told her mother about Joshua's nightmares and her mother sat down, very pale and trembling. To Jane's surprise her mother began to cry. She remembered her mistress being with child years ago. Nobody knew who had fathered the child and the furious master had her hidden upstairs throughout the pregnancy. He told the neighbours that his daughter had travelled north to care for her late mother's sister. Eliza was confined to her rooms and not even allowed in the garden. When her time came, the old housekeeper delivered the child. The labour had been long and Eliza suffered greatly. Maria had seen the housekeeper quickly pass the limp child to the master who left the room. He returned a short time later and informed Eliza that the baby was dead. Eliza never spoke of it again.

Maria and Jane stared at each other. Joshua did not bury the child and she may still be alive and living only a dozen miles away.

Eliza was now approaching forty and still a striking woman. She was tall and slim with very unusual pale blonde hair. She had rebuffed many suitors and seemed to foster a deep suspicion with regard to men. She led a solitary life, keeping the books and riding around the estate on her horse. Jane was keen to discover if the child had survived, to visit the village and make enquiries. Maria advised caution. The following day she travelled to the tiny cottage inhabited by the retired housekeeper, who was well provided for by Eliza. Old Florence was delighted to see Maria and welcomed her inside for tea. But her face puckered into sadness when Maria told her of Joshua's nightmares and confession.

'My poor little Eliza.' She cried. 'I should have killed that old bastard years ago!'

Florence had cared for Eliza after the death of her mother, when she was still a small child. She had noticed a change in the previously happy child at about the age of eleven. Eliza had become clingy and was reluctant for Florence to leave her alone at night. Florence thought it was just a phase and due to the premature loss of her gentle mother. Eliza would have periods of being withdrawn and tearful. At times she would return to her happy self for a few weeks. Then Florence realized that the periods of happiness invariably coincided with her father's trips away on business. Finally Florence noticed with horror the unmistakable smell of her father on the sheets of Eliza's bed when she changed them. Eliza told her everything. Her father had been creeping into her bed in the dark, smelling of whisky and grunting. He never spoke to her but he rubbed himself on her body and then left. Next day he behaved as of nothing had happened and she often convinced herself that she must have been dreaming. Florence had protected her as much as she could. She moved the girl's bedroom but he found it. She invented periods of sickness where she would sleep in Eliza's room. But over the years, his drunken night visits persisted and Eliza was unable to fight him off. She spent many years lying awake, dreading his approach, praying that tonight he would not arrive. Eventually, inevitably poor Eliza was with child. From the night he took away her dead child she had barred the bedroom door and Florence believed she would have killed him if he had ever gained entry.

Maria returned and told Jane and Joshua the awful circumstances surrounding the birth of Eliza's daughter. They were at a loss to decide what they should do. Several days later they hitched a horse to the old cart and travelled to the village that Joshua had only seen in the moonlight. There was an Inn at the top of the hill near to the house he had left the child. They chatted to the local inhabitants. It seemed a nice, friendly place. After refreshments they took a stroll down the street. Joshua saw the church tower. They saw a carpentry shop owned by a man with an unpronounceable name. Then they saw a well-dressed young couple emerge from the building where Joshua had laid the near dead baby. He was a tall, dark, swarthy young man and she was a slim, pale young woman with distinctive almost white blonde hair and her mother's soft hazel eyes. They laughed as they walked down the street and smiled at each other. As they passed Joshua, his wife and her mother, they said 'Good afternoon.' And the young man bowed. It was obvious to the three of them that this young woman was Eliza's daughter and Joshua had saved her life. Back at the Inn, Maria asked after the couple.

'Oh.' Answered the Innkeeper. 'That would be young Isabella Martin, she's from the big house, own 'alf the village they do, and sail round the world in ships and the lad is Mustapha the Magician's grandson. Them two work in the sick house, freely 'elping them as is sick. A lot of strange foreign people in that family, but they're the kindest people you could 'ope to meet and this village would be the poorer without them.'

So, Isabella was now part of a rich family, famous for its kindness to others. How might that life change if she were made aware of the unfortunate, sinful circumstances that led to her birth. As for Poor Eliza, she had buried the child sixteen years ago along with the disgusting memories of her father's unwanted attentions. The three of them left the village and they decided to take that awful secret with them to the grave and mother and daughter, oblivious to each other's existence, continued to live the rest of their lives a dozen miles apart, and Joshua's nightmares ceased.

Chapter 42

Matthew completed his studies and took up his position as doctor to the village. The villagers were largely unsettled by this event. For generations they had placed their trust in Mustapha and Mary and were gradually getting used to Anna, who had now taken on the responsibility of most of the births. Very few people in the village were old enough to remember a time before Mustapha the Magician. Matthew Knightly, son of the vicar, was a virtual stranger to them. Attendance at the sick house plummeted and the frantic hammering on the door of the big house at all hours increased. As word slowly filtered its way around the village that little Mustapha was working with the new doctor and that they both possessed the potions and at least some of Mustapha's vast knowledge, a few of the more adventurous inhabitants arrived at the sick house, driven as much by curiosity as ailment. They discovered that the doctor charged for his services although the destitute still received treatment free of charge. They learned that Mustapha's potions and remedies remained free to all. Consequently, little Mustapha was inundated with people wanting to see him, whilst poor Matthew sat in his consulting room staring at the walls.

Mustapha explained to the distraught Matthew that the transition would take time.

When he had arrived in the village with his potions, he was viewed with great suspicion. It had been the women who first sought his help in childbirth, after hearing that he could reduce their pain. The men had remained intransigent. The devout thought he was the devil, or at least in league with him. It had taken him many years, and several unfortunate disasters, in which his skills were witnessed first hand, to slowly gain the trust of the people. Matthew was crestfallen. He knew what Mustapha said was true.

Matthew's first patients arrived from outside of the village. They were from the rich farming families. The locals continued to prefer little Mustapha, whose name evolved haphazardly into young Mustapha as he was now taller than Mustapha by virtue of the latter losing a couple of inches in height as a result of his great age.

The dark clouds of the storm in November had an unexpected silver lining for Matthew and his standing in the village. As Mustapha had said, it often takes a disaster for people to revise their views. The storm was not as severe as the one that had devastated the village years ago. There was very little lightening and no lightening strikes. It was the tremendous force of the wind that wreaked the most harm. It blew trees over and pulled roots from the damp soil. It blew the sheep into the air, knocked cows over and lifted roofs. The villagers suffered an extensive amount of minor injuries, cuts, bruises and a few broken bones. The morning after the storm the sick house was full to bursting. Even Mustapha and

Mary were in attendance. The Mustapha's, Mary and Matthew tended to the broken bones first. Isabella was busy running to and fro collecting the pain remedies, bandages and balms from the cupboard. Paulo and the chippies fashioned the splints. By mid afternoon, all the bones were set and splinted and most had been ferried to their homes. Harry and Big Ern carrying them home like babies. The cuts had been stitched and bandaged. Mary had taken Mustapha home to rest. Isabella was making more hot tea for Matthew, the chippies and young Mustapha. The door burst open and a small girl struggled through carrying a dog, almost as big as her in her arms. Her face was dirty and tear-stained.

'Please Sir, 'is leg is busted!' she cried.

The animal's back leg was dangling and he was whining with pain, his eyes wide and terrified.

'Please Sir, can you mend 'im?' she burst into a renewed bout of tears and the dog howled with her.

Matthew took the dog and laid him on a table, young Mustapha gave the dog a bowl of warm sweet tea laced with pain relief, equivalent to the dosage for a child. The dog stopped whining and closed his eyes.

'Sir! Is 'e dead Sir?' she cried.

'No.' answered Matthew.' He's had some medicine so that he feels no pain.'

The tearful child held tightly onto Matthew's coat and watched as he carefully realigned the broken leg. He bound the leg with two thin splints and a thick bandage and told the child not to let the dog bite off the bandage and to bring him back in a week. He gave the child a small bottle of pain relief and told her to put two drops into the dog's water twice a day. Isabella gave her a warm cup of tea and when Matthew was satisfied that the dog was conscious, Harry and Big Ern, who knew where she lived, carried them both home.

The news of Matthew's kindness to little Maud's dog meandered its way around the village, briefly earning Matthew the title of 'dog doctor'. Fortuitously, the title was short-lived and he finally became doctor Matthew and young Mustapha became doctor Mustapha. The villagers cared little that Matthew had studied for years in London to earn the title. To them, as both men did the same job, they deserved the same title. Besides, doctor Mustapha was the one in charge of the remedies.

When Maud returned to the sick house, her dog hopped in behind her, managing well on its three good legs. Matthew changed the bandage and checked for any swelling or heat and then put on a clean bandage. After two months the dog's leg had healed and he was able to put weight on it, but for the rest of his life, he would demonstrate his three-legged walk whenever Maud said. ''E's a good boy, yes 'e is!'

Chapter 43

It was at Christmas that Mustapha noticed, with a grim disappointment and a dreadful sense of foreboding, the object of James's obsession. Isabella was blissfully unaware and failed to notice his tortured eyes follow her wherever she went. Young Mustapha had not failed to notice and watched James with a suspicious cold, black stare.

It was Holly's birthday and she was the centre of almost everyone's attention and she basked in the attention, proudly demonstrating her week old skill of unstable walking.

Mustapha and Mary retired early in the evening. They sat each side of their fire, waiting for the kettle to boil, grateful for the shared solitude. Mustapha told her what he had seen. That James's reaction to Isabella was not like a normal young man's crush, he did not arrive with a bunch of flowers or write her sentimental notes. He did not light up when she spoke to him, but retreated further into himself, like a spider enticing her into a web. To Mustapha, this was more sinister, more devious. Mustapha made plans to minimize her exposure to James.

Mustapha spoke first to his grandson. Without preamble, he asked young Mustapha if he intended to marry Isabella in the future. Mustapha said he did.

'Granddaddy, who else would I possibly

want to marry? She is the other half of me!'

'And is she willing?'

'Of course, we have already decided what we shall name our children, should we be blessed!'

The forthcoming marriage was announced on New Year's Day. Mustapha hoped that the announcement would avert a difficult situation from developing. He hoped that James's awareness of the forthcoming marriage may cool his ardour and encourage him to set his sights elsewhere. The family decided that late summer would be a good time for the wedding, just after the chaos of harvest. Sophia and Olivia begged to be bridesmaids. Isabella lost her favourite handkerchief, the one that Ivy had embroidered with tiny purple poppies. She hunted for it in the big house and in the sick house. She asked the family to watch out for it. She was not unduly alarmed by its loss and believed it would turn up. Then she lost her silk scarf. She tried to remember when she last wore it. Then her tortoiseshell hairbrush disappeared. Anna thought that excitement due to the wedding could possibly be responsible for her forgetfulness. Mustapha thought not and feared it was something more serious.

James was ruined by the news of the wedding. His moods swung violently between overwhelming self-pity and cataclysmic anger. At times he was maddened by jealousy and believed that young Mustapha stood in his way, and but for him, Isabella would be his. At other times his hatred centred on Isabella, the young woman that disturbed his nights. A battle raged in him, between his animal instincts and his religious upbringing. His father had largely ignored James, the first two sons having fulfilled his needs as a parent. By the time James was born, the Reverend Knightly had transferred his attention to his parishioners and his scientific studies. His mother had tried to hide from James that he was a sore disappointment. She had always wanted a daughter and as each son was born the discontent increased. Faith had cared for him physically but she failed to love him. Her despondency increased when she did not have other children and she believed that god was punishing her for her selfishness. James's eldest brother John had always been his father's favourite and Matthew, the sensitive, clever one that had made everyone very proud, was his mother's. James had been nobody's esteemed child. He had worked hard at his religious studies, believing that if he followed in his father's footsteps, he would gain approval. Nothing had prepared him for the impact of Isabella. Her unwitting intrusion into his life had unleashed terrifying, insatiable, unspeakable desires that he was unable to control. James prayed fervently, but even his prayers were invaded by visions of her, behaving in a way that traumatised him further. He could smell her on the scarf and handkerchief that he kept under his pillow at night, careful to hide them during the day. He pulled the long fair hairs from her hairbrush and licked them. Helpless, he defiled the objects during the night and in the morning he was destroyed by guilt and he smashed his head against the wall until the searing pain overcame the guilt.

His parents were at a loss. They had no idea how to deal with the sullen, secretive creature that their son had become. They both prayed for him, but God did not appear to be listening. The Reverend James confided in Mustapha, and begged him for some kind of remedy or tonic for James. Mustapha was loath to tell the Reverend what was ailing his son, which he believed that James would naturally grow out of in time. He gave him a potion to aid relaxation and sleep, which had the adverse effect of enhancing his desires and rendering them more sublime, glorious and infinitely more powerful, and his feelings of guilt disappeared. James spent his days with Isabella's scarf tucked inside his undergarments and surrendered to his rampant desires and defiled it whenever the urge came upon him. His parents mistakenly assumed that the enigmatic smile on his face was an improvement in his condition.

Little Maud had taken it upon herself to arrive at the sick house after school and sweep the floors and tidy up. She tied Spot in the stable at the rear of the building alongside the horses. It was Maud, alerted by Spot's frantic barking, who discovered the prostrate doctor Mustapha, unconscious and bleeding from a head wound, lying on the stable floor. Matthew and Isabella carried him inside. There were two substantial cuts to the back of his head, both in excess of an inch long, exposing the bone of the skull. Isabella washed the cuts with boiled salted water and Maud held the pad of bandages firmly in place as Matthew gathered together his stitching equipment. He sterilized the needle and thread and examined the largest cut whilst Maud continued to put pressure on the other. Young Mustapha remained unconscious and Isabella was struggling valiantly to hold back her tears. Matthew closed all the curtains, cutting out as much of the light as possible. He pushed the table, with young Mustapha on it, as close to the window as he could, on the sunny side of the building. He held young Mustapha's eyes open and asked Maud and Isabella to open the curtains on his command. As the sun streamed in directly on young Mustapha's face, Matthew was greatly relieved to see both of his pupils constrict.

'That is a good sign.' He reassured Isabella and Maud. 'I think he will recover well.'

He sent Maud to Paulo's workshop, and Paulo obtained a horse and cart and Harry carried the still unconscious young Mustapha outside. They made him as comfortable as possible and Paulo drove slowly to the big house. Isabella sat in the cart and cradled young Mustapha's head. Sal saw the cart approaching slowly across the field. Curious, he went outside calling to his brother. Sam and Sal carried young Mustapha to the sofa beside the fire and Paulo ran to find Mustapha. Isabella told Mustapha that

Matthew had already tested his eyes, and that they had responded to light. Mustapha repeated the process with a mirror. Then he pottered off to find a potion that would help numb the pain when he regained consciousness. Young Mustapha opened his eyes after almost two hours and was confused to find himself at home beside the fire with most of the family staring at him. He had no recollection of what had happened. He remembered being at the sick house earlier, but could not remember being in the stables. Isabella told him that little Maud had found him lying on the stable floor, bleeding from a head wound. He tried to sit up, but the pounding in his head increased and Mustapha gave him hot, sweet tea laced with potion. Young Mustapha fell asleep again and Mustapha said that that was the best thing for him.

Matthew arrived in early evening and he and Mustapha went into the garden to talk. Matthew did not believe that the cuts were accidental and they were not caused by a fall. He explained to Mustapha, who as yet had not seen the wound, that the two cuts were deep and caused by something sharp, like a nail. Yet he could find no protruding nails in the stables. He wondered if it could have been a wandering vagabond trying to steal the horses and who had run off when Spot barked. Mustapha was doubtful. He hoped that young Mustapha would be able to recall more of what happened in the next few days. He did eventually remember going to check on the horses around midday, but nothing else.

James had intended to pulverize the head of young Mustapha, but after the dog began barking, he feared discovery and hid behind the stables. He was exasperated to discover that young Mustapha was recovering well. He even had the audacity to visit young Mustapha and offered to escort Isabella on a walk in the woods. A sudden, piercing, ferocious glance from Mustapha prompted her to decline. James asked Mustapha for more of the sleeping remedy. Mustapha gave him some but warned him that it was not a long-term solution and that remedies of this kind, containing poppies, could cause problems if used for too long. James stated that he was feeling much better and did not envisage needing it for much longer. Mustapha looked deep into his eyes. James felt momentarily naked and turned away. Mustapha knew without doubt that it was he who had attacked his grandson.

Chapter 44

Mustapha called a meeting of the men in the family. They all assembled in the dining room around a large tray of tea. There were the twins, Joseph, Gabriel and his sons Charles and Aziz, Paulo, Jack, Robert and young Mustapha. Everyone knew it must be something very serious. Lily remembered the last time there had been a meeting like this. It had been about Jacob nearly thirty years ago, and the women were allowed in then. Mary, the only woman who knew what the meeting concerned sat outside the door to make sure the others did not eavesdrop.

Mustapha considered the subject too distasteful to have the women present. He told the men that he believed that James had developed an unhealthy obsession concerning Isabella and that he was convinced that James had attacked young Mustapha in the hope of removing his rival. He said that they had announced their marriage to deter James, but it had the opposite effect and forced his hand. He also told them that Isabella had no knowledge of this, and that several of her personal possessions had disappeared and he thought that James had taken them. He was adamant that Isabella was now in danger and must not be left alone at any time, and that a member of the family must be with her at the sick house, particularly until young Mustapha was fully recovered. A Rota was worked out, minus Mustapha and Joseph who were considered too old for the task. Paulo included Harry and Big Ern as he trusted them and he knew they would be keen to help.

If anyone had any doubts regarding James, they were allayed a couple of days later when he visited the sick house unannounced, when he knew that Isabella would be there. He explained he had come to see his brother, but remained in the room with Isabella and was busy encouraging her to go for a stroll as she was not busy. Harry, who was on protection duty quietly asked little Maud to fetch her dog inside. When Spot caught sight of James, his hackles rose instantly and he lunged across the room, snarling and baring his teeth. Harry grabbed for the enraged animal, managing to be just slow enough that he was able to sink his teeth firmly into James leg. Matthew came out of his room as a response to the commotion and was horrified to see Harry and Maud struggling to remove the unusually aggressive Spot from his brother's bleeding leg. The bite was a nasty one, requiring cleaning and stitching. Harry reported the incident to Paulo, who went to the butcher's shop and purchased the juiciest bone he could find, and gave it to Harry to pass on to Spot.

Matthew helped James onto his horse and they rode home to the vicarage together. Matthew had the distinct impression that Harry and little Maud had been amused by the incident. Isabella had the same feeling, especially when the door closed behind Matthew and James, and

Harry and little Maud roared with laughter as they cuddled and kissed Spot. Harry had told Maud that James was, 'a very bad man who hurt doctor Mustapha.' Little Maud knew he must be right, as Spot had never bitten anyone before and she knew that Spot had seen what happened in the stable.

James's wound did not heal well. Dog bites frequently develop infections, as did James's. The Reverend James volunteered to collect the balm from Mustapha. Mustapha had been tempted to mix either an ineffective balm, or one containing poison, but found he was unable to do either, and still be able to live with himself, so he gave the Reverend the correct one. The Reverend James had an uneasy feeling on his journey home. The family had been different tonight, almost as though they were silently closing ranks. They were closing ranks. Unfortunately there were several members of the families with feet in both camps, destined to be unwitting casualties of James's antics.

Anna had been shielded from the dilemma, as she had spent the last few weeks with Faith at the vicarage. She was aware that James was not well and had trouble sleeping and eating. She found him a strange, furtive individual, but of late had appeared to be somewhat better. Faith had no idea what was going on and Ellen Lily, who still visited regularly, knew that something very significant was afoot but had no idea what, despite having spent several fruitless evenings trying to prize the information from Gabriel. She had no idea that both her sons knew what was happening. As soon as James was up and about again, the protection squad swung into action again. Isabella, who everyone was trying not to enlighten, thought they were there due to the attack on young Mustapha. She had no idea that they were protecting her from James. Isabella rode home with Paulo in the early evening and went upstairs to see Mary and Mustapha. They were both asleep in their armchairs so she quietly went to her room and closed her door. She sat on the edge of the bed and reached for her book. Her ankles were suddenly grasped in a vice-like grip, and before she managed to shout out, she was wrenched from the bed, landing face down on the floor with a resounding thud. Then a hand grabbed her by the throat, stifling her shout for help. She was thrown roughly onto her back, and held down by the throat as her attacker ripped at her clothing. Then she saw it was James. He was red in the face and dribbling, his breathing was laboured and heavy. She was stunned. James was on his knees above her, leaning on her throat. She felt his hand, claw like, searching for her undergarments and he ripped them away in one vicious movement. He stared into her eyes victoriously as he began to hurriedly loosen his trousers, sneering and panting like a dog. Isabella shut her eyes tightly and brought up her right knee sharply, with all the strength she could muster. James was thrown up and to one side. He plummeted into a vacuum of breathless paralysis, instantly usurped by excruciating, tortuous agony as the pain exploded from his desecrated testicles to the pit of his stomach. Isabella jumped to her feet and kicked him as hard as she could in the stomach and was about to kick him in the face when Mustapha burst in and bashed him firmly on the head with a stout walking stick. Mustapha and Isabella quickly tied his feet and hands together and lashed him to the bed. Mary ran downstairs to find help. Sam tied James more securely and Paulo rode off to collect the Reverend.

'It's James.' he said to James's father.

They rode to the house quickly, the Reverend frantically going through a terrible list of alternatives in his mind. None of them were as bad as the scene he was presented with. His youngest son was lashed to the legs of Isabella's bed and he was screaming the most loathsome, sickening profanities at Isabella, who despite her ordeal, stood defiantly in front of his face as they stood him up, and she spat in it!

The men assembled in the dining room again, this time with the Reverend, his son and Isabella. Young Mustapha was cornered in the bathhouse by the five women of the house to prevent him from attacking James. The poor Reverend James listened to the list of accusations. The thefts, the attack on young Mustapha, the dog bite and now the disgusting attack on Isabella. James denied nothing. He continued to bay at Isabella like a wolf to the moon.

'There's my scarf!' she shouted as the thin

silk slithered from James half undone trousers.

Reverend James looked slowly up at her, like one woken from a dream, then he dejectedly pulled the out the rest of the scarf and proffered it to Isabella. Her eyes flashed.

'I never want to see that again for the rest of my life!' she hissed.

A lengthy period of deliberation ensued. Eventually, they all agreed that the Reverend James could take his son home, as long as he was locked up and unable to leave the house until a suitable institution could take him. The Reverend asked Mustapha for more of the sleeping remedy.

'As far as I can see, that remedy has done more harm than good, he'll have no more from me!' he said coldly.

The Reverend and his son rode home in silence, a rope around James's waist attached firmly to his father's saddle. The poor Reverend prayed for guidance and wondered how everything had gone so wrong and James began planning his escape.

Within minutes of the Reverend arriving home, and relating the whole sad series of events, Faith was sobbing, and Anna was galloping off to the big house, closely pursued by her husband. They burst into the kitchen just in front of Ellen Lily, who had finally extracted the facts from Gabriel. The whole house, having just settled down, erupted into a new round of excited discussions, imaginative explanations and tea. Everyone was proud of Isabella, the once shy little girl terrified of spiders who had found the strength to stand up to a monster. Far from being frightened, all Isabella experienced was a severe bout of murderous indignation. From that day, she barred her bedroom door and window each night and slept with a large stick under her pillow.

Chapter 45

The Reverend James locked his youngest son in his bedroom, An hour later Matthew apprehended James as he was climbing down from his bedroom window, so they barred the window with fence posts nailed across the frame. As the effects of Mustapha's remedy gradually abated, James's guilt returned with a vengeance. He screamed and howled and pleaded with his father to allow him to go and apologise to Isabella. The Reverend James refused. He pleaded with his mother, who sobbed and ran away. Matthew, the one 'caught in the middle' more acutely that most, could not bring himself to speak to James. The Reverend James knew of several madhouses in London, run by clergymen of his acquaintance. He was aware of the stark conditions in many of them. The majority of the mentally ill, the 'feeble minded' were often taken care of by their families or housed in workhouses and poor houses. The dangerous, the category that included James, were placed in madhouses and generally chained to walls or placed in straightjackets and received harsh treatment from the staff. The Reverend James was loath to expose his youngest child to a life of abuse and imprisonment. He decided to care for him at home. The Reverend spent his nights with James, whose vivid hallucinations caused him to scream in terror and wake the household. The hallucinations gradually abated and the Reverend was hopeful that his son was recovering, until the night that James, emboldened by his father's lassitude, bashed the poor Reverend over the head with a cricket bat. Leaving his father unconscious, spread-eagled on the wooden floor, he made his escape. He took provisions from the kitchen and a horse and rode to the big house. Due to Mustapha's vigilance, all the doors were securely barred, so James rode into the woods to bide his time.

At first light, the Reverend rode over to inform Mustapha of James's disappearance. Mustapha was not surprised. He looked at the beleaguered man, devastated by events and felt great sympathy for him. He took him into the kitchen and made tea. The two men discussed the alternatives and the Reverend was adamant that James would be transported to a madhouse following recapture. He knew that there was no other solution, no other way to protect Mustapha's family. All day they searched for James. They searched the outbuildings and the village. That night Isabella was woken by the sound of hammering on her barred window. It was James on a ladder, demanding to be admitted. She ran to the far end of the house and woke Sam. He woke his brother and they ran outside to see James descending the ladder. They gave chase and Sam briefly caught him, but was unable to hold onto the enraged, kicking, biting James for long enough for his brother to help restrain him.

Paulo enlisted the help of Harry and Big Ern the following day and they searched the woods behind the big house. They found evidence that James had been there but no sign of him or his horse. Harry and Big Ern volunteered to stay overnight at the big house and enlisted the help of little Maud's dog Spot. After the family had retired to bed, Harry un-barred the kitchen door, extinguished the candles and laid in wait. On the third night of the vigil, when they were beginning to think James had left the area they were alerted by Spot. He rose to his feet, hackles rising, growling very quietly. Harry and Big Ern listened, but heard nothing. The dog stood still, ears twitching, nose raised, quivering in expectation. Harry and Big Ern rose silently, made for the kitchen door, stood one each side and waited. Spot followed them and stood beside Harry. They watched as the latch rose silently and the door began to open slowly. Harry grabbed James's arm, still attached to the latch. Spot grabbed his leg and Big Earn slammed the door hard onto the rest of him. James fought back with the monumental strength of the deranged. He spat, bit, gouged and wriggled, immune to pain. Eventually, after a great deal of crashing around the kitchen, Harry pulled his arms behind his back, Spot still had his leg and Big Ern pushed him down and sat hard on his chest, emptying his lungs of air. The commotion had woken Paulo, who slept above the kitchen and he arrived downstairs as Harry and Big Ern were tying James to the leg of the heavy kitchen table. Within minutes, most of the family joined them, including Mustapha with a large dose of sleeping remedy that Big Ern forced down the throat of the choking James who was still trying to kick anyone within range with the leg unencumbered by the diligent Spot. Within minutes James was comatose. Everyone relaxed, with the exception of Spot who had to be enticed from James's leg with the tastier option of a lamb bone. Some of the family returned to bed, Harry and Big Ern watched over the prisoner until Paulo returned with the Reverend James. Mustapha gave the Reverend enough sleeping remedy to sedate James for the next week, during which time his removal to a madhouse could be arranged. Mustapha estimated that a teaspoonful three times a day should keep him drowsy enough to be manageable, but on no account exceed the dosage. Three days later, the night before his removal to the madhouse, James was found dead in his room. Nobody ever knew exactly what happened, whether the Reverend had accidentally left the sleeping potion in James's room and he had drunk it all, or whether the Reverend exceeded the dose, damning his own soul rather than committing his son to the horrific ordeal of a madhouse. It was a very quiet funeral conducted early in the morning. Mustapha insisted that he attended, out of respect to Knightly family, and to initiate the healing of the bond between the two families, made fragile by the distasteful misfortune of James's illness.

Chapter 46

Ellen Lily, familiar with the loss of a son, was the first to visit the vicarage after the tragedy. She and Faith shared a tearful reunion, paving the way for Anna and Holly's return to the vicarage. The Reverend James was humbled and impressed by the support and the warm, ready forgiveness of the whole family. He thanked God that James had not killed anyone and he thanked him for the genuine friendship of an extraordinary family.

Less than two months after the death of James, and two weeks before the start of Khalid's second voyage, the wedding of young Mustapha and Isabella took place. The Reverend James conducted the ceremony and Jack, her brother and godfather, gave Isabella away. Young Mustapha waited for her with the Reverend. He was dressed in a long pale gold silk shirt and matching baggy trousers. His long black curls shone in the rays of sunlight coming through the stained glass. As Isabella walked down the aisle, dressed in ivory silk, her long, fine hair shimmering and swaying as she walked, carrying a bunch of white poppies, the Reverend could see why his unfortunate son had confused her with an angel. Sophia and Olivia were both dressed in deep gold dresses, their dark curls dotted with tiny white flowers. Mustapha sat beside Mary in the front pew, he remembered the day he had set the target of living long enough to see the two of them married and he quickly set a new target of seeing their first child. They were so dramatically different, he was unable to imagine what their child would look like, and it would definitely be a surprise. The celebration was the usual lavish, extravagant affair that the villagers had become accustomed to and they arrived in droves to wish the couple good luck and happiness. Even the Knightly family were able to smile, especially when Anna quietly confided that she was with child again.

When young Mustapha and Isabella finally retired to their room next to Mustapha and Mary, they found their bed covered in the violet quilt of a thousand stars and the room lit by dozens of candles and perfumed with jasmine. It took several months before Isabella allowed young Mustapha to remove the defenses that she had erected on the window and door.

The ship sailed in early August, bound for the Cape of Good Hope, East Africa, India and China. They would be gone for two years. There were some tearful goodbyes at the dock and Joey made Sam promise him that he could go on the next voyage.

The villagers were busy harvesting the fields and Mustapha and Mary were harvesting the poppies. It had been an abundant year with warm sun and gentle overnight showers. Young Mustapha, Isabella and Matthew were busy at the sick house with seasonal injuries caused by scythes and sharp knives and the occasional fall from a haystack. Little Maud was now the official cleaner at the sick house and earned a small wage.

Paulo and the chippies were very busy with an order for two-dozen new pews for the church. Pip was busy with tiny pieces of veneer, completing a large panel containing the Lord's Prayer constructed from an oak base, with mahogany and ebony lettering and a complex border of stripes and squares. This was a secret endeavour and destined to be presented to the church by the family.

A severe drought arrived in September, followed by high winds that robbed the trees of their shriveling, parched leaves earlier than usual. By mid October the trees were bare and it felt like winter. Mustapha prophesied a harsh, prolonged winter. Gabriel, Paulo, Harry and Big Ern took his advice and began collecting the dead and dying trees from the woods and stockpiling them ready for transportation to the village, should they be needed. Harry and Big Ern and the long saw made short work of the trees and they filled the empty stables both at the big house and Gabriel's farm with neatly sawn and chopped wood for the winter fires. Everyone liked Harry and Big Ern, who worked hard with smiles on their faces, glad to put their phenomenal strength to good use. In particular, Mary Ellen was very fond of Harry and rushed out with refreshments whenever he was around the farm. Harry invariably blushed crimson and struggled to find the right words to thank her.

Gabriel recognized himself in Harry, during his first years at the big house, when he fell in love with Ellen Lily and assumed her to be out of his reach. Gabriel liked Harry. He was honest, loyal and blessed with a cheerful disposition. He watched him carrying vast amount of heavy logs into the stables as though they were mere matchsticks. Gabriel followed him into the stables and helped with the stacking of the logs.

'Harry.' He said, causing Harry to look up in alarm. 'I would like you to know something.'

'Yes Sir.' Answered Harry with a blank expression.

'When I was your age, I was a penniless workman looking after Aziz Shadi Rashad Salamar Badr al din's horses.'

'Oh.' Harry chimed in, wondering where this conversation was going.

'I fell in love with Ellen Lily. She was one of the beautiful daughters of this very wealthy family.'

'Yes Sir.'

'I said nothing, I believed I was far too poor to ask for her hand in marriage.'

'Hmm.'

'I'm telling you this as I want you to know that I was mistaken, and to advise you not to make the same mistake.'

Harry stared at Gabriel, not sure of quite what he meant.

'What I mean Harry, is that should you ever consider walking out with my Mary Ellen, I would be happy about that.'

Harry went very red and was unable to manage more than a grin.

Mary Ellen appeared at the door of the stable, flustered and smiling and carrying a tray of tea and little cakes she had made especially. As Gabriel left the stable, he winked at Harry, who managed to turn an even deeper shade of red. The following Sunday, Harry arrived at Gabriel's farm and asked if Mary Ellen would like to visit his mother. Mary Ellen spent a frantic ten minutes donning her best frock and brushing her thick chestnut curls. Gabriel and Ellen Lily watched them as they walked towards the village, hand in hand. Harry towered over Mary Ellen and was twice as wide. She looked very small and fragile beside him, and Gabriel knew she was in safe hands. Harry's widowed mother had been avidly cleaning and washing everything during the three day warning that he had given her. She put on her best apron after he left to fetch Mary Ellen and ran to and fro in panic, trying to catch sight of them across the fields. It was only the end of October, but she had lit the fire for Mary Ellen, not wanting her to think them poor. In fact, since both her sons were working for Paulo, they had been able to eat every single day. The widow Richards was exhausted with excitement by the time Harry and Mary Ellen arrived. Not knowing quite what to do the poor widow attempted a curtsy, which made Harry and Mary Ellen both laugh.

'Good afternoon Mrs. Richards, I'm very pleased to meet you.' Said Mary Ellen warmly, clutching the widow's hand, which caused her to wobble precariously with surprise. They had tea and biscuits and the widow was taken aback when Mary Ellen got up and helped her to clear the table. She was still in a state of shock when they left several hours later. She liked Mary Ellen, but she had not been what she expected. When Harry returned from escorting Mary Ellen home, he told his mother that one day, he was going to marry Mary Ellen and his bewildered mother fainted clean away on the hearthrug.

The widow Richards gradually regained her composure and she and Mary Ellen got on well, but she was thrown into a new bout of panic when Mary Ellen invited her to tea at her parent's farm. The poor woman had nothing to wear, and was unaware that at Gabriel's farm, nobody cared what she wore. Her sons, understanding her discomfort, bought her the first new dress she had ever had, from the little draper's shop, and she burst into floods of tears. She was welcomed in by Gabriel and hugged by Ellen Lily, her old coat was taken and hung up by Aziz and Charles took her arm and led her to the tea table. Tea consisted of cold meats and pickles, cheese, bread, cakes and biscuits. The widow had never seen so much food on one table. Everyone was so kind that she felt like crying, but managed not to until she and Harry were walking home. He asked her what was wrong.

'Nothing son, I am so very proud of you and I know that your poor father is too.'

Harry squeezed her hand as they walked home.

.

Chapter 47

Mustapha's weather forecast was accurate and the snow began to fall in early November. The shepherds took his advice and moved their sheep from the marshes. They housed them in backyards or on the village green that had been enclosed with sturdy fences. This gave the sheep some shelter from the wind and made the chore of providing them with hay easier. In the past, sheep had starved to death on the marshes when the shepherds had been unable to reach them or even find them in the deep snowdrifts.

Gabriel borrowed Harry and Big Ern from Paulo to help him transport the wood to the village. Mary Ellen, who was working at the school, often visited Harry's mother on her way home, throwing the widow into a frenzy of activity, moving clothing or a plate left on the table. It took her several visits before she accepted that Mary Ellen had come to see her and not to inspect her little home.

Mustapha persuaded Joseph to arrange extra deliveries of flour, salt, sugar and potatoes from the town before the roads became impassable. The sacks were delivered to the kitchens at the school and the sick house, in case the provisions in the village ran low. The snow continued to fall. There was no wind and the snow fell gently but relentlessly and getting about the village became hard work. Mary Ellen decided to close the school, but the local women who worked there offered to continue to cook the midday meal for the children aware that it was often the only hot meal they received. The school became the warm oasis for the children, who fought their way through the snow to sit beside the big hot stoves and wait for their meal. Then their mothers began arriving to help with the cooking, cleaning and keeping the fires roaring. Even some of the men dropped in, taking a break from chopping and sawing the wood from the woodpile, to warm their hands and feet and drink a welcome cup of hot soup. Harry and Big Ern cleared the paths that led to the school and when they told Paulo how many people were using the school, Paulo told Joseph and Lily. Just before Christmas, Harry and Big Ern cleared a path from the big house to the school, so that Gabriel and his heavy horses could drag a sledge, fashioned from a cart, to the school. It was laden with joints of beef and mutton, chickens, a dozen large Christmas puddings, sacks of onions, carrots, swede and parsnips and a message from the family to keep the school open over Christmas for everyone and wishing them all a very happy Christmas. The villagers brought more large cooking pots from their homes and whatever food they had intended for Christmas dinner. It snowed heavily on Christmas Eve. Christmas morning was bright and still, without a breath of wind. The blanket of pristine snow silenced the landscape and dazzled anyone who went outside. Almost a third of the villagers spent their Christmas in the school. The women cooked and the men kept the fires alight. They even lit the fires upstairs, that had rarely been lit since Aziz Shadi Rashad Badr al din and his family had moved to the big house. Everyone was warm and well fed and in the evenings they sang songs and read stories. Nobody could remember a more joyous Christmas.

Harry, Big Ern and their mother spent Christmas at Gabriel's farm and during the afternoon, Harry and his brother and Mary Ellen battled their way through the soft, deep snow that had made the track to the big house impassable for weeks. The majestic silence of the beautiful woodland was shattered by the invasion of the three young people who shouted and laughed at each other as they struggled, fell over and pulled each other along. They arrived at the big house, red-faced and laughing, Mary Ellen riding on Harry's shoulders, to wish a happy Christmas to the astonished family. Harry hugged Paulo and thanked him fervently for changing their lives. They stayed for a cup of hot sweet tea and then set off again through the snow, Mary Ellen's laughter ringing through the trees. They stopped to pay their respects to Aziz Shadi Rashad Salamar Badr al din and Elijah. Mary Ellen had been very young when he died, but he had been kept alive by the stories of his generosity and famous parties. Harry remembered seeing him when he was a little boy, riding his big black horse through the village.

Matthew and Anna spent Christmas at the

rectory. They had intended to be at the big house, due to the imminent birth of their second child, but the snow had made the journey hazardous. Mustapha, who had preempted that possibility, and had given Matthew a potion some weeks before Christmas. It was Holly's second birthday and her happy chatter and spontaneous hugs helped to heal the wounds inflicted by the disturbing events of that year. Anna got up in the early hours of Boxing Day, feeling restless and uncomfortable. She crept downstairs, made some tea and sat beside the kitchen fire. Faith had heard her pass the bedroom door, grabbed her dressing gown and joined her in the kitchen. By the time Anna had drunk her tea she knew that the baby was coming. Faith wanted to wake Matthew, but Anna decided to leave him asleep a little longer. Twenty minutes later, without any warning, Anna leant forward in her chair and knelt on the floor and to Faith's stupefaction and sheer wonder, and in the long tradition of the women in Anna's family, deposited her second little daughter onto the hearthrug. Faith sat transfixed, her cup of tea in her raised hand, her mouth open, staring at the wriggling baby. Anna sat on the rug and lifted the child. She had to call to Faith several times before the spell was broken and Faith eventually managed to find towels and wrap the baby and cut the cord. When the Reverend James and Matthew came down several hours later in search of their wives, they found Faith and Anna, baby at her breast, sitting beside the roaring fire drinking tea. They called the child Lucy.

In January the snow began to fall again, this time accompanied by strong winds that blew the snow, and several unsuspecting villagers, into deep drifts. Many families remained at the school, unable to return to their homes. Harry and Big Ern remained undaunted by the wind. They trudged around the village checking on the old people, a few of whom they wrapped up and put on their rudimentary sledge and moved to the safety and warmth of the school. Their mother Elsie, on the insistence of Ellen Lily stayed on at the farm. Harry and Big Ern arrived at irregular intervals at the farm and the big house. They loomed unexpectedly out of the blizzards, caked with snow, still smiling and checking that everyone was well. When Harry realized that Mary Ellen was worried about her sister, he and his brother made the arduous journey of several miles to the rectory. They walked in a straight line, as the crow flies, clambering over hedges, skidding on frozen ditches and wading across the fields. The Reverend James opened the door in surprise, to be confronted by two colossal snow-caked individuals politely asking after everyone's health. They sat in the kitchen drinking steaming tea and the snow thawed and dripped into puddles on the floor around their chairs. Holly, startled by the two massive men steaming and dripping in the heat of the kitchen, ran to her father. Anna proudly showed them baby Lucy. After three cups of tea, several mince pies and a large slice of Christmas cake, Harry and Big Ern set off again, following their rapidly disappearing tracks. They called in at the big house on the way, with news of the baby Lucy and then trudged off through the woods to Gabriel's farm, where they peeled off their soaking wet, heavy clothing. Mary Ellen gave them some blankets and they warmed themselves in front of the fire and slept soundly on the hearthrug for several hours, snoring contentedly.

Chapter 48

Following an uneventful navigation of the west side of Africa, the ship encountered heavy seas when rounding the Cape of Good Hope. Even Khalid was alarmed by the vast expanse of dark grey water that towered above the ship and threatened to engulf them at regular intervals. After two days of battling the elements they sailed into calmer waters and the crew could finally rest. As they sailed north the weather became warmer and they were soon in emerald waters of the Indian Ocean. Khalid saw the whales and dolphins that his father had told him about. He heard the songs of the whales and stood on the bow and watched as the dolphins raced the ship and leapt out of the clear green water to get a closer look at him. They sailed into a busy port, searching for ebony for Paulo. Sam decided to stay there for a week or so to give the tired crew a welcome break. They stayed in a building erected on stilts, with a roof thatched with palm fronds and were regularly entertained, and sometimes robbed, by a hoard of vervet monkeys. Khalid loved them and pleaded with his father to take one with them. He bribed a little monkey with tasty treats until it was brave enough to take food from his hand, then the day before they were leaving he tied a string round it's neck, named it Bill and carried him to the ship. Bill was less that delighted by this development and shrieked and jumped about frantically trying to bite him. Undeterred, Khalid tied him to a mast and gave him some fruit. Bill was dejected for the first few days at sea and even refused food, but he eventually made the best of his new circumstances and spent much of his time sitting on Khalid's shoulder, picking inside his ears and carefully grooming his hair, eating anything he found. Bill was less than popular with the crew, due to his tendency to climb up the rigging and urinate on passers by. The ship meandered slowly in a northeasterly direction, past the numerous little islands covered in palm trees, surrounded by white sand and turquoise water. This area remained Sam and Sal's favourite place and they were in no hurry. Khalid watched the brightly coloured fish swimming in the clear, sparkling water. Bill sat on his shoulder chattering gibberish and scratching himself.

Khalid excitement began to mount as they sailed the Arabian Sea to their next destination, India, the land of his mother's birth. His father had promised to take him to his mother's village where he would meet relatives, possibly his grandparents if they were still alive. He remembered the stories she had told him about her childhood in a land of hot sun and warm monsoon rains, where cows were sacred and never eaten and could wander freely about the countryside. A land where people rode about on elephants and where there was not just one God, there were hundreds of them. She had said it was a land of vivid colours, where bright purple, cerise, red and yellow flowers bloomed all year round and grew up the sides of houses. It was the land of enchanting perfumes where people painted intricate designs on their hands and feet, and at marriages, painted their whole bodies. It was a land of castes, a position in society that was recognized as permanent. Whatever caste you were born into would last throughout your lifetime. Each caste designated the jobs available to you. She had been born in a lower caste, just above the 'untouchables', who dealt with the funeral pyres of the dead. She said she would have remained poor, but his father Sam had not cared what caste she belonged to, he married her for love and she became rich. This could not have happened if she had remained in India. It was a land where magnificent tigers roamed and ate you if you got in their way and highly patterned snakes that could kill you with one bite.

Sam, Sal and Khalid travelled inland on a donkey cart to Mina's village. As soon as they left the coast the heat became intense and they were plagued by hundreds of flies. It took two days to reach the village. They stopped overnight at a dilapidated shack. Their meal was a hot goat curry that made Khalid's eyes and nose run and he was convinced that he could see tiny worms swimming in his water. They slept on filthy mattresses that made them itch and Khalid did not think very highly of the land of his mother's birth. The situation improved a little when they reached his mother's village. His father was recognized and welcomed as the man who lifted Mina from a life of hard work with little reward. Her parents were still alive and made a great fuss of Khalid, who was glad that he had spent time with Mustapha learning the language. He understood most of what was said, but was the cause of much hilarity when he spoke. He met cousins, aunts and uncles and was plagued with questions about his mother and younger brother. But the flies continued to crawl all over him, the food was too hot and the burning dust, that blew around everywhere, got into his clothing, his hair and made his eyes sting. The only relief he could find was sitting in a muddy little stream that flowed sluggishly past the village, but even that became unbearable in the evenings when the mosquitoes returned. The depth of poor Khalid's misery reached an all time low, when on top of his general discomfiture, he suffered a disabling bout of diarrhoea, without consuming even a single orange. After two days of stomach cramps and passing nothing but burning hot yellowish water that seared his anus so fiercely he was unable to sit down, he had had enough. He lay in the muddy stream, tears trickling through the thick dust on his distraught face, his feet and legs speckled with insect bites.

Sam had little sympathy for his son, who whined and pleaded incessantly to return to the ship. He informed him that were he not able to rise above such minor discomforts, he was not cut out to be a travelling merchant. They remained in the village for several weeks, awaiting delivery of sacks of ginger, turmeric, chilies, peppercorns, cloves, coriander seeds and cardamom pods. Khalid made an effort to suffer quietly and tried not to look too delighted when they finally loaded the carts in preparation for returning to the ship. He said goodbye to his relatives. He lied, and thanked them for making him welcome, instead of telling them that he had hated the flies, the goat droppings, the continuous putrid stench and stifling heat, the dust, the food, the water and that he vowed never, ever to set foot in his mother's foul, loathsome, abomination of a village for the rest of his life. Khalid prostrated himself on top of the sacks of spices on the journey to the coast as sitting and bouncing on the wooden seats proved excruciating. As soon as they reached the docks, Khalid slid down from the spices and struggled across the sand and threw himself into the cool clear waters of the Arabian Sea. He lay spread-eagled in the shallow water, the gentle waves lapping over his body, bringing the first infinitely pleasurable relief to his tortured, swollen, smarting anus. Sam and Sal laughed so much they almost fell from the cart. Khalid remained lying in the water until the ship was about to weigh anchor. The ship's cook gave him a pot of Mustapha's soothing balm and he spent the next few days, sulking, lying in a hammock with Bill, who he had forgotten about during his ordeal. Bill found quite a number of tasty morsels secreted in Khalid's tangled hair.

Chapter 49

The snow stopped falling in late January, but the thaw failed to arrive until mid February, by which time Charles, Ernest and Henry, Joseph's last three brothers had died, within weeks of each other. Joseph had them laid in the charnel house until the earth was soft enough to dig their graves. The last camel also died from extreme old age and sheer boredom, as nobody took much notice of him since Khalid had gone to sea.

The thaw resulted in the usual slippery thick mud of late winter, but due to the early, dry, sunny spring it dried up earlier than expected and encouraged a bumper crop of new shoots to erupt all over Mustapha's garden. The sheep on the village green began to lamb before the shepherds had a chance to move them to the marshes and the village was inundated with escaped bleating lambs, able to squeeze through the fences. The snowdrops, celandines and primroses bloomed in the hedgerows and wood, which was carpeted with the spikey, bright green leaves of the imminent bluebells. Anna took Lucy to meet the family and Mustapha took her outside to present her to the sky, with an apology for being two months late. Pip, who had diligently struggled into the workshop to light the fires throughout the winter, had finished the prayer for the church. The school reopened and everyone began to look forward to the wedding of Harry and

Mary Ellen, planned for midsummer. Harry and Big Ern had gained the respect of the villagers throughout the winter. They had worked tirelessly, shoveling snow, delivering wood, rescuing people and distributing the hay to the sheep buried in the undulating snowdrift that the village green had become. The family arranged a celebratory meal for them at the big house in the late spring and Paulo introduced them to the bathhouse. They watched, fascinated, as Paulo and young Mustapha filled the marble troughs with steaming water, perfumed with oils. Piles of warm towels were laid on the shelves. When the baths were full, Paulo and young Mustapha left the brothers alone. Harry and Big Ern stared at one another in disbelief. Harry was first to remove his clothes and gingerly dip a toe into the water that was a great deal warmer than he had expected. Big Ern watched his brother as he climbed into the bath and slowly lowered his considerable bulk into the water, which rose dramatically, almost reaching the top of the bath. Harry sat very still, worried that the water would overflow. The sensation was amazing, Harry had never in his life experienced the lightness that water brought to his large body and he lay back and relaxed with a huge smile on his face. Reassured, Big Ern undressed and climbed into the other bath, he had never ever felt both wet and hot at the same time. The brothers wallowed. They submerged themselves completely and blew bubbles out of their noses. They were astonished at the amount of bubbles generated by flatulence. They laughed and chattered to each other across the steamy room and promised themselves that one day they would build their own bathhouse. Paulo tapped gently on the door and delivered a tray of tea and warm biscuits. He laughed at the crimson, sweating, smiling faces of the brothers who felt like they were in paradise. When Big Ern reached for his tea he became seriously alarmed by the demise of his hands and feet that had become wrinkled and puckered like walnuts. Paulo laughed even more and assured him that they would return to normal quite soon. The brothers remained in the water until it was almost cold, wondering why it was only the soles of their feet and the palms of their hands that shriveled and why hair floated on the surface. Eventually, they dried themselves on the warm, soft towels, dressed and rejoined the family who were beginning to think they had drowned.

'I have never been so wet!' exclaimed Big Ern.

Harry and his brother talked about their night in the bathhouse incessantly. So Paulo and Gabriel decided to have a bathhouse built at the farm as a wedding present for Harry and Mary Ellen who would live there after their marriage. They told them they were building a new feed store.

Rose was with child again, to the delight of Paulo who was hoping to add an 'S' to his sign on the workshop.

Due to Anna being busy with her daughters,

Isabella accompanied Mary when she delivered the village babies. Young Mustapha went with them, as his knowledge of the potions was almost as extensive as his grandfather's. The village women admitted doctor Mustapha, trusting him as they had the original Mustapha. Many remained uncomfortable with the idea of allowing doctor Matthew to attend their births, as he was an ordinary man.

One evening, a stranger knocked frantically on the door of the big house. He had recently moved to the village with his wife and his neighbour had directed him there after hearing the screams of his young wife. When they arrived, the neighbour was trying to comfort the distressed young woman. Young Mustapha gave her a potion and within minutes she was free of pain but remained very anxious. The husband, named Albert, explained that they had lost a child at ten months of a fever and then his poor wife had given birth to a dead child that had arrived legs first. Mary, Isabella and young Mustapha stayed with her all night. Her labour was hard, but slow and young Mustapha gave her a remedy for strength and stamina as well as for pain. At first light, after prolonged straining the child's feet arrived first. Isabella supported the exhausted woman in a sitting position on the edge of the bed and Mary and young Mustapha gently pulled and turned the baby as Mustapha had done when Rose had her second twin. Mary told young Mustapha to pull down the tiny arms, one by one. Then they carefully turned and tipped the child, young Mustapha pushed his fingers between the cord and the baby and pulled the cord over the chin and the large, robust male child fell into Mary's waiting hands. He yelled immediately, and his mother burst into tears at the beauty of the sound. Young Mustapha fetched her husband. He had tears in his eyes and would not stop clutching young Mustapha's hand in abject gratitude. Mary dealt with the mother's needs and Isabella took the baby and his father Albert to make some tea. Mustapha asked Albert if he would object to him saying a prayer for the child. Albert would have agreed to anything at that moment. He handed his son to young Mustapha and Isabella opened the door and beckoned to Albert. He followed them outside, where the tall, stately young Mustapha lifted the child high above his head and recited a strange language to the sky. As Isabella watched her husband, tears welled up in her eyes. It was like he had suddenly become a man. Mustapha would be so proud. Albert had no idea what had been said, but he knew it was a prayer and he was glad that it was for his wonderful son. They drank their tea and Albert produced a small box containing his savings and asked Mustapha how much he owed him.

'There is no charge.' Said young Mustapha.

'But you have done so much, you saved them both. I must pay you something!' begged Albert.

'The medicine is a gift from God and carries no charge.' Mustapha explained 'It is the rule of my grandfather.'

'But, all your time…..' Albert pleaded.

Young Mustapha took his hands in his.

'Are we all not gifts from God?'

.

Chapter 50

Mary Ellen spent the last few days prior to her wedding at the big house, to give Ellen Lily and Anna time to prepare her bedroom, and to give Gabriel and the workman the chance to put the finishing touches to the secret bathhouse. Elsie was beside herself with nerves and excitement. Lily and Rose had made her a new dress to wear at the wedding in deep blue silk with paler blue cuffs and collar. Mary Ellen dress was a pale shade of lavender blue that matched her eyes.

Elsie felt like royalty, as she stood beside Mary and Ellen Lily in the front pew of the church. Her two immense sons stood side by side in front of the Reverend waiting for Mary Ellen. Gabriel proudly led her up the aisle, where she was dwarfed beside her future husband. The church was full to bursting. This was the first time a villager had married into the family and nobody wanted to miss the special event. Harry was bursting with pride as he and his beautiful Mary Ellen walked from the church to the cart decorated with summer flowers. The party was held at the big house as Gabriel's field was too small and nobody was sure how the highly-strung horses would respond to the inevitable uproar. Mustapha and Mary sat up in the tree house and watched the children running around and the adults dancing to the music. The lambs turned slowly on the spits beside the house and the smell made everyone ravenously hungry. The hot bread and roast vegetable began to emerge from the house. There were vast trays of cakes that had taken the women several days to bake. The musicians took a break and eat with the villagers. Gabriel, Paulo and Big Ern disappeared to set up the new four-poster bed that the chippies had made for the couple. Maria and Mina had made the curtains and bedspread from a patchwork of silks in violet, blue and cerise. Following the fireworks at midnight, Harry picked up Mary Ellen and carried her, squealing and giggling through the woods to her father's house. They were overcome with passion halfway there and the marriage was consummated on a bed of wild flowers under the stars.

The evening after the wedding Mary Ellen noticed her parents bustling about, exchanging furtive smiles and wondered what was afoot. Then Gabriel invited her and Harry to go and see their wedding present from the family and took them to the new feed store and left them standing outside of the door. Confused, Harry opened the door, to discover the new bathhouse, full of steam and housing two large troughs full of hot water.

Big Ern took to visiting every week to share the bathhouse with his brother, Charles and Aziz where the young men organized flatulence competitions, invariably won by Big Ern. Try as she did, Mary Ellen never managed to persuade

Elsie into the bathhouse, who maintained 'it would be the death of her.'

After the chaos of harvesting, when the men watched the skies suspiciously for any signs of rain, the village settled down to make ready for a quiet autumn. Mustapha had been watching Rose and decided that she would soon give birth. With her family history of twins, coupled with her feet first delivery on the last occasion, he wanted to be ready. Rose woke Mary and Mustapha in the early hours at the beginning of September. She left Paulo fast asleep due to his squeamish disposition. Mary woke young Mustapha and Isabella as Mustapha took Rose downstairs. He gave her a mild remedy to help her to relax and they sat on the sofa whilst young Mustapha and Isabella heated the water in the bathhouse. Mary made a large pot of tea. By the time they took Rose to the bathhouse they had decided that young Mustapha and Isabella would deliver the baby, with Mustapha and Mary intervening if necessary. Rose, on her second potion that made her laugh uncontrollably did not care who helped. Lily, sensing her daughter's time had come, got up and took over the tea making. Two hours later, Rose's waters ballooned into the bath water and young Mustapha helped her onto her knees, gave her the potion for stamina and Isabella got into the water to check what part of the child presented first. Young Mustapha knelt in front of Rose and quietly reassured her and encouraged her to push deep and strong. To everyone's relief it was a head that protruded, covered with black curls, rapidly followed by the rest of a strong healthy boy. He spluttered as Isabella lifted him from the water to hand to Rose, but young Mustapha shook his head, so she gave the baby to Lily. Rose's belly remained tight to the touch and young Mustapha knew it was twins again. He and Isabella looked at each other and prepared themselves for the next child. Mary made to get up and help, but Mustapha caught her hand and she sat down again. Fifteen minutes later, Isabella, her hand underneath Rose, looked up to young Mustapha with a smile and he knew that this child's head had come first. It was another boy, only slightly smaller that the first. Rose sat in the bath with a smile on her face as she remembered that Paulo would now be able to add his 's'. By the time Paulo came downstairs, Rose was sitting on the sofa and his two new sons lay in the crib beside her. He stared in disbelief, wobbled momentarily and then, despite having been spared the messy aspects, fell to the floor in a faint. Mary and Mustapha sat in the kitchen, leaving Isabella and young Mustapha to empty the bath and clean up.

'They are ready to take our place.' Said Mustapha with tears in his eyes. 'We can die in peace now Mary.'

'Not yet we can't.' answered Mary in alarm. 'Don't you forget your wish to meet their child!'

'Ah yes.' Smiled Mustapha wistfully.

When young Mustapha came out of the bathhouse, he and Mustapha took the babies outside, and for the first time, they presented them to the dawn, together. Mustapha remembered when he had presented the first set of twins with young Mustapha's grandfather, when young Mustapha's father was just minutes old and realized that he had lived a very long life. Lily had tied a ribbon on the wrist of the firstborn as, like their uncles, were impossible to tell apart. They named the twins Edmundo, 'protector of prosperity' and Estavo, meaning 'crown'. Paulo was impatient to revise his sign and wanted to add two 'S's' , but everyone said that was silly and the whole village would die laughing at him. So he settled for just the one.

.

Chapter 51

By the time the twins were born, the ship had sailed across the Bay of Bengal, collected mahogany from Burma and was entering the South China Seas. Khalid, like Mustapha before him was entranced by the precarious, tall rocky islands of the South China Sea that appeared to be growing up out of the water, capped by dense forests. They spent several weeks sailing around, occasionally stopping for fresh water and provisions. They arrived in China in December as planned, as Sam wanted his son to experience the Chinese New Year celebrations. Khalid had recovered his shattered equilibrium and self-respect severely dented by his experiences in India, but he was anxious with regard to what would be China's unsuspected surprises. The climate was to his liking, as was the lack of flies. Encouraged by these developments he went ashore with his father and a light heart, only to be utterly demolished by the food. Strange creatures cooked on the ends of sticks, creatures that he would have trodden on at home. Crisp insects in bowls, dead snakes coiled in watery gravy. Soup full of long thin worms that were actually noodles and became his staple diet throughout their stay. He knew better than to complain, and coped reasonably well with his father's hilarity at the expression on his face when presented with yet another new monstrous edible atrocity. Bill was less fussy and attached by a string to Khalid, he ate anything given to him and stole a great deal more.

They purchased bolts of silk and crates of blue and white porcelain and chests full of tea. They visited the markets and bought presents for the family, beautifully carved ivory hair adornments and new silk hanfus for the newer members of the family. Khalid enjoyed the New Year festivities and became fascinated by the Chinese tradition of naming years after twelve different animals and that the Chinese Gods had made them all swim a river in order to settle the argument about what the first year would be called. Khalid was born in the year of the rat that had ridden across the river on the back of the ox and jumped onto the opposite bank at the last moment. Dismayed, Khalid was unsure whether to be proud of being first or ashamed of being a cheat. He would have preferred to be born in the year of the dragon, like his father and uncle or the year of the horse like his mother. He persuaded his father to buy a set of tiny jade animals depicting each year and a calendar so that he could work out everybody's animal year at home.

There were many more beggars in the streets than on their previous trips and the general atmosphere was unsettling. Sam discovered that there had been a rice famine that had resulted in a mass exodus of people from the countryside into the busy port. Piracy was becoming commonplace and many merchants had suffered losses. Sam and Sal decided to leave before the end of the New Year celebrations, joining forces with several other merchant ships as they sailed in a westerly direction through the South China Sea. They spent the spring in the Indian Ocean, waiting for better weather in the Atlantic. They dropped anchor off an uninhabited island and rowed ashore. They fished, collected fruit and cooked on open fires on the beach. Khalid learnt to swim in the shallow warm water and discovered a number of strange creatures inhabiting the patches of sea grass. Bill climbed the palm trees and kept well away from the water. They saw pods of dolphins and in the distance the plumes of spray emitted by huge whales searching for the shoals of herring. When their fresh water ran low they sailed to the coast, several hundred miles to the south from where Bill had joined them. Sam suggested to Khalid that it would be kinder to let Bill return to his natural habitat and join the dozens of monkeys near the shore, rather than subject him to the cold winters at home. Very reluctantly, Khalid released Bill under the trees, within sight of the other monkeys where he was unceremoniously attacked by the less that welcoming locals, so the rejected, disheveled Bill returned to the ship with a cut on his ear.

Rounding the Cape of Good Hope was less daunting on the return journey and Khalid saw dozens of vast whales swimming beside the ship, their sudden bursts of spray startling Bill. The Atlantic Ocean produced the usual strong winds and heavy seas followed by days of flat calm. It was not until they were approaching the Iberian peninsular that the storm hit. They had seen it coming from the west. They could not outrun it so the hatches were battered down, the sails furled, the storm ropes attached, the cargo secured with extra ropes and Bill shut in the cabin. The heavy rain coincided with nightfall and the thunder and lightening followed. Sam and Sal hung onto the ships wheel. Khalid was tied to the bridge holding a lantern and struggling to stay on his feet as the ship pitched and rolled. A crewman was swept over the side and hauled back aboard spluttering and choking. The storm moved on and at first light the wind abated and the crew had no idea where they were. They sailed on and adjusted their course by the stars when night fell. They arrived home two weeks later and Khalid had developed a deep admiration for his father and uncle. Prior to this voyage, Khalid had merely thought of them as his father and uncle, but now he knew they were extraordinarily brave, resourceful men who faced danger and discomfort without complaint and he felt ashamed. The voyage had changed Khalid, he had embarked as a headstrong young man, full of his own importance and lacking in empathy, much like his grandfather Salamar had been as a young man, and had returned much humbled and a good deal less sure of himself. Mustapha saw it as a welcome improvement.

Chapter 52

Paulo and Rose's twins were eight months old when their uncles and cousin returned and had just embarked on their crawling adventures, necessitating the return of Paulo's fenced enclosure. Mary Ellen was waddling around the big house about to give birth. Mary and Ellen Lily were praying that she had inherited the family trait of easy deliveries, due to the enormous size of both her belly and her husband.

Maria and Mina were busy preparing a welcome home meal for their husbands and Khalid was questioning everyone about the year they were born in and making a list of the animals. Mina could not wait to hear about her village and if her relatives were still alive. She was tearful when he told her that her parents were still alive, as she knew she would never see them again. He lied to her when she asked if he had loved her wonderful, vibrant village, transformed into paradise by a twenty-year absence and selective amnesia. He could not bring himself to tell her that it had constituted the most abhorrent experience of his entire life and that he had detested the foul place. Bill, initially welcomed into the family, soon queered his pitch by scampering across the kitchen beams and urinating on Mina who pursued him and pelted him with potatoes until she knocked him off. Bill ambushed the children and stole their food, he hid kitchen utensils and when Mustapha discovered him cavorting in the microscope room knocking bottles over, he declared war on Bill. He made him a harness and a lead and imposed a strict training regime. Mustapha knew that monkeys were pack animals with strict social codes where each monkey was certain of its place. This monkey, undisciplined and spoilt, assumed it was the leader of the pack and did exactly as it pleased, with alarming consequences. Mustapha asked Paulo to construct a cage with a 'Bill proof' method of closure. He was sitting in the tree house and waiting for Paulo to return home with the cage when Mary Ellen informed him from the base of the tree that she thought her pains had started. The family swung into action. Mary lit the stoves in the bathhouse and Maria and Mina put the water on the heat. Sam rode over to the sick house to tell young Mustapha and Isabella and Sal walked though the woods to tell Ellen Lily and Gabriel, who took two horses and rode to the workshop to collect Harry. They all forgot about Paulo as he was of no use during this type of crisis. Harry arrived first, followed closely by Gabriel. Harry's horse had the bemused expression of a creature fearful of gently rising into the air after he dismounted. He ran indoors to find Mary Ellen. He found her outside walking through the garden chatting to Mustapha and thought he had been misled. Mustapha had given her a mild potion and he explained to Harry that walking about would help the baby to descend.

So Harry took over the shepherding of Mary Ellen, and Mustapha went to the bathhouse with a rope to attach to the large loop he had had inserted into the bathhouse ceiling for the occasion. By the time that young Mustapha and Isabella arrived, Mary Ellen was still circumventing the big house on the arm of her husband. She had told him not to worry when her waters broke on the west side of the house, so he didn't. When Mustapha went to check on Mary Ellen, his keen nose detected the smell of her fluids and he marched her straight to the bathhouse and put her into the water, mindful of these women's tendency to expel babies with little or no warning. She was in little discomfort but Mustapha could see that her belly was contracting strongly. She had no urge to push and was content to relax in the hot water arguing with Harry about names for the child. Mary brought in the tray of tea and after two cups Mary Ellen needed to push. Mustapha had her kneel in the water and hang on the rope, explaining that the position speeds delivery. He believed that she was carrying a large child and even she might encounter some hard work pushing it out. He gave her the strength and stamina potion. Harry sat on the floor beside the bath watching his wife's face contort with supreme effort as she pushed, sweat trickling down and dripping off her nose and chin. Between pushes she relaxed into the water and caught her breath. Young Mustapha and Isabella arrived to help as Mary Ellen pulled herself up on the rope, said 'Ooh1' and deposited the large child into the bath water with a resounding splash. Harry jumped up in surprise as Mary Ellen sat down and fished the spluttering baby out of the water. Everyone was taken by surprise and stared at Mary Ellen, who stared back smiling, proud of her achievement. Then the whole bathhouse juddered and reverberated to its very foundations as Harry thundered onto the floor in an elephantine faint. The women all looked at one another.

'It must be something to do with carpenters!' remarked Mary.

It was a boy and they named him Gabriel Harold after his grandfathers when Harry finally recovered from his faint. Then everyone adjourned to the sofas and left Isabella to help Mary Ellen. The two Mustapha's took little Gabriel outside as the sun was setting into the woods. The young Mustapha held the baby in the last rays of sunshine and recited, word perfect, the message to the sky. Mustapha beamed with pride. Bill, who Paulo had found anchored to the table leg, was in his new cage wearing an expression of major defeat. Paulo showed great sympathy for Harry following his fainting episode, unlike the rest of the family, who at best regarded it as mildly funny.

Mustapha put Bill in his cage overnight and when he was naughty. The rest of the time he sat on Mustapha's shoulder and groomed his hair. Mustapha used dried fruit as a reward and perfected two signals with Bill, a soft chattering sound for when Bill got something right and a sharp, high-pitched shriek that would stop Bill in his tracks and cause him to run to Mustapha's shoulder. When Bill developed an unhealthy romantic interest in people's ears, neither of Mustapha's signals worked, and an hour in the cage was required. That usually reduced his ardour.

Khalid announced that the baby had been born in the year of the horse, which pleased grandfather Gabriel enormously.

Chapter 53

The summer grew fiercely hot and the whole village slowly became submerged into a sweltering, steaming, wilting torpor. The slightest exertion soon resulted in fatigue. There was no drought as it frequently rained at night, dawn was pleasantly warm but by nine o'clock the relentless sun evaporated the water and increased the high levels of humidity. Even the animals became lethargic, with the exception of Bill. The sheep made their way slowly across the marshes to stand on the sea wall and catch the slight breeze from the estuary as the tide turned. Mustapha and Mary sat in the tree house fanning each other with a tea tray and watched the children sprawled on the field and even Joey lacked the energy to run about. It was harvest time and the farmworkers suffered the most from the excessive heat. Several collapsed where they worked. Mustapha prescribed salt. He had barrels of water, laced with sugar and salt delivered to the workers in the fields several times a day with instruction to drink as much as they could. It worked, they were still hot and tired but they stopped collapsing and their heads stopped aching.

There were a significant number of cases of sunstroke in the village. The symptoms were giddiness, nausea and severe headaches. Mustapha had treated sunstroke many years ago whilst at sea but rarely in the village. He instructed young Mustapha and Isabella to administer a pint of water and lay the patient flat on their backs for twenty minutes, by which time the increased blood supply to the brain succeeds in cooling the overheated organ. He advised everyone to keep their heads and the back of their necks protected from the sun's direct rays and the men went to work with handkerchiefs and pillow cases attached to the back of their caps. The women wore headscarves and covered the heads of their children.

The cases of vomiting and diarrhea increased, caused by the rapid 'turning' of food in the unusual heat. Mustapha prescribed starvation for two days and a lot of water with sugar and a pinch of salt. He advised eating only meat that had been killed the same day and advised against stews being reheated and the importance of keeping flies from foodstuffs by covering them with damp, clean cloths.

Maria and Mina dragged out the old tin baths from the stables, not used since the building of the bathhouses, placed them in the shade of a tree and filled them with water for the children to play in. Bill went to investigate, but objected to being splashed and returned to the tree house.

The heat wave lasted almost two months and people began to dream about frost and snow. It ended with a dramatic storm during an afternoon at the end of September and instead of everyone sheltering indoors, they ran outside and stood in the cool rain and watched the lightening and the children jumped about in the rapidly forming puddles. The following day the stifling heat was replaced by the pleasant warmth of early autumn, and the family decided to throw a party in the front field. They lit the fires for the spit roasts early in the morning. Harry and Big Ern were in charge of the fires and turning the sides of beef and the numerous whole sheep required to feed the village. The women had been baking bread for two days. Mustapha and Mary supervised the baking of cakes laced with cinnamon and vanilla and containing Mustapha's candied peel that had been forgotten about at Christmas. There were baskets of apples and pears and a table of cheeses. Edmundo and Estavo were starting to walk and safely corralled in Paulo's fenced enclosure and Mary Ellen proudly introduced her big chubby three-month old Gabriel, with his chestnut curls and bright blue eyes, to the villagers. The local musicians played for the crowd, who sang their best loved songs and the younger ones danced to the lively gigs. When it got dark, Big Ern lit the bonfire. Mustapha, with Bill on his shoulder, watched the faces in the firelight. There were the old people who were children when he had arrived, their children and their grandchildren, many of whom he had delivered with Mary. He felt very old and exceedingly weary. He went to find Mary who was laughing with a crowd of old women. He caught her eye and she was concerned. She said her goodbyes and took Mustapha to their bed and shut Bill in his cage. She made tea and they sat together in bed.

'I can feel death in this house tonight.' Said Mustapha quietly.

Mary felt her chest tighten in fear and her eyes filled with tears. She wanted to argue with him, tell him that he cannot leave her. Instead she put the tea tray on the floor and enclosed the old man, built mostly of bones and skin, in a warm embrace and stroked his hair. She could feel his warm tears dripping onto her breast and she knew that her heart would break. At first light, she was woken up by a miraculously, spritely Mustapha, with a broad smile on his face and a tray of fresh tea in his hands. She threw a pillow at him and burst into tears.

At nine o'clock, Rose took a tray of tea to her mother and Joseph who had not joined the family at breakfast. She discovered her mother staring at the ceiling and shaking uncontrollably, with her cold husband at her side, his face discoloured and contorted by death. Rose dropped the tray and ran to find Mary and Mustapha. Mustapha knew by her face that death had visited the house. Unable to speak she led them to her mother's room. Mary pulled the traumatised Lily from the bed and with Rose's help she took her to hers and Mustapha's sitting room. Mustapha joined them a few minutes later with a potion for Lily, who remained staring blankly and had not uttered a word. Mustapha said it was severe shock. He estimated the time of death around midnight, due to the stiffening of the body. Nobody knew how long Lily had lain beside him awake, whether she had witnessed the death or whether she had woken to find him dead. Lily's eyes closed and she curled up and slept on the armchair. Joseph had dealt with death for most of his life. He was comfortable with death and had always arranged everything and nobody else knew what to do next. Due to the faint, but unmistakable sweet, suffocating vapours of putrefaction seeping from room to room and pervading the house, Mustapha had Sam and Sal carry the body he had wrapped in sheets out to the stable. Mina and Maria opened the windows, stripped the bed and scrubbed the mattress and the men took it outside to dry. Mary lit candles and heated jasmine oil that woke Lily, and caused a bout of hysteria when she finally accepted it was not a vile dream and that both of her husbands were dead. Mustapha gave her more of the potion and she slept again. She never recovered. Unable to enter her room again she slept in the room near Maria and Sal vacated by young Mustapha when he married. She stood silent and pale at the funeral and gazed straight through the people offering their condolences. Rose tried to raise her spirits, reminding her how much her eight grandchildren loved her and needed her. Lily remained impassive. She felt desperately lonely and isolated. Mustapha watched helplessly as her light faded and she withdrew into herself and died quietly three weeks after Joseph. Sam and Sal carried her coffin to the churchyard and she was laid to rest beside Aziz Shadi Rashad Salamar Badr al din, who had waited a long time for his beloved Lily to join him. From that day, visitors to the churchyard noticed a warm fragrance wafting through the graves. Some of them recognized the unmistakable aroma of jasmine oil.

Chapter 54

The sudden deaths of Lily and Joseph stunned the family. They had dealt with the finances for years, so nobody else had bothered. Sam and Sal were very successful merchants and barterers but had little interest in bookkeeping. Gabriel had helped in the past and he and Paulo tackled the meticulously kept ledgers. Young George, Paulo and Rose's eldest son was eleven and had demonstrated a gift for mathematics at an early age. He deciphered the numerous ledgers with ease. There was one for the farm and another for the proceeds of the import business and a third for Paulo's carpentry business. There was another listing the incoming funds from the farm, Paulo's workshop and the imports, and all the outgoing expenses for the school and the sick   house. George soon discovered that all of the ventures were very profitable and according to the figures, the family was very rich. However, nobody knew what, or where these riches actually were. The large expenditures, like the purchase of new vessels every ten to twelve years and the funds to pay for imports had all been provided by Joseph, who subsequently collected in the money paid for the cargo when it was sold. He sold the grain, the crops and the fleeces and paid the wages of the farm workers.

George found several letters from Barings

Bank in London and it appeared that Joseph had on occasions used the Bank to exchange gold for currency and vice versa. Gabriel and Paulo watched George as he scribbled a list of figures in the margin of a ledger, added them up and announced calmly that the family was worth in excess of five hundred thousand pounds in gold and currency and owned half of the land in the village. Gabriel shook his head in disbelief and Paulo felt faint. George, with the air of someone who knew what he was talking about, explained to his father and Gabriel that it was all very simple and although he was only eleven, he was able to keep the books for the family, and if they didn't believe him, they were welcome to employ a bookkeeper who may well swindle them out of a considerable amount of the money that they didn't even know they had! All that remained, said George, was to locate the whereabouts of the fortune. Paulo and Gabriel stared at each other. George surveyed them impassively.

'I think we need a family meeting.' Suggested Gabriel.

By the time of the meeting the following day, George had located the fortune in a large cupboard in Joseph and Lily's bedroom. There were three tea chests, two containing bundles of currency, the other containing gold. George struggled into the meeting lugging the heavy ledgers and placed them on the dining table. Everyone looked at him and waited so he explained which ledgers contained which information. He gave the figures for outgoing and incoming expenditure for the last two years and the amount of profit made. He began to inform the stupefied audience of the projected figures, based on the productivity of the farm and the high price for imports, when Mustapha stopped him.

'Does anyone here have any idea what this boy is talking about?'

'Um. No.' said Sal and several others shook their heads and the rest looked at the floor.

'Do *you* know what you are talking about George?' Mustapha asked hopefully.

'I do Sir. I have calculated that this estate is worth in excess of five hundred thousand pounds in currency and gold. That figure does not include the value of the land owned by the estate. I would estimate, at todays price for..'

'Please stop.' Wailed Mustapha. 'And just tell us what we need to do.'

'Nothing at all Sir, I have told my father that I can keep the books, but if the family feels I am too young, then I would advise you to hire a bookkeeper. I also warned him that a bookkeeper could easily swindle a family that possesses such little knowledge of its own assets. It is up to you all to decide.'

The family collectively felt inadequate and admonished by George, with the exception of Rose, who felt exceedingly proud of her confident young mathematician with his black curls and intense blue eyes.

'Also.' Added George.' I am almost

twelve!'

The family dissolved into a round of applause and George blushed. He was given complete control of the family's finances and told he was only to call a family meeting should he encounter any problems. They declined his offer of a full monthly report. George left school and he took his job very seriously. He kept the family's finances in order for the rest of his life, expanded their land holdings, arranged for the ship to carry copper and brass to Turkey for their expanding ship building industry, doubling the profit of each voyage and made some very profitable investments that the family had absolutely no interest in at all.

Chapter 55

It was the first Christmas without Lily and Joseph, but largely due to the amount of children in the house, sadness was kept at bay and the family, assisted by a small army of women from the village, enjoyed several days of celebrations. There was a light fall of snow followed by a hard frost that grew on the trees and the layers of straw protecting Mustapha's garden like shards of glass. Mary and Mustapha sat on their sofa looking at the glittering woodland discussing death. Mary missed Lily and was saddened that the last few weeks of her life had been so unbearable for her. The thought of losing Mustapha was both inevitable and unthinkable for Mary. Their lives had become so irrevocably entwined, like old vines, and neither of them could distinguish where either one of them ended or the other began. The idea of dying first was just as unthinkable. She could not bear the thought of leaving Mustapha alone, with nobody to care for him the way she did. They had become two halves of the same person.

'It's not death that frightens me, it's being separated from you Mustapha.' She said quietly.

'Then we will die together.' He answered, putting his arm around her shoulders.

She looked into his black eyes that sparkled the way they had when he first entered the kitchen when she was a young woman. She had spent many years loving him like a father. During their years of caring for the sick and tending the garden, she had loved him as a mentor and best friend. At the death of Aziz Shadi Rashad Salamar Badr al din she had loved him as a son. Mustapha was not merely her husband he was everything else as well.

'And.' Added Mustapha. 'I intend that we are also buried together!'

He smiled at her and she sniffed, trying not to cry.

'Trust me.' He whispered. And she did, unconditionally.

Satisfied, Mary set aside the thoughts of death and lifted the singing kettle from the fire and made the tea. Mustapha watched the woodland and made plans, for he too could not entertain the inconceivable terror of being separated from Mary. The only way he could explain how he felt, even to himself, was to experience the pitiful agony of the most exquisite butterfly, trying in vain to fly, after someone had pulled out the wings from one side of it's body.

They drank their tea.

'I also think that as we are all so very rich, we should build better houses for our farm workers!' he announced with glee and scuttled off purposefully with the suggestion to Sam, Sal and George.

Everyone agreed that it was a splendid idea and after an hour of animated discussions they had decided to build twenty substantial roomy cottages on the edge of the wheat field just outside the village. They would call it Lily Lane, as ultimately, Lily was the one that had attracted such good fortune to the village.

Plans were made, materials ordered and by spring, the labourers and stonemasons arrived. Paulo and the chippies provided the carpenters. As it was Kent, they chose to build the cottages with bricks and peg tiles, manufactured in the county. The building work generated considerable interest and speculation as to what the family was up to now. When the workmen arrived on Friday afternoon for their wages, Mustapha was waiting to tell them what was happening. He explained that the family was building new cottages for local families. However, absolute priority would be given to those employed by the family to whom the cottages would be rent-free. A small rent would be charged to villagers employed elsewhere. The farm workers, most of whom lived in cramped old properties, were very impressed and after work each day would arrive at the building site to watch the steady progress of the houses and offer help. Their wives and children delivered refreshments and looked inside the half-built structures and wondered at the large spaces and big windows that opened and shut like cupboard doors. They marveled at the kitchens, with built in sinks and cooking ranges and even shelves for pots and pans. They crept across the floors made of new solid wood. Each cottage was different. Some were built solely with bricks, and others had the upper floor clad with weatherboarding.

The doors and windows were in different places and the smallest cottage had two rooms downstairs and another two above. The largest was double the size with four. Some had more rooms in the attic. Every house had a door at the front and another at the back. Each had a long fenced garden for growing vegetables, a wooden shed for storing tools and produce, a water pump and an outside lavatory. The workmen were left in peace to finish the houses at harvest time when every pair of available hands had work, including the children. Another structure appeared along the back of the gardens, a long, one-story stone construction. It contained six separate sections. Four were the bathhouses, each containing four large baths a stove and a water pump. The other two contained rows of large sinks, a stove and water pump and was designed for the women to wash their clothes and linen. The six doors of the bathhouse opened onto a raised communal area, sheltered by a protruding roof, where the women could hang their washing if it rained, and the men could sit together in the evenings, smoke, play dominoes and look out over their gardens. The cottages were allocated by the size of family and the numbered keys were given to the men during the big party held in the field outside the big house when harvesting was over. Many of the men were immediately hauled away by their excited womenfolk, armed with lanterns and a burning desire to see inside their new homes. The following day, which was Sunday, Harry and Big

Ern, great advocators of the bathhouse, arrived to show the residents how to use them. Paulo and Gabriel, equipped with horse drawn carts, spent the rest of the day moving furniture from around the village to the new cottages.

The largest family, containing three generations and numbering a total of twenty-one individuals, ranging from ten to seventy three, had been allocated the cottage containing the most rooms. For the first time in years, they were able to sleep less that ten to a room.

Mary and Mustapha visited the new cottages, after giving the residents a couple of weeks to settle in. Everyone wanted to show them inside their cottages that smelled of new wood and polish. The women were so pleased and proud of their homes, but Mary was troubled by how few possessions these women had, and how full the attics were of discarded furniture in the big house. She drove Mustapha home, enlisted the assistance of Sam, Sal, Paulo, Harry and Big Ern and had them search the attics until they found twenty hearthrugs and as many chairs, tables, and other useful items as they could find, bring them downstairs and load them onto carts. They loaded three carts and drove them to the new cottages, where she gave a colourful hearthrug to each family, had Harry and Big Ern unload all of the furniture in front of the cottages and told the staggered women to choose what they needed most. A few days later, two children arrived at the door of the big house asking to see Mary. They presented her with a cake, numerous bunches of wild flowers and six lace handkerchiefs from the women in the new cottages.

'They said to say 'thank you so very much Miss Mary'.' Said the little girl.

Chapter 56

Young Mustapha and Isabella had been married for over two years. They spent all of their time together, at work and at home. Mustapha envied them, their steadfast, exclusive relationship as yet undiluted by either the joy or the heartache of children. Mustapha was pleased, as they had married so young and needed time to themselves before embarking on parenthood. Mary Ellen and Harry, whose first son was already running around, were expecting their second child and Anna and Matthew their third. It seemed to Mustapha that life's major events were getting closer together, although, in reality he knew that he was getting further apart. He was delighted to be relegated, along with Mary, to the garden and to their rooms at the end of the house. Now they were no longer afraid of death, they spent all of their time together, chatting, playing chess and drinking tea, making the most of every moment.

Isabella confided in Mary just before Christmas that she thought that she might be with child. The sickness that began a few days later, confirmed their suspicions and Mustapha made ginger root tea. She was unable to cope with the aromas from the kitchen, so at Christmas the two Mustapha's and their wives spent their time in the rarified atmosphere of jasmine oil behind the closed door of their rooms at the end of the house. Isabella, whose complexion was always very pale, took on a transparent, spectral quality. Young Mustapha fussed over her, running to the kitchen for biscuits, cake and boiled eggs whenever she thought she could eat something. He banned her from returning to the sick house after Christmas, even after her sickness stopped and she was eating like a horse. So Isabella spent her time in the garden with Mary, Bill and Mustapha, who calculated that there would be a new child in June, July and probably August. Judging by the size of Mary Ellen, she would produce the first.

The ship sailed in March, bound for North Africa, Crete and Turkey. Sam kept his promise and took Joey as well as Khalid. They sailed directly to Turkey to unload the brass and copper and Sam and Sal took the brothers to the hamam where Aziz Shadi Rashad Salamar Badr al din had taken Lily shortly after their marriage. They visited Hagia Sophia and saw the Topkapi palace where the sultan lived. Joey fell in love with Constantinople and believed that it was the most beautiful place he had ever seen. They bought sweets, a number of silk bedspreads and a crate of coloured glass lanterns, ordered by Mary before they left. They purchased crates of tea and bolts of silk and sailed to Crete, where they bought crates of porcelain delivered from China. Joey was impatient to reach North Africa as so far, they had not traveled more that a mile from the ship and he was eager to camp overnight in a desert. Joey got his first close sighting of dolphins the day before they docked. Joey had never shown a great deal of interest in the lazy old camel at home. It was so neglected nobody could remember whether it was Lumpy of Humpy. The camels they were to ride through the desert on were livelier, grumpier and prone to spit and bite. Joey toppled off his camel during its jerky ascent, much to Khalid's amusement, but managed to remain attached on his second attempt. His camel remained truculent throughout that day. Sometimes it ran off in a random direction, other times it just stopped and once it sat down in the sand. The man leading the camels, resembling Mustapha, grew impatient and tied the beast to his own mount and glared at Joey and said something he did not understand. The next day Joey was provided with a different camel that, within minutes, behaved exactly the same as the first and the camel man spoke with Sam. Apparently Joey's constant, restless fidgeting was upsetting the camels. He spent the rest of the trip tied to the irritated camel man, trying to keep still. When Joey asked his father what the camel man had said, Sam translated the conversation.

'Is the boy sick?' the camel man had asked him.

'No, that is how he always is.'

'Then I am truly sorry for you Sir!'

Khalid collapsed with laughter and Joey decided that camels were stupid creatures.

They went to the tannery and purchased as many hides of various thicknesses to fill the hold and this time, Khalid did not hold his nose. On the return journey, the camel man tied Joey's camel to his own at the outset and shook his old head sorrowfully in Joey's direction.

With neither Anna nor Isabella available to work in the sick house, Matthew and young Mustapha hired a young woman from Lily Lane, the eldest daughter of a farm worker. Beth was a strong, energetic young woman with light brown hair, worn in a thick plait that reached below her waist, and hazel eyes. Armed with a bucket, mop and wet cloths, she cleaned the sick house from top to bottom, reorganized the cupboards and caught the eye of Big Ern when he delivered a new set of shelves. By the time he had drunk the tea she gave him and watched her wiping down the new shelves he was besotted.

'I've just met the woman I am going to marry!' he told his brother when he returned to the workshop. 'Her name is Beth.'

Despite it being early summer, Mustapha constantly suffered from the cold and shivered in the slightest breeze, so Mary and Maria made him a long, hooded coat of lambs fleece, similar to the one made by Lily when she was a young woman. Mustapha wore it all summer without overheating and was a source of amusement to Mary who told him he looked like a sheep when he bent over in the garden.

Mary Ellen delivered her daughter in the bathhouse at Gabriel's farm in the early hours of the morning, with the help of her mother and did not need the potion that Mustapha had left on the kitchen shelf. Harry did not faint when Daisy emerged from the bath water and he ran all the way to the big house and woke everyone, hammering on the door with tiny Daisy rolled in a towel, so that young Mustapha could present her to the stars. Three weeks later Anna gave birth to John Matthew, attended by her husband and Faith.

Big Ern had developed the habit of lurking at the workshop door around the time that Beth walked past on her way home to Lily Lane, to wish her 'Good Evening.' He even arrived at the sick house with a splinter in his thumb, that he would normally have extracted himself, hoping that she would remove it for him. Young Mustapha poked the splinter out with a needle and Big Ern did not even catch sight of Beth, who was busy in another room. One evening he missed her passing the door of the workshop. He walked very fast down the road to catch up with her to wish her good evening. He caught up with her quickly, said good evening, and continued to walk at the same high speed, leaving her behind in the road. He then walked a considerable distance out of his way, as he was too embarrassed to turn round and walk back. Beth, an astute, spirited young woman with seven brothers knew exactly what was going on and she found Big Ern's hesitancy amusing. She let him suffer for weeks, and then she arrived unannounced at the workshop with a box of cakes and introduced herself to Paulo and the chippies. Big Ern almost fell over struggling to hide himself behind a pile of lumber.

'Would you like a cake?' Beth inquired, peering into his hiding place and startling the red-faced Big Ern. He rose clumsily and tried to pretend that he had been searching for something. He could hear his workmates woefully concealed laughter and grinned sheepishly. Beth, unable to control herself any longer, laughed so much she was forced to sit down. Big Ern took a cake from the box and then began to choke himself as his mouth, due to nervousness, was utterly devoid of spittle. Beth rose from the chair, leant over to Big Ern, kissed him on the cheek, told him he had suffered enough and he was welcome to walk her home at six o'clock. He choked so much that most of the cake crumbs exited via his nostrils, violently propelled by a momentous sneeze. Beth dodged the cake crumbs and returned to the sick house laughing. Big Ern was mortified, but by six o'clock, he had recovered his good humour and was standing outside the sick house waiting for Beth, who took his arm with a smile and he walked her home to Lily Lane. Beth's long plait swung rhythmically as they strolled down the road and when it brushed Big Ern's arm he could feel his legs go weak.

Chapter 57

Mustapha experienced a remarkable new lease of life during Isabella's pregnancy. He was incredibly excited, as he had been at the unexpected birth of his precious Maria. He had wanted to stay alive to see his grandchild born and even he found it almost unbelievable that he now awaited a great-grandchild. He followed her everywhere, around the house, in the garden and on her afternoon walks in the woods. Mary regularly cooked him spicy chicken and cinnamon puddings to tempt him away and give the poor girl a moment's peace. Isabella's health improved dramatically once her sickness stopped. She had boundless energy, her hair and eyes shone and she even developed some colour in her pale cheeks. Young Mustapha, who was as protective as his grandfather, refused to allow her to return to work in the sick house in case of germs.

During August, Mustapha, Mary and Isabella replenished the stocks of potions and Mustapha made ready a little box of remedies for all eventualities that he kept on the top shelf of the bathhouse. August came and went and Isabella became impatient. Mustapha was apoplectic when he found her climbing up and down the tree house stairs in an attempt to start her pains. He sat her at the bottom of the steps and held her hand in his and begged her to wait until the pains started naturally as he believed that the child knew when it was ready to come better than she did. Mary saw them through the upstairs window, rocking gently on the bottom step of the tree house, Mustapha's thin arm around her shoulders, and she was momentarily overcome with emotion. In early September, Mustapha made certain that the stoves in the bathhouse were laid ready to be lit, that the woodpile was replenished and all of the big pots filled with water. At night he took on the qualities of an alert spider and constantly disturbed Mary as he suddenly sat up and listened intently to the slightest noise. Isabella's labour began in late morning when she remarked that her belly had become very tight and hard several times in the previous hour, and Mustapha changed from the fidgety, tightly coiled spring that he had been for the last month, into the calm, capable man they were more familiar with. Mary breathed a sigh of relief. During the afternoon Isabella's belly continued to tighten and when her back began to ache in the early evening, Mustapha lit the fires in the bathhouse. He gave her a mild remedy to relax her and ease the backache and by the time that young Mustapha had returned from the sick house, Isabella was dozing on the sofa. By ten o'clock she reported that she had slight pain with each tightening and Mustapha offered her a potion but she declined, preferring to wait until they were stronger. Mary attempted to send Mustapha to bed for a sleep, pointing out that he would require energy later on and she would wake him when he was needed. The best she achieved was for him to agree to lie on the sofa and rest his eyes. Isabella moved to the bathhouse in the early hours and submerged herself in the hot water that obliterated the residual discomfort remaining after a stronger remedy. She suffered a bout of giggling and said she could hear the poppies talking to one another. Mustapha could see she was having strong contractions, but after several hours still had no urge to push the child out. At six o'clock he woke Mary, who was asleep on the sofa and announced it was time to intervene. He had examined Isabella and believed that they needed to break her waters to speed the birth, as both she and the child were tiring. He administered another potion and guided young Mustapha's hand as he felt for the bulging sack of water and burst it with his fingernails. As soon as Mustapha saw the greenish tinge in Isabella's waters he demanded that young Mustapha fill the other bath with clean, hot water as quickly as possible. Mary could see by Mustapha's eyes that something was wrong even though his manner remained calm. As soon as the bath was full and Mustapha had added a handful of salt to the water they lifted the surprised Isabella from one bath to the other. He gave her the strength potion as soon as she had the urge to push. This bath had no attachment for the rope so Mustapha resorted to the twisted sheet method. He quickly gave the other end of the sheet to young Mustapha, as

Isabella pulled so hard that Mustapha, with the ballast of an insect, was fearful of falling into the bath with her. Mustapha knelt beside the bath and held Isabella's arm, whilst he quietly reassured her and encouraged her to push long and hard. Mary knew he needed this baby to come out fast. She climbed into the water behind Isabella and supported her in a kneeling position. She could feel the hard dome of the child's head beginning to emerge and nodded to Mustapha, who pushed the sheet away and grabbed both of Isabella's hands, looked into her eyes and with every ounce of his own strength urged her to push. He counted to ten, told her to breathe in and push again. Young Mustapha held his breath and prayed as he listened to his grandfather. On the third count to ten the baby's head emerged, but it took poor Isabella two more desperate pushes to pass the shoulders. When Mary lifted the disgruntled, spluttering child from the water they could all see why. He was one of the largest babies they had ever delivered. Mustapha flopped to the floor with exhaustion and relief. Isabella had no strength left and young Mustapha supported her limp body to prevent her from submerging herself. Mary remained marooned in the bath holding the baby, still attached to its mother, who protested loud enough to summon the urgently needed assistance of Maria and Rose. Maria lifted her father, who weighed little more than a bag of sticks, from the floor and carried him to the sofa, collected the noisy infant after young Mustapha cut the cord, and rolled him in a towel and laid him beside his weary great-grandfather and returned to help Rose extract Mary from the bath. Exhausted and soaking wet, Mary hobbled from the bathhouse, though the kitchen and collapsed onto a sofa, pleading for tea. Rose put the kettle on to boil and returned to the bathhouse to assist young Mustapha and Maria. Twenty minutes later young Mustapha carried his very tired, smiling wife in and sat her in the armchair. Rose poured the tea. Mustapha was fast asleep, despite the newest member of the family bellowing in his ear. Maria passed the baby to Isabella and once he was attached to her breast he was thankfully quiet. Young Mustapha waited for his grandfather to wake, as he wanted him to present his great-grandson to the sky. Mustapha was greatly relieved to see the sleeping Isabella in the chair opposite with the baby asleep in her arms, as when he was waking up he briefly feared it had all been a dream. Mary was asleep on the sofa. Young Mustapha passed him a cup of very sweet tea and when he was sufficiently revived he gave him the child and asked if he would present him to the bright, early autumn morning.

When they returned indoors they unrolled the child from the towel. His skin was slightly paler than his father and his eyebrows were dark brown, a sign that when he grew hair it would be dark. As yet he had been too busy yelling or feeding and had not opened his eyes. Out of sheer curiosity, due to his phenomenal size, they took him to the kitchen scales to discover his weight. They weighed a mixing bowl first, then the mixing bowl and child. He weighed in at eleven pounds and six ounces, once they had subtracted the weight of the bowl. The cold surface of the bowl started him awake and he opened his eyes and glared at them with the glistening black eyes of the Mustapha's.

Maria sent them all to bed for the afternoon and she and Mina began cooking in anticipation of the amount of visitors that would arrive later to see the baby. The, as yet, nameless child woke them all just after six o'clock with the enthusiastic bawling of a hungry baby. Isabella fed him and they all went downstairs, enticed by the smell of food. The room was full of family waiting to see the new arrival. As he was passed around, he stared long and hard, scrutinising each individual with his black eyes and no one could imagine him being named anything except Mustapha.

A week later, the ship returned and Khalid informed everyone that this year's babies had been born in the year of the goat and would be clever, tender, kind-hearted and compassionate.

Chapter 58

Big Ern took Beth home for tea with his mother. Elsie had made a huge effort to provide a spread like Ellen Lily had when she had tea at her home for the first time. There was cold meat, cheese, bread, pickles, a fruit pie and little cakes. She almost wore her best frock, and then changed her mind, not wishing to show off. Beth was impressed and assumed that carpenters families ate like that every day. Her own parents had welcomed Big Ern and were proud that their only daughter was walking out with a tradesman who was related by marriage to the family in the big house. After a month of walking out, Big Ern asked Beth to marry him, she agreed and the wedding was to take place in the spring.

As soon as Paulo told everyone that Big Ern was marrying Beth, the family, who had not had a wedding for almost three years, decided to give them a wedding like Harry and Mary Ellen's as a wedding present. Mustapha set himself a new goal, to live to see them married.

Mustapha and Isabella had taken several weeks to recover from the exhaustion they suffered after the birth of the baby. Mary noticed that Mustapha took longer to recover from exertion and he seemed to be getting thinner. She cooked his favourite foods and made him rest in the afternoons. For once, he did as he was told, which concerned her even more. Mustapha himself was well aware of his own increasing frailty and took young Mustapha into his confidence and together they secretly began to lay in place the plans for his inevitable death. Young Mustapha would need an accomplice and they chose Harry, who was given instructions to have two coffins made in the workshop and hidden at the back of the unused stable where the camels had once resided.

Autumn was wet and windy and the trees lost their leaves early. The family was always aware of the seasons passing, but took little notice of the actual date, month or even the year, until Khalid reminded them that the next year would be the start of a new century, and it would be the year of the monkey. Bill glared morosely from his cage, in which Mustapha had imprisoned him, due to lack of trust, since the birth of the third Mustapha.

By Christmas the weather had changed. There was a light dusting of snow, a hard frost and brilliant sunshine. Beth, Big Ern and Elsie spent Christmas with Gabriel and Ellen Lily and during the afternoon Big Ern and Beth walked through the silent crystalline woods to wish the family a happy Christmas and the family took the opportunity to tell the couple that they would provide the wedding, as they had for his brother, and asked what colour dress Beth would prefer. Bewildered, Beth eventually admitted that since early childhood, she had dreamt of wearing a red dress. Rose, Sophia and Olivia took her upstairs to the room where most of the sewing took place and showed her the array of coloured silks, including several reds and asked her to choose. There was dark red, like blood, bright red like ripe apples, an orangey red like the sunset and one the colour of ripe raspberries. Beth loved the soft raspberry red, so they measured her and told her to come back for a fitting in mid January. Olivia, who had measured Beth and noticed she was of a similar size to her grandmother Lily, quietly asked her mother if it would be impolite to offer Beth some of Lily's clothes, that were clogging the cupboards. Rose asked Beth if she would be offended, but she would be doing them a favour if she could make use of some of the clothes. Beth was not offended and when they opened the cupboard doors and she saw the row of beautiful clothing, she was speechless, and far too overwhelmed to choose anything. Sophia, sensing her discomfort, lifted out a thick, deep red winter dress in soft wool, and held it against Beth.

'Try this on.' She suggested.

In a daze, Beth removed her old dress and Sophia helped her into the new one. It fitted her well and when she looked into the mirror she failed to recognize herself.

'It looks beautiful on you.' Said Sophia as Rose and Olivia quietly left the room.

Poor Beth was speechless. Sophia removed two more winter dresses from the cupboard, a violet one made of velvet and a cerise one with black collar and cuffs. She wrapped up the two dresses along with Beth's old dress and tied the parcel with string.

'Perhaps you could make use of this?' asked Sophia, as she opened another cupboard and pulled out a long black wool coat with thick light brown fur on the collar and cuffs. She held it up and Beth, still lost for words, slipped into the most wonderful coat she had ever seen. She followed Sophia back to the sewing room.

'Are you sure…? She stammered to Rose.

'Beth, you will be doing us all a great favour if you can make use of them, and I must say they do look well on you!'

Beth smiled then, and flung her arms around Rose and thanked her so much that Rose butted in.

'Promise me that when the weather is warmer that you'll come back and take some of the summer dresses, there are a great deal of them!'

Beth skipped down the stairs and Big Ern was so impressed that he stood up. They had a cup of tea and said their goodbyes. Beth was so overjoyed that she forgot all about her old coat, and ran all the way through the woods and Big Ern, carrying the parcel, had difficulty keeping up with her. Ellen Lily gave Beth a parcel of food to take to her brothers and Big Ern, Elsie and Beth walked to her house and when her mother saw her, dressed like a lady, she became very emotional and was forced to sit down. Her brothers demolished the food and Beth was unable to stop smiling.

On the Century's eve, the family threw a big

party, with music, food, a massive bonfire to warm the crowd and the biggest display of fireworks the village had ever witnessed. Rose was searching for Beth in the crowd as she had found the fur hat that matched her coat. She found her with Big Ern, who was difficult to miss, and her parents, warming themselves beside the bonfire.

'You forgot this.' She said with a smile, placing the hat on Beth's head.

Beth smiled and gave Rose a hug, and knew that her life would never be the same again.

Chapter 59

The snowdrops bloomed early due to the mild, damp winter. By February both Daisy and John were crawling and when they visited the big house, little Mustapha made heroic, but unsuccessful attempts to keep up with them. Mustapha spent hours quietly watching the child as he began to explore his world. He was a happy child with a ready smile for anyone that spoke to him and a tenacious curiosity. In the spring, Isabella returned to the sick house and Mustapha and Mary enjoyed hours of fun playing with the baby, whilst the family set about arranging the wedding. Beth's dress was finished, designed by the artistic Sophia and constructed by Rose and Olivia. Beth had worked at the sick house for over a year and proved to be a good nurse and had attended several births with young Mustapha. She had taken young Maud under her wing, helped her to improve her cleaning skills and asked her to be her bridesmaid. Maud was beside herself with excitement about the wedding and about the dress she would wear, especially when Beth told her she would be able to keep the violet silk dress.

Spot, adorned with a red ribbon around his neck, waited outside of the church on the day of the wedding. Beth was stunning in her raspberry red dress with matching ribbons pinned to her long wavy hair. Big Ern had never seen her hair brushed out loose and it reached to her thighs in thick undulating waves. Maud had been scrubbed, brushed and dressed and her own family barely recognized her.

Paulo and his chippies had repaired and extended Elsie's house in the weeks leading up to the wedding and Mary Ellen had prepared the bedroom for the couple, with a red silk bedspread and red glass lanterns from Turkey.

Mustapha and Mary watched the party from their perch in the tree house and Beth's father, cap in hand, found them and profusely thanked them for giving his girl such a wonderful day. Mustapha shook his hand warmly.

'Thank you Amos, for allowing us to share your lovely Beth, she is an incredible young woman!'

Beth moved in with Big Ern and his mother. Elsie kept house and Beth and Big Ern returned to work. Elsie tidied their bedroom every day, she stroked the bedspread and dusted the lanterns and never tired of standing in the beautiful room that was part of her little house. Summer was pleasantly warm and largely dry. Sophia and Olivier parceled up Lily's summer dresses and delivered them to Beth in case she was too embarrassed to collect them.

Mustapha and Mary spent the days in the garden with little Mustapha who had mastered the art of crawling. Bill demonstrated no aggression towards the child and his incarceration ended. Little Mustapha intently watched the little monkey and regularly burst into gales of laughter at his antics. Bill appeared to like the child's company and often sat beside him for long periods, sharing food and studying small stones, worms and pea-bugs. Mary kept watch as little Mustapha had a tendency to eat unfamiliar objects. Mustapha delighted in observing his great grandson, grateful for every day he spent with the happy child with dark brown curls and chubby limbs. Mary did most of the work in the garden as Mustapha's vigorous days were coming to an end. He had good days, when he managed to climb the stairs in the tree house unaided and potter for a while amongst his poppies. Some days Mary had to carry him. As his strength failed, hers increased. Maria smiled as she saw the incongruous procession through the window, Mary laughing as she lugged Mustapha up the stairs of the tree house, followed by a little Mustapha crawling slowly behind her and Bill running up and down the handrail, chattering loudly. She took them a tray of tea and biscuits. Her father's skin had darkened, his hair and beard were silver and he resembled a mummified corpse, but his mental faculties remained undiminished. Mary's hair was streaked with grey and she had retained her indomitable strength and energy but was increasingly forgetful. Maria realised that as time had passed and their interdependence increased, they were evolving imperceptibly into one functioning individual. They became a common sight in the kitchen, Mustapha sitting comfortably in an armchair whilst Mary listened to his instructions and successfully produced tasty puddings. Little Mustapha followed them everywhere, even when his parents were home and Bill followed little Mustapha.

The family had, for the last few years, made an effort to make Christmas special, aware that it may be Mustapha's last one. That year was no exception. When Maria took a tray of tea to Mustapha and Mary on Christmas morning, she was startled to find their bed empty. She found them outside in the snow, laughing like children, Mustapha in his lambskin coat lashed to the sledge, clutching his great grandson as Mary pulled them around the big field. Young Mustapha and Isabella looked out of their bedroom window onto a scene they would remember for the rest of their lives. They watched as Mary parked the sledge near the front door and lifted little Mustapha from the sledge and stood him in the snow. She untied Mustapha and picked him up and slipped over. Maria opened the door to see both Mary and Mustapha in a giggling heap in the snow and little Mustapha tugging at their hands, trying to help them to their feet. Maria helped the cackling pair into armchairs beside the fire and hoped she herself would be as happy when she was old.

'No! no!' exclaimed the excited little Mustapha to anyone that would listen.

It was Mustapha who explained it was his best effort at saying 'snow'.

The thick snow kept most people indoors over Christmas and the family had a quieter than usual, but very happy Christmas, and Mustapha was grateful for the peaceful atmosphere, surrounded by the people he loved most. After dinner Mustapha fell asleep in the armchair, and little Mustapha, exhausted by the excitement of snow climbed up and fell asleep curled up on his great grandfather. Sophia ran and collected her drawing paper and pencils to record the scene for little Mustapha.

The snow persisted throughout January and much of February. On sunny days Mary would heat up a number of large stones in the oven and wrap them in cloths, put both of the Mustaphas and the hot stones on the sledge, cover them in a blanket and drag them off. Sometimes they went as far as the village. Little Mustapha loved the snow and was most perplexed when he took a snowball indoors and left it on the rug beside the fire. When he returned it had gone so he made another one that he sat beside. He watched it change from white to transparent and disappear into the rug.

'No gone!' he said, turning to Mustapha, who had been watching, fascinated. He explained to the child that snow was made of very cold water, and when it got warm it returned to water. Little Mustapha seemed satisfied with the explanation, but cried when he looked outside one morning and all of the snow had disappeared.

Chapter 60

Mustapha, reduced to a wisp, rarely made it unaided up the steps of the tree house that summer and Mary carried him, refusing all assistance. He knew he was getting weaker and were it not for Mary, and his promise to her, he believed he would have died by now. Despite his struggle to keep on living, they shared a happy summer with little Mustapha whose speech was becoming more coherent. In late summer Mary caught a cold that developed into a cough. Young Mustapha and Isabella insisted that she rest indoors and mixed a poultice to relieve her chest. The old couple made it downstairs for little Mustapha's second birthday. In October Mary's cough was better, but the illness had taken its toll on her and she was happy to sit quietly on her sofa with Mustapha and watch the woods.

Young Mustapha was woken at first light by a deafening stillness in the house and a compelling need to check on his grandfather and Mary. They were lying in their bed, Mary's eyes were closed, her head rested on Mustapha's chest and her left arm encircled his body. Mustapha lay on his back with both of his arms around Mary, exactly as he had told his grandson they would be on the morning of their deaths. Young Mustapha crept quietly from the silent house and ran through the woods to implement the plan that

Mustapha had concocted in life. He woke Harry by throwing small stones at his window. They ran back through the woods, entered the sleeping house and rolled the bodies in the bed sheets and Harry carried them downstairs, across the yard and into the stable, young Mustapha quietly opening and closing the doors. They pulled out the coffins that had been stored there for over a year, and placed the couple inside and nailed the lids on and placed them in the garden amongst the poppies. It had been Mustapha's strict instruction that no one except young Mustapha and Harry was to see them after death. They wanted everyone to remember them alive.

Young Mustapha and Harry went to the kitchen and made tea and waited for the dreadful moment when they would have to break the news. They were instantly assaulted by a barrage of questions from the shocked family, until young Mustapha silenced them all with the list of the wishes of Mustapha and Mary, that they had made before they died. They did not want to be seen. They wanted to be buried on the day of their death. They wanted to be carried from the house, through the village and to the church and on the first Saturday after the funeral they wanted the family to throw a party for everyone with food, music and fireworks. They wanted their lives to be celebrated, not their deaths.

Harry went home through the woods to tell the rest of the family.

The slow procession left the big house in early afternoon. Harry and Big Ern carried one coffin. Gabriel, Charles, Aziz and Paulo carried the other. They headed across the fields to Lily Lane and turned left into the road that led to the church. The edges of the roads were lined with every man, woman and child that lived in the village. The men held their caps on their chests and the women bowed their heads. As the procession moved slowly past, the villagers quietly joined the swelling crowd as it followed the coffins to the churchyard. The two coffins were laid side by side, near to the grave of Aziz Shadi Rashad Salamar Badr al din. Only Harry and young Mustapha knew that Mustapha and Mary had been buried in the same coffin, still locked in their final embrace and covered with Mustapha's lambskin coat. The other coffin contained two bags of soil, and nobody, least of all Mustapha himself, knew that he had been one of the very few individuals that had been alive in three different centuries. He had been born in 1699.

Out of respect for Mustapha and Mary the family threw a big extravagant party and the villagers arrived, unsure of what to do. Young Mustapha stood on a table and shouted that Mustapha and Mary wanted everyone to party like they always did, and that they would be watching to make sure they did. Once the musicians started playing and the food was served, the rather morose party eventually livened up and several people, at different times during the evening, out of the corner of their eye, swore they saw the old couple sitting in the tree house.

Over the years, little Mustapha spent hours sitting in the tree house with Bill, chatting and smiling and waving his little arms about. People assumed that he was talking to the monkey.

THE END

Made in the USA
Charleston, SC
29 November 2014